I USED TO BE AN ANIMAL, BUT I'M ALL RIGHT NOW

I USED TO BE AN ANIMAL, BUT I'M ALL RIGHT NOW
ERIC BURDON

faber and faber
LONDON · BOSTON

First published in 1986
by Faber and Faber Limited
3 Queen Square London WC1N 3AU

Photoset and printed in Great Britain by
Redwood Burn Limited, Trowbridge, Wiltshire

British Library Cataloguing in Publication Data

Burdon, Eric
I used to be an Animal, but I'm all right now.
1. Burdon, Eric   2. Rock musicians – Great
Britain – Biography
I. Title
784.5'4'00924   ML420.B/

ISBN 0–571–13492–0

Library of Congress Cataloging-in-Publication Data

Burdon, Eric, 1941–
I used to be an animal but I'm all right now.

1. Burdon, Eric, 1941– . 2. Rock musicians –
England – Biography.   I. Title.
ML420.B883A3 1986   784.5'4'00924 [B]   85–29193
ISBN 0–571–12952–8
ISBN 0–571–13492–0 (pbk.)

To Alexandria Mirage
Thanks to Ronni Money for research

CONTENTS

INTRODUCTION

Over the years I did not keep a diary. Most of what you are about to read are memories, dreams, feelings and even hallucinations, but that's rock'n'roll.

I tried to live out my rock'n'roll fantasy as best I could from the very first day I heard the music. I knew it had a special power. What kind of power we are still waiting to find out. Only time will tell.

This music was born amidst the pain and hardship of the poor, black and working-class peoples of the United States of America. Over the years white men have turned it into a multi-million dollar business, as vast and as complex as any other business in the world today. Little wonder it is easy to forget its beginnings – three simple chords and a back beat. Its roots were in gospel music, Negro spirituals, blues songs, field chants, hollers and work songs of the Old South. It spread to the big cities and is still spreading – it may end up in Outer Space.

I guess I knew a long time ago that rock'n'roll could carry me away, or even destroy me, and that's why I've attempted to keep my feet firmly on the ground. I ignored and turned my back on the business aspects, at great cost and expense to myself. But at least I've survived to tell the story. 'Money can't buy me love' The Beatles sang in the sixties, and I believed it.

My story is true. Everything you read happened, although not always in the right chronological order. There's no way it could be, as even after only one or two weeks on the road with a touring band, life becomes a blur. One town is much the same as another, one hotel room the same as the next. I present my point of view in an attempt to recreate the feeling of life on the road with a rock'n'roll band, and to tell what it was like growing up in post-war England. I came from working-class stock. Suddenly I was projected into a new world and became one of the privileged few. 'The experience is the important thing,' a friend of mine once said. That's all I ever did, go out and grab at the experience. As one of the first blues I heard points out 'This story ain't got no moral, this story ain't got no end, this story only goes to show, there ain't no damn good in man.'

ERIC BURDON
Newcastle upon Tyne, England

ONE
OUR STREET

I was weaned on war. I was born in 1941, when the whole world was in flames. In the East the Japs were tearing across towards the west coast of the United States; the Germans were clawing their way across Russia towards Stalingrad and Moscow; and the British had recently had the shit kicked out of them in Dunkirk. War, war, war. The first ten years of my life seemed to roll by like one long, grainy, black and white newsreel film from the front. I was born in Newcastle upon Tyne – a hard, proud city. I'm known to the rest of my countrymen as a Geordie. I'm in a business that has made countless millions for many people and yet at this time I have to borrow money from my parents to survive. What's the reason? What have I given, what have I taken and what have I learned? There's something about being born and raised in this particular part of the British Isles that just won't let you forget. Wherever I am – Japan, California, France or Sweden – I'm constantly reminded of my heritage and what I'm supposed to represent. It's a good place to be from. Yet for as long as I can remember I have wanted to leave.

Music – the talent to get drunk enough or out of my mind enough to climb on to a stage in front of a club full of people and sing with emotion is what was deeply rooted inside of me. Letting it out and getting across how I really felt was what helped me escape from Newcastle to see the rest of the world. But human nature being what it is, well, that's why I'm back here in Newcastle penniless, beginning this journey back into my own personal history, trying my best to lay down the truth for what it's worth.

Marondale Avenue is a cul-de-sac on a housing estate built just before the Second World War to accommodate workers in the shipyards and other heavy industries that lay along the banks of the river Tyne. Cul-de-sac is a chic way of saying dead-end street, but this little community was far from dead. When I was a kid it was like a little village and it still is today. Everybody knows everybody else. Around the time I came into the world my father was an electrical engineer employed by the naval yard on the riverbank about a mile from where we lived. From my bedroom I could see the heavy cranes that were used to move the huge iron plates that would be welded together to make the big ships and the big guns. They looked like dinosaurs to me, monsters from a time long gone.

This cul-de-sac was circular with a row of neat, red brick, semi-detached houses. We lived at Number 31, and an adopted aunt of mine, Nora, lived next door. My parents' door was open day and night to both friends and strangers. We knew nothing of the fear of being burgled. Everyone looked out for each other: the best security system in the world.

Each house was behind a small brick garden wall, with a wooden gate. This was a perfect little playground; in those days there weren't any cars. When it was dark and the streetlights came on, the circular brick cul-de-sac became an arena for us kids. Five-a-side football, snowball fights, baseball, imaginary Roman contests, war games, bonfires and bike races. You name it, we played it, right outside my front door. The kids from the adjoining streets would come over to Marondale to play out their contests. Like all kids, we'd run wild, the games getting harder and harder until something had to give, like a high-aimed ball crashing into a bedroom window. That was it! An extremely pissed-off neighbour would come to the front gate yelling and shouting and we'd disappear into the inky black night. Then we'd creep back one by one and the games would start again.

My father, Matthew Baird Burdon, was a small, dapper man with a shock of white hair, a small moustache, and an even

4

temper (except with my mother). He was an easygoing, fair-minded individual, who did his best to live and let live. He was always a man of strong convictions, if you dug deep enough to find them. He wanted no part of the war, although he wasn't about to make himself a conscientious objector – that in itself would bring trouble. He quietly made sure that he was not involved in the military and served his war years, after I was born, working on the big guns in Dover as an electrician. This was his contribution without actually having to pull any triggers on anybody. He was also an atheist in his own way. He absolutely hated organized religion of any sort, except for the Salvation Army, whom he felt were above the normal religious organizations. They did something for the poor people. (He must have had many a hot soup or cup of tea, in the middle of miserable nights during those war-torn years, provided by the Salvation Army.) He was a steady drinker, but I only ever saw him drunk once. I don't think I ever heard him swear. I guess what I'm trying to say is that he was a good old man and I had a lot of respect for his attitudes.

My mother is also short, well built, hard like a lion but loved by everyone. She has a big, broad face, with large eyes inherited from her mother, Clara. I did some wild things when I was a kid, but I was hardly ever physically punished, something I'm grateful for. I firmly believe that it does no good. I was physically thrashed just once. It must have been one of those periods in my father's life when things were really tough and he found himself at the end of his tether. I walked home in my new bottle-green coat, and new shoes, caked in mud and slime. They were horrified that I should come home from school in such a state; they'd worked hard to buy me clothes. I was so covered in mud and filth I couldn't enter the house. I stood there at the bottom of the stairs, in the yard, tears in my eyes, knowing that I was in for a good hiding. I was never given a chance to explain that on the way home from school I had accidentally fallen into some building foundations. The earth was soft below my feet and I had sunk. I'd begun to panic and scream for help. Someone on a nearby building estate heard my cries and the fire brigade had come and rescued me. That's how I came to be covered in mud.

I didn't forgive my father that beating for years, but it was the only one. Other times, when I got out of line, my mother had a simple answer: she'd just sit on me, her full weight, right on top of me and I couldn't move. My anger would eventually disperse and I'd end up with her sitting on top of me, tickling, turning my tears into hysterical, uncontrollable fits of laughter.

Clara, my maternal grandmother, was a grand old Scots lady. She was as hard as nails and feared by her family. She ruled the roost. But on New Year's Eve she'd sing Scottish folk songs, Celtic and Irish ballads, alone in the middle of the room bringing everyone to tears. My grandfather, her husband Jack, was over six feet tall. Always immaculately dressed, he'd been a miner since he was fourteen, losing his hearing in the First World War. He was billiards champion for the north-east of England. He smoked and swore like a trooper, but I loved him. I used to love to go along with him to one of the two jobs he held down. One was in the flies of the Empire Theatre at Newcastle and the other was backstage at Newcastle United Football Club.

Around the time I was born my grandparents had a small lodging house just across the street from Newcastle's football ground. The clientele was a mixture of the athletic football crowd and the theatrical crowd from the Empire and Theatre Royal. On Saturdays a mixture of the two factions would meet, pints in hand, watching Newcastle United hammer another team into the ground from the rooftop of my grandmother's house. It was a world of pigeon fanciers, snooker champions and back-alley bookies. Many evenings I'd spend with my grandfather up in the flies, high above the performers in the Empire Theatre. Looking down through the drapes, curtains and ropes, I imagined I was the Phantom of the Opera (one of the earliest movies I ever remember seeing).

The First World War had contributed to my grandfather's deafness, but the Second World War made my father's ears more acute. I remember walking home from the swimming baths on a warm summer evening, when I was about four or five. My father and I, towels and swimsuits tucked under our arms, were munching away on a newspaperful of fish and chips. I was skipping along happily, not a care in the world, when suddenly my father stopped dead in his tracks. In the distance somewhere we could hear a shriek that was all too familiar to his ears.

'Good God,' he said.

Quickly he picked me up, my fish and chips spilling all over the road.

'Dad,' I cried out, 'me chips.'

'Never mind your bloody chips.'

He grabbed hold of me and slammed me into a doorway, pressing my body against the wall with his, as flat as possible. The screech became louder: a Stuka bomber. The terrifying howl of the Messerschmitt engines penetrated the night. Then all of a sudden, he stopped and broke out laughing. I didn't know what was going on. I was confused, but then I realized it was a cinema with its doors open on the hot summer night. The Movietone News soundtrack had leaked out into the street, scaring my father into believing it was a real attack.

'I'm sorry, son, I'll get you some more chips,' he laughed. 'I'll away back to the fish shop, we'll get some more.'

Gas masks and bomb shelters were a part of our everyday life. I had a rubber gas mask which was actually a full-size baby crib, with a Plexiglass screen to look through and an airtight seal all the way round. In the early days of the war, I was no doubt carried at regular intervals up and down the stairs of 31, Marondale Avenue during air raid alerts, whether it was an exercise or the real thing.

On the night I was born there was an air raid, although Newcastle got off lightly. We were up in the far north-east, away from most of the prime targets in the south. There were only two air raids in Newcastle, one on the night I was born, one much later when they hit Newcastle's Central Station goods yard. During the latter raid my other grandmother, my father's mother, had a railway wagon and a section of railway line land on her rooftop and backyard. They lived some three miles away from the goods yard that was hit; such was the blast from the German bombs that night.

My father had been born and raised in that house, which overlooked the Tyne. One of my earliest memories is watching a small tug rammed and sunk by a larger ship, one New Year's morning, on the river, right below my grandmother's back window. The crew scrambled for safety in the icy cold polluted waters of the Tyne. Another memory comes to mind, perhaps imagined. I remember creeping across my grandmother's living room in the darkness, peeking through the curtains, a full moon in the sky and the ghostly shadow of a Junkers 88 flying the length of the

'on the night I was born
I swear the moon turned a fire red'
Jimi Hendrix

river, dodging the searchlights, the black and white cross of the Luftwaffe on the side of the plane.

On Saturday afternoons we made shopping sprees over in the town, the West End of Newcastle. I can recall the NAAFI club, the American soldiers, the faces of the black GIs. I recall my amazement at their black skins and strange hair. Other soldiers wandered around in groups, with a small black diamond patch on their uniforms. They were German prisoners who had been put to work on the farms in the outlying districts. They were allowed into town at weekends to do their shopping. There were rumours of a German spy loose in the woods. Everybody was looking furtively for this elusive master spy. I asked my father about this recently. Rudolph Hess had stolen a private airplane from the German High Command and had flown himself across the North Sea and landed in Scotland to find sanctuary. He had tried to negotiate with the British Government to end the war. Then quite suddenly, the hostilities were over. Victory day. I remember the celebrations in the streets as if it were yesterday. I think my first taste of romance was under one of the huge wooden tables that were put out in the streets for the massive celebrations. The tables were draped in Union Jack bunting. Hiding under the wooden tables, I held hands with a small red-faced blonde girl. We sat there, copying our elders, by toasting each other with our victory mugs filled with bright green pop.

Food and clothing were rationed; the currency of the day was cigarettes and nylon stockings. They were impossible to obtain other than via the black market. I watched with wide-eyed fascination as my mother painted false seams to her sister's legs. She was courting and brought home a blond-haired Tommy, whose name was Alf. He was a motorcycle enthusiast. He took me riding and thus began a lifelong love of motorbikes. 'The faster you move, the longer you live,' said my now-favourite uncle, his AJS gleaming in the sun.

The war ended, the boys came home. There were a lot of divorces, a lot of broken families and a lot who didn't come back. There were kids in the West End of Newcastle with no shoes on their feet. There was a lot of poverty and a lot of unemployment. I never felt it; my parents cocooned me. I was lucky. Luckier than most. My uncle Jack returned. He was a Regimental Sergeant Major in the Durham Light Infantry. He'd been off in the East somewhere. He was in Singapore when it fell, and was captured for a while. Before the war he'd been the Head Warder of Changi, the British military prison. Although the war was over he continued to fight. He was a lifer. He returned, via a residency in Hong Kong, in about 1951.

I recall on one of his visits back home on leave, he brought with him a Gurkha corporal and between them they lugged a Bren gun into the house. It was placed on the table at my grandmother's. It smelled of oil and looked like death; I was fascinated by it. I guess I got on the men's nerves, hanging around asking questions, but they couldn't get rid of me. After asking about twenty times to let me see his knife, the Gurkha corporal finally got rid of me. When nobody was looking, he quickly whipped out the weapon. I looked at the fantastic huge blade. His big brown eyes lit up, he took my left hand, and passed the blade swiftly across the thumb, drawing blood. I screamed and jumped back in horror. Tears welled in my eyes at the sight of the blood and I began to blubber. No sympathy from Uncle Jack.

'Let that be a lesson to you.'

(Gurkhas never draw their knives unless they draw blood.) Even worse ... if ever I related this tale to any of my mates, they would laugh it off as bullshit!

My school was nestled between a boneyard slaughter house on one side and Vickers Armstrong Shipyard on the other, so between being sick from the smell of the slaughter house and deafened by the heavy machinery from the shipyard, it was no wonder I was thought to be a slow learner. There were times when one student after another would have to leave the room in order to puke if the wind was blowing in the wrong direction. On hot summer days the windows would have to be closed because of the noise from the welding machines. Between the school on the river bank and where I lived in Marondale, there was a huge field of undeveloped wilderness. Part of it still exists today. Back then, to us kids in the neighbourhood, it was as wild and as immense as the open ranges of the early West that we'd read about and seen in movies. This was the place where the Catholic and Protestant kids did serious battle on the way home from school. Our armouries, our battle plans, and our hideouts were fashioned from the disused and forgotten paraphernalia left over from the war. The countryside was pock-marked with concrete bunkers, machine-gun posts, anti-tank barriers, reels of dangerous rusty old barbed wire. In weekend searches we'd dig up everything from live .303 rounds to hand grenades. Older kids would bring airguns, BB guns and now and again the real thing – .22s. I remember one kid bringing along a .303 Lee Enfield. They'd set up bottles and cans as targets and pink away to their hearts' content.

At school I was an avid comic-book collector and I recall giving away five of my prime American coloured comic-books for one Daisy airpistol. I knew my father would go crazy if he found out. It was my biggest secret to date, as my father was so anti-war. He wouldn't even let me go to see the war movies that most of the kids regularly enjoyed. I can especially recall having a massive argument with him over the fact that I wanted to see James Mason, my favourite actor, in the movie about Rommel. This was strictly forbidden. So the airgun was a hot issue. I returned home from school with it hidden in my jacket pocket. I'd been given one or two pellets and darts to try it out. You pressed the muzzle against a hard surface and the barrel retracted providing the compressed air to project the pellet. When you pulled the trigger the front end of the barrel shot out and the pellet followed.

I was downstairs in the hallway of the house checking it before I went upstairs. Suddenly I noticed a huge bluebottle fly buzzing around in the hallway. The curtains were drawn at the foot of the stairs so nobody could see me. I didn't put a pellet in the spout, I just wanted to down the bluebottle with the rush of air. The bluebottle, aware that he was a potential victim, tried his best to escape. He landed in a corner of the porch window with its opaque fancy glass. I had him cornered. I pulled the trigger, the barrel leapt forward out of the gun and crashed into the glass, smashing it to smithereens. I went white. I heard my father upstairs.

'What the bloody hell – ?'

I was thrown into total panic. I quickly stuffed the airgun down the back of my pants. My father came bounding down the stairs, pulling the curtain back. He saw the broken glass. 'What happened 'ere?'

'I was just trying to swipe a bluebottle, a huge big fly in the window and I tried to swipe it and . . .'

Suddenly his concern changed: 'Are you hurt?' I felt even worse seeing his concern for my safety. When he had established I was all right, he took me upstairs, sternly lectured me and told me that I'd have to contribute money from a paper round that I was about to take to pay for the damage. This was the first of many problems I'd get myself into because of my attraction to firearms and weapons. Next day I took the gun out to the field to one of our concrete bunkers, one of our gun hideouts. I wrapped it in an oily rag and buried it in the ground in a corner. It would be safe there until I needed it.

When enough time had elapsed between the dreadful accident with the bluebottle and the airgun I decided to go and retrieve the weapon. I hoped and prayed it was OK. I met Alan at the crossroads on the way from school and we took off down the trail towards the bunker. The huge half-inch thick iron door on hinges was ajar. Alan and I prised it further open and stepped into the cold, foul-smelling darkness. We pulled the gun excitedly from the ground and dusted it off, overcome with excitement. All we had to do was buy some slugs or coloured darts and dartboard and we could come out here and shoot to our hearts' content and nobody would worry.

My father was never one for going to the cinema. I used to beg him to take me. One day he volunteered. I might not like the movie he said, but I could come along anyway. When I saw Marilyn Monroe on the screen in Technicolour, I understood what he wanted to see. *Niagara*. It had a profound effect, both upon me and my father. We left the cinema in silence. All shook up. We knew we'd seen something special. Marilyn Monroe.

Then television came into our world. When someone in the street got a set, a whole gang of kids would do acrobatic formations in order to get a peek through the curtains at the TV. My uncle Joe got one and invited me across to look at it. It was in the afternoon. When the picture came on the screen, at first all I could see was lines. Then I saw something! Yes, there were formations, recognizable things that were moving. It was an empty cricket pitch, without a commentary. Just an empty cricket pitch, nothing else. It must have been an interval during one of the Test series. Suddenly, a little white dog came on to the screen, cocked its leg, and took a pee against a post. That was the first thing I ever saw on television.

But already it was beginning to change people from a nation of radio tuners and listeners – another hangover from the Second World War – to a nation of watchers, gazers and seekers. Events like the Coronation of Queen Elizabeth II brought families, tribes and streets of people around the tube to watch. One evening the Tiller Girls were dancing, high-stepping in a row. The whole family was glued to the box. The Tiller Girls finished their routine and a man in a bow-tie announced that a brown-skinned girl was going to sing. Black and white in colour. It was Billie Holiday. The black and white blues! I felt as if she was singing just for me, pushing her feelings towards me. It wasn't a very joyous occasion, I think I could sense she was dying. I felt a great sympathy toward her. I fell in love with her, and as soon as she appeared she was gone. The Tiller Girls were back again, high-stepping in their fishnet stockings. My aunt and my mother were making remarks about how disgusting it was for females to show so much of themselves. All the men in the house were lapping it up. But all these images were in black and white, there seemed to be little colour in my life. Except Billie Holiday and Marilyn Monroe.

The first real woman in my life didn't appear on any screen. Newcastle's town moor is a huge expanse of wide-open green, lush land belonging to the freemen of Newcastle in the city centre. Each year at race week, gypsies and show people from all over Europe and the UK assembled there for one week of full-tilt carnival. I approached an old style caravan with wooden cart-wheels, old-fashioned springs, a slatted wooden box with a roof and a stove pipe. Through the rows of sheets hanging out to dry on the line I could see a fireplace with a huge black metal pot upon it. A gypsy woman lifted the metal pot off the fireplace and dumped it into a steaming iron tub. She stepped backwards to avoid the steam burning her face; her blouse was loose and fell open, her naked breasts exposed themselves. I could see the hard brown nipples. I was transfixed. She didn't see me for a minute. Then she caught sight of me standing between the sheets hanging on the line. Her bright brown eyes looked straight at me. She grabbed her breast with her right hand, squeezed it at me and made a face and growled 'Grrr . . . Git'. I took off like a bullet. I never forgot it. I masturbated for the first time over the memory of that incident. It has stayed with me for ever.

At school, I excelled in some things and was dreadful in others. Anything to do with people, like history, art, religion, geography,

I loved ... anything to do with facts and figures, I was easily bored by. I hated exams and when I sat my 11-plus I remember spending the examination period gazing out the window, wondering what difference it would make if I failed. I didn't do a thing through the whole examination and then, typical of me, tried to make up for lost time in the last fifteen minutes. Needless to say, I failed. In the long run it didn't make much difference, it was a stupid system anyway.

So I ended up at Wharrior Street Secondary Modern, a place that struck fear into my heart. I'd heard terrifying things about the school and the name alone conjured up a tribe of warriors that were separate from any other school in the neighbourhood. I'd heard that the initiation rite was to throw all newcomers over the goal-post. I wasn't there to find out. I got there early and hid in a toilet until classes started, and avoided any confrontation. It was a tough school, emphasized by the many occasions I saw police cars outside of the school, coming to pick somebody up. Staying out of trouble presented more of a hassle than learning.

One teacher who did reach me was Bertie Brown, a Second World War veteran with some wonderful stories. Bertie's war was altogether a different kettle of fish to the one that I'd seen on Movietone News or that had been related to me by my uncles. Bertie described his job in the War as a cross between a civil engineer and a combat pilot. We sat there with our mouths open as he talked of his work in the Pacific operation flying on recon. missions on enemy positions; taking photographs, making reports and even landing sometimes on strange South Pacific Islands to take soil samples to see if these places were suitable for huge bomber runways in the future. He had some hair-raising tales of being at close quarters with his Japanese adversaries. I began to think of things in terms of colour, but it was still the old war game.

It was Bertie Brown's magnificent stories about his adventures in the RAF in the Far East at war with the Japanese that made me think in terms of something else other than black and white. Because of the shortage of teachers at the time, Bertie taught several different classes. As well as being our art and mathematics teacher he sometimes taught English too. But whatever he was supposed to be teaching us, we'd just trigger him off by asking him some irrelevant question about his war exploits and he'd be gone. 'I remember one day, I think we were off the coast of Malaya...' and we'd be transported off into his Technicolor wonderworld of war in the South Pacific or Indian Ocean.

It was Bertie Brown who saw something a little extra in me. He put my name forward to be considered as one of the Secondary Modern students to attend further education as an experiment. It's an everlasting example to me of how one individual's interest in another can totally change the course of life. At first I was given a year's test of attending extra studies every Saturday morning at Newcastle University to see whether I was really interested in further education. After completing this course I sat another exam and gained entrance into Newcastle College of Art and Industrial Design, Clayton Road, Newcastle upon Tyne. Here I was to begin a whole new era in my life; a great awakening period for me.

I met other young people who were interested in something more than the black and white of war, the shipyards or the coal mines. I would actually get to be in the same room and share the day's education with girls! I was about to enter the most enjoyable period of my life.

Through all these events growing up after the war, I had instilled in me, and still carry, an enduring obsession with guns. At art school I began to come to terms with it all. But Bertie Brown, the teacher who saved me from the shipyards and the mines, had first appealed to me as a war hero. My first air pistol was a toy, but it allowed me to feel a sense of the power weapons can provide. It does seem at odds with the repulsion I felt when faced with the spectre of war, but I have had to live with this contradiction all my life.

TWO
SCHOOL LEAVER

My mother and father were proud of me. They were relieved somebody actually thought they could make sense out of the crazy things I came up with.

On my first day in class at college, I heard somebody yell from the back of the room: 'Is anyone here interested in jazz?' I turned around and three or four seats behind me I saw the smiling face of John Steel, who would one day become the drummer with The Animals.

'Yeah sure, I am,' I called back. I made a deal with the guy sitting next to John. He moved so John and I could share desks. John had a world of information at his fingertips about jazz and musicians. He would teach me a lot. It didn't take us long to get into heavy rap sessions where he would turn me on to who he felt were the best players.

Johnny Steel and I became close friends. The first year of college was a mandatory basic course in general Art History, which John didn't seem to be too interested in. After the first year he was to take a class in technical drawing which would put him in a different part of the college faculty to me. But we got together almost every lunch-time, and also between 4.30 p.m. and 7 o'clock when the day classes had finished and we were waiting around for night classes to begin. It was during these periods that jam sessions would happen in the common room along with two other senior students who were in the exhibition design class, Winston Scott and Philip Payne.

The four of us evolved into quite a little clique of movie and music *aficionados*. In fact it's safe to say that most of our studies took place in the cinema when we were supposed to be out and about filling our sketch books with drawings and information that would be relevant to our studies. John Steel and I felt that we learnt more from Marlon Brando's performances and from the exciting American movies that were being produced at the time, particularly by United Artistes, than we could in college. After seeing Marlon Brando in his film version of *Julius Caesar*, the following day John Steel was bold enough to turn up with a haircut that was then considered outrageous. His hair was usually combed backwards and trimmed short. Now it was combed forward Brando-style and twisted in small curls around his ear. This, you must understand, was the mid-fifties and for boys to be innovative about their looks was outrageous on any level. He walked through the classroom door to the screams of the girls and whoops and hollers from the class. 'You like my haircut, man? Nice huh, cool. Marlon Brando?'

I could do nothing but admire Johnny's boldness and I began to realize that underneath the surface of this quiet, conservative little guy there was a bold, courageous, innovative thinker. He was also a friend enough to me to guide me through at least one rocky romance. There was a Greek girl in my class. Her name was Maria and she was stacked. Not only was she stacked but she had an attractive, cute little face, long brunette hair half-way down her back and the most shapely pair of breasts I'd ever seen anywhere. She had a steady boyfriend, outside of the college, but that didn't stop me. Every chance I got, my greedy little hands were all over her and of course I was making an absolute fool of myself. John was man enough then to take me aside and tell me in no uncertain words, 'Hey man, what is it between you and this chick? The whole class is laughing at you. Why don't you just cool it?'

I never did. I kept on at her and at every possible chance I was seducing her behind the blackboard in class, in the dark-room during photography lessons, in the corridors, in passing between classes. When John took his technical drawing class and moved away from the studio, I had no one to guide me or restrict my little assaults on Maria. It became particularly hot and sticky during life classes when a nude model was used. Although I must admit, it wasn't just down to me. Maria loved my attention. She loved to get me at it. Just when I'd seem to be behaving myself and getting on with my work, I would pass her desk and she would stop, smile, look at me, swivel round on her revolving chair, move her skirt up past her knees showing a shapely pair of gams encased in nylon stockings, smile and say, 'Ooh, legs!' Of course, I was straight in there, not caring who was watching or what anybody thought. It was disgusting, but I had a great time. So John was off to technical drawing and I began a year's course in commercial art before going on to specialize in exhibition and interior design.

My little sexual assaults on Maria ended rather sharply one day, when she brought her boyfriend up to the college to sort me out. He didn't really have much sorting out to do, as he stood about six foot four. One look at him was enough to make me leave college by the back exit, and from that point on I left her well alone. Ah, hot memories.

Long tall, lanky Philip Payne had an extensive record collection which rivalled mine, and I must admit that Philip was responsible for turning me on to people such as Gene Vincent, Johnny Burnette, Chuck Berry and Little Richard, and as the college was lenient enough to allow us to have a record player in our studios during the day as we worked, there was often frantic activity in exchanging, buying and selling records. But somewhere along the line we had to get it on and perform and get involved in this wild rock'n'roll music ourselves. There were one or two happening clubs in Newcastle at that time. The most happening was the New Orleans Jazz club which was a meeting place for many different musical and artistic fashions in Newcastle. The club was great because almost every night of the week there was a different kind of music. Not only guest stars from down in the smoke such as Ronnie Scott and Ken Colyer's Jazzmen, Chris Barber, Ottilie Patterson, etc., but the local jazz talent of a pretty wide range would play there too.

On Saturday night Mighty Joe Young's Jazzband played with Joe on guitar, Ian Carr on flugelhorn and trumpet, his brother Mike Carr on piano and vibes and John Walters on trumpet and vocals. John is now a top BBC radio producer and worked for many years with hip DJ John Peel. Then he was a student at Newcastle art school. We had the same holidays, and I worshipped him as a top local jazzer. John called me up to sing and the first week it went down a storm. I went back each week and they started paying me in pints of beer. First of all I had begged Mighty Joe Young to allow me to sing a couple of songs. It was unheard of then for jazzmen to allow young rock-influenced punks like me to clamber on stage. But I got along with the band, as my jazz background had turned me on to Count Basie and Joe Turner, the Kansas City Five and Jimmy Witherspoon. His songs had beautiful head arrangements which I learnt from memory and the Mighty Joe Young Band knew by heart. I could holler with them to my heart's content. The band would rip out Basie riffs and we'd tear the joint up.

I bought a copy of Ray Charles' single 'What'd I Say', parts one and two, and played the record till it wore out. There was something very sexual, sinful and erotic about Ray's music. The relationship between the Raelets, his back-up group, and his own voice made it obvious that Ray was having musical sexual intercourse with his back-up singers. It fascinated me. And in my wildest dreams I went looking for the girl with the red dress who could do the birdland all night long. I never ever dreamed that I'd get to see her, not in Newcastle anyway. But I did, in a club called the Downbeat.

I was there with some of the guys one night hanging out, getting loose, getting drunk, having a good time, when in the middle of the floor there she was, a light-skinned negress wearing a tight red dress, jiving and bopping to her heart's content with another girl, another black girl. I couldn't believe it. I walked straight up to her and asked her for a dance. It didn't take me long to get through to her. She was from North Shields which was on the other side of the river and she had to go home by the last train, so I walked her to the railway station. Her name was Doreen Caulker and I fell madly in love with her.

My whole love affair with Doreen was orchestrated by that one record, 'What'd I Say'. It epitomized the way she moved and the way I fell for her. I played the record continually. I sang it continually. I lived it.

I came out of the fish and chip shop one night and was walking up the hill towards a Methodist church hall which was on the cusp of the hill. I was standing there underneath the lamppost, eating my fish and chips which were swimming in vinegar when I heard that riff, that Ray Charles riff, being played at intense volume coming from the Methodist church hall. I couldn't believe my ears. It certainly wasn't the record. I knew it wasn't a recording, but the movement was correct, it was real. I made a bee-line for the doors, paid a shilling entrance fee and stood there in the middle of an almost empty dance floor. At the end of the hall there was a small combo playing, the Thomas Hedly trio – bass, piano, and guitar. I stood there, munching on my chips, listening fascinated. This was the basis of the band that I'd been looking for. After they'd finished 'What'd I Say', to my amazement Thomas Hedly got up, walked away from the piano down to the end of the hall to order himself a soda pop, and the bass player, who turned out to be Alan Price, put down the bass and got on the piano himself, and launched into a medley of Jerry Lee Lewis songs. He played even better than Thomas Hedly and I knew from that moment on that this was one musician I'd have to get together with.

I waited until they'd finished their set, and introduced myself to Thomas Hedly, who looked not unlike Jerry Lee Lewis himself. Alan Price and the guitar player, whose name I can't recall, just hung out in the background and watched myself and Thomas talking. They had been gigging around for some time on the other side of the river doing the club circuits and hoped eventually to get on to the Carol Levis Talent Show.

Before I left I got a chance to talk to Alan Price. I told him that I felt he was much better on piano than on bass. He grunted his thanks and walked away.

The appreciation of this music, my love for Doreen Caulker and my constant reading up on jazz and the history of American black music was pushing me further and further towards a real appreciation of black culture.

I can't place exactly when in early life I got my nut cracked. I had played around at school and had what I called 'sexual experiences'. I could convince myself that I'd actually done it all, that I'd 'gone all the way'. But in all honesty I had not yet been laid by a willing lady in a conducive atmosphere, without interruption, all night. I still had that joyous experience to look forward to. Somewhere along the line, during that long hot summer between leaving school and beginning college, it happened.

There was a jazz club in Nelson Street run by a guy called Mike Jeffery on behalf of Newcastle University Students' Union. It was three floors up on the edge of a big market. It was a hot club. Mighty Joe Young played there regularly, as did the Clyde Valley Stompers. The best of the north-eastern music scene was represented at the club. It attracted a cross section of Student Union and street people. Even the squatters had given it their approval. One of the many characters it attracted was a miner known as Geordie. He was five foot three, dark and handsome, with jet black hair, and dark eyes to match. He had an incredible physique for a guy who put away so many pints of Newcastle Brown Ale.

Geordie had a scar which stretched across his skull from ear to ear, and was only just covered by a new growth of black hair. He had been seriously injured while illegally racing a pit pony underground in a quarter-mile stretch of tunnel. He wasn't wearing a helmet and he struck his head on a crossbeam. He was in a coma for three weeks and hospitalized for a year. Then he was permanently retired and paid off with a lump sum. He was enjoying the benefits of early retirement when I first ran into him at M.J.'s jazz club. He had a girlfriend, a blonde who wore skirts so tight she looked as if she had been poured into them. And she obviously spent a lot of time working on her highly polished fingernails. In the dim light of the jazz club, her blonde hair looked like silver. She puckered her lips, even when she wasn't talking.

I was spell-bound. She was like Brigitte Bardot. Christ, how I envied Geordie and his dark good looks and physique. And being a miner too, all the girls were attracted to him. I thought to myself . . . just wait until I grow up.

That was it, that was the problem, I just didn't feel fulfilled. On one level I'd left school, I could swagger down my own street with the mark of a school-leaver upon me, but when I got with the older guys (and they weren't that much older), I felt like I was standing there at the bar drinking my pint of Newcastle Brown Ale with short pants on. It was horrible, I had to get fucked. Now finding a girl was relatively easy, you understand. I mean I'd seen her, I knew what I wanted, there was always a chance that I could pull it, but where were you gonna pull it to? Now there was the

big problem. Charlie was a mate of mine. He had been in a bad
road accident and lost the use of his right leg. He'd been in hospital for months. Now he was back home and his folks were only
too happy to have him back. They'd do anything for him, even
trust him to stay in the house all alone while they went on holiday
for two weeks. I was glad that I'd confided in him and made him
understand that I had to get my cherry busted. 'Yeah, the house is
empty all this week,' he said, 'just let me know what you come up
with and you're on.' It was up to me now.

I was leaning against the jukebox about one o'clock one
Sunday afternoon in the Spanish City down at the coast. I focused
in on the blonde walking towards me. As she got closer my heart
leapt in excitement. It was her — Geordie's bird. The selec-
tor arm moved along the jukebox mechanism too slowly for
me. I stood there, my eyes open wide with my hands pushed deep
down the pockets of my suit. Come on, come on, come on. It
stopped at 43 – got it! She was now level with the doorway of
McKinley's amusement stand. The needle hit the first groove on
the record. Chuck Berry's guitar leapt out of the grooves, across
the tarmac and pulled her like a magnet towards the jukebox
where I was standing. She peeled off the top part of her suit,
shook her hair in place and said, 'Wow, it's hot'. 'Yeah, innit,' I
said, as I mouthed along with Chuck's lyrics. I now stood straight
in front of her, rocking forward from left to right on my toes, my
huge purple crêpes, their soles bending on the hardwood floor,
whilst my hands and arms and legs kicked into my standard
Chuck Berry imitation. Her blue eyes opened behind the
mascara, the pale purple mouth formed an 'ooo'. 'You're good,'
she said, 'you can rock and roll.' I had to have her.

I searched wildly through my pockets for more coins. Thank
God, a shilling hiding in my back pocket from last night. I
dropped it into the slot and selected 'Blueberry Hill'. As I
searched for another record I was suddenly aware of her perfume
drifting up my nostrils. Then, the killer, I could feel two hard, yet
soft, firm forms just beneath my shoulder blades. Her lips must
have been less than two inches away from my ear when she whispered 'Do you have "Digging my Potatoes" by Lonnie Donegan?'
I was knocked out. She actually considered the jukebox mine. I
turned to talk to her and got the full effect of her daytime make-
up job.

Along with the aromas and the close-up view of her firm breasts pressing against her delicate silk garment, the evil length of her nails, which appeared to be dipped in fresh blood, screamed out to be taken. I couldn't resist it. I kissed her on the lips.

'I'm down here at the coast with me Ma,' she said. 'They're just around the corner. I remember you from Nelson Street. I used to go out with Geordie.' 'Used to?' I said. 'Aye, well he's a bit funny you know. Changeable. Very strange lad,' she said. I blurted out quickly, 'How about this Tuesday? You gonna be there this Tuesday?' 'Aye, I might be,' she said, chewing wildly on the gum in her mouth, looking now towards her mother with the kids who were coming round the corner of the amusement park. 'Well I'll be there, too,' I said. 'How about it?' 'Aye, do you dance, like?' 'Oh yeah, I dance,' I said, lying through me teeth.

Tuesday night. Me best pair of Levis were freshly washed and even had a crease down the front and I wore the new imitation leather black jacket with 'Johnny' written on it. Even when it was hot I didn't take it off. I was posing. When she asked me to dance I nearly died, but when the Clyde Valley Stompers kicked into 'Tiger Rag' I was off and bopping. Suddenly I found my feet on the floor and danced my arse off. Then they played the blues. I danced with the blonde until I was crippled. She recognized the sign. 'I need a cigarette,' she said, grabbed me by the hand and pulled me towards the side of the dance floor. Charlie stood in the darkness with the keys to the empty house in his pocket. Winston Scott promised to drive me over there in his car, and when he dropped us off outside the door underneath the streetlight, it was beginning to rain.

'Eee, it's a nice big house,' she said as she strode down the corridor as if she owned the place. 'What a lovely kitchen.' I stood there in the doorway, slowly taking my coat off. I could see her all the way down the end of the corridor in the kitchen upon a chequered floor. She stood beneath the bright spotlight, everything I'd ever dreamed of. A sexy bitch in the kitchen, somebody else's kitchen, somebody else's bitch. I was being evil at last, I loved it, it drove me on. 'Is there owt to eat?' I said. 'I'm starving.' Peeling the potatoes underneath the spotlight over the sink, her platinum hair now looked like chromium. I hung in the doorway, made small talk with her, opened two beers and just looked in amazement, eventually sliding down the wall next to the door, sitting on the floor, getting a wonderful floor-level view of her shapely legs, trim ankles and full hips, the wonderful colour of her lithe legs encased in her light tone nylons. Sense upon sense, layer upon layer of femininity, I'd never been so close, so involved, been able to take my time, been given the time to see, feel, smell and be fed by a woman.

'Here you are, beans and chips,' she said. 'Do you want any HP sauce?' We sat down to dine, at the almost empty table, beneath the chandelier of electric lights. My bare foot moved across the floor, found her foot, felt the soft calf-hide of the high-heeled shoe, and the silken flesh of her leg. I kept up the pretence of being hungry, ate against my will and trembled holding the fork, scooping the Heinz tinned beans into my mouth, burning my mouth, blowing it completely, scoffing down the plate of food. Before she was finished I was behind her, my arms around her shoulders. 'Going to make a cup of tea, then?' she said, turning to look at me, smiling. She crossed her legs, the top of her stocking revealed, smiled as she recognized the ever increasing lump that was emerging uncontrollably between my legs. 'Now for dessert,' she said, unzipping my pants but leaving me there suspended, smiling again. 'But I would like a cup of tea, dear.' She stood up, smiled, looked at me and moved the back of her hand across my face, her long nails trailing off as she did so, sending electrical impulses through my system. 'Sure, I'll get it.'

I stood there alone in the kitchen, the door open, waiting for the kettle to boil. I went to the cupboard, fetched the teapot, tea-bags, milk and sugar. I turned and looked down the corridor. A white high-heeled shoe lay on its side, beyond that the thin silk wisp of a nylon stocking draped over the banister. I stepped into the corridor. 'Tea!' I yelled up the stairs. Silence. 'You want some tea?' I said. Still nothing. I walked along the corridor, picked up the white shoe, looked at it, then moved on to the stocking. Before I knew it I was half-way up the stairs, following a trail of underwear which ended in the bedroom.

She lay there naked, arms open, one leg up in the air. I quickly climbed out of my jeans and T-shirt and threw them on the floor. She opened her raised leg as I moved in next to her. The light and dark shadows from the shade now illuminating an area of soft, delicate blonde hair. One of her hands grabbed for my rigid bone and the rivers flowed.

I had a quick, sudden, black and white photographic flash of Charlie's mother standing with a desperate look on her face, over a washing machine with a packet of Omo. She hooked me with her right leg underneath my arse and sent me speeding towards her. We lay there together in the soft crisp white pillows and sheets, our tongues frantically searching for each other. Her breathing grew wilder. Her cries of 'Yes, yes, yes' and 'Give me, give me, give me,' eventually slid into a moan, a low and soulful moan. I was drowning in her lips, lost in her hair. Outside of her, at that very moment, the world didn't exist. I was wrapped up totally in this fantasy that I had at last fulfilled.

Eventually I felt warm and comfortable around the groin. She went silent for a few moments, then gave out a strange, long, deep sigh. Suddenly she asked me: 'Well, did you like it?' 'What about you?' I said. 'Are you kidding? I don't do this sort of thing all the time you know? What do you take me for? I asked you anyway, did you like it? Did you get off?' 'Yeah, really, I enjoyed it, it was terrific.' 'Have you done it before?' she asked. 'Yeah, I do it all the time,' I lied. There was no reaction. She let it ride. I'd passed the test, although I must admit I wasn't sure what I'd done. Her strong left hand was now still moving, more slowly, but definitely up and down my semi-hard shaft. I went to work on her breasts. They were wonderful, I'd never really seen a pair of breasts this size this close up before. Although they weren't big, a total handful or mouthful, whichever way you looked at it, I worked hard on them till they changed colour and shape and this excited me even further. I stayed there for what seemed hours. She lay back and enjoyed it and whispered in my ear, 'Again, again, let's do it again!' She sank further into the bed. This worried me. I wondered if it was going to be even harder to find my target. But no, now she was wet and soft.

This time I could really feel what I was supposed to feel. This time it lived up to all those stories that I'd heard at school, in the toilets, behind the wall, over illegal cigarettes, over pints with the guys who worked in the factories. This time I was feeling it. This time I knew it excited me as much as it excited her. I wanted to stay there forever. I pushed myself away from her face, bending my back, my legs searching for the edge of the bed, my feet digging into the carpet. I knew, at that time, that I'd never ever forget what's-her-name, and that this woman, whoever she was, would have a profound effect on me. The role model for just about all my sexual exploits in the future.

After this period, girls seemed to be available everywhere. There was nothing to stop me, or so I thought anyway. My second flame was the wife of a miner, but by this time I was so cocky it didn't put me off – not in the least. 'Anyway,' she explained, 'he works nightshift and sleeps during the day,' which gave her plenty of opportunity to sleep around.

She was a dark, brown, lithe, skinny, healthy-looking girl, who was so proud of the state of her body after giving birth to her first child that she often would just lift up her sweater, fondle her breasts, stare across the room at me and say 'Do you like them, do you really like them, do you really think they're good?' I usually had no reply for such a question, such an action – within seconds I was buried in flesh. She'd follow me to the gigs and if she had to be home on time to see her old man, she'd give me a knee-shaker in the back alley in between sets or just before she caught the last bus home. She went out of her way to make a profound effect upon me and I dug it, she was beautiful and I knew, somewhere along the line, dangerous. I didn't seem to grasp back then what marriage meant to two people, nor was I concerned, and I didn't know it then, but it was time for 'the big lesson'.

She drove me crazy, to the point where, although there were other chicks available, I went looking for her one night. I'd been told to stay away from her on Thursday nights as that was the night her old man was off and they went to a dance together at the Rex, on the seafront of Whitley Bay. I went creeping there. I had to see her.

On arriving I met Red Alex. 'Oh aye, she's here,' he said, 'you mean that dark bird I've seen you in the Go-Go with?' 'Yeah, that's right.' He leant forward, 'She's here with her old man.' 'Yeah, er, that's what I heard. Married, huh?' 'Oh, married to the max. He works at me brother's pit. One of the lads at the face. You want to be careful,' said Red Alex, waving a finger at me as a warning. I must have looked around nervously over my shoulder as Alex laid this warning on me, a tremor of fear running through my system for the first time.

Underneath the red exit sign next to the ladies' toilet I saw her, in a purple evening dress, devastating, every inch a witch. The next thing I was aware of was her eyes – dark, flashing, as she stepped in through the swing doors to the ladies' room. I climbed from the stool and went towards her.

'Me old man's here, you know.'

'Is he?' I said. 'Well, why are you following me, then?'

'I'm not following you,' she said. 'Don't you want to speak to me, just 'cos my old man's here?'

'Why, what are you saying, what are you talking about, you mean he doesn't know?'

'Well, he didn't. I told him tonight.'

'You did what?'

'I had to tell him, Eric, I couldn't go on like this. And he's here and he wants to see you.'

I pushed her aside, fled, heading through the swing doors, out on to the seafront and the beach. I felt the cold, damp sand beneath my feet and turned to head up the beach, to find my path blocked by a huge human form. 'Hold it!' I stopped dead in my tracks.

'Are you the geezer who's singing up in The Downbeat Club in Newcastle?'

'Yeah, I am. What about it?'

'Well,' he said, his voice lowering, 'I hear you know me missus real well. You know, the bird in purple, the one you were just talking to on the way out.'

'Oh, I didn't know she was married.'

'You liar,' he said.

'Oh no I'm not,' I protested and then realized it was hopeless. I'd been caught red-handed. God knows what the sentence would be. There was a stormy silence. I waited, expecting to feel blows raining down upon me, a boot in the groin, or my jaw being blown away from my face – anything.

'Listen, man,' he said, his voice choking, 'please don't take her away from me, just don't encourage her. She's a wild one I know, but I love her, she's all I've got.'

I turned and looked towards him, his fists clenched in anger down at his side. As for me, I felt like I wanted the sand to eat me up or the waves to come and wash me away. He shook me to the point of real shame and from then on I had a new-found respect for another man's property. I'd got the slap on the wrist I needed.

One day in 1958 during a college lunch break I picked up my favourite magazine, *Jazz Monthly*. Flipping through the pages I was excited to see something I'd been awaiting for years. The Antibes Jazz Festival would be presenting no less than Ray Charles and his Orchestra. I couldn't believe it. He'd be down there this summer with the Raelets and his original band. Where to get the money and time and how to get there! The festival was due to happen in the middle of my summer recess, so I had the time and somehow got the money together. I took off on the road with my 'bindle' on my back, in search of Ray Charles. I bought the tickets through the mail order coupon in *Jazz Monthly*. I was on my way to live out a dream. For years I'd sat at home listening to albums like *Ray Charles At Newport* and *The Atlantic Live Festival*. Now I was going to be in the South of France on a hot summer's night actually digging Ray Charles 'live'. It was all too perfect.

I made my way across the Channel and hitch-hiked south. I realized that if the hitch-hiking didn't get better I wouldn't make it in time. I reached the south coast with one day to go. Next day lifts were bad. Nobody seemed to want to give me a ride. I didn't know where I was. The concert was on Saturday night and now it was Friday.

I spent the night in an old railway station, curled up in my bindle. At midnight a car arrived. A Frenchman walked into the station, looked around then was about to leave. I staggered after him and it seemed he was in desperate need of directions. In halting French I tried to help, showing him my road map. It seemed he was going my way. I tried to explain I needed a ride but he tried to drive off without me. I was so angry I grabbed hold of him, yelled and screamed and threatened him. 'OK, OK,' he said, 'you come.' I grabbed my belongings, got into his car and took off. But I knew I wasn't going to make it. I arrived in Antibes just as the last act of the festival had finished. Ray Charles had packed up and gone.

So I had missed my chance to see the greatest innovator and performer in a field of music I loved.

I turned around and started hitch-hiking towards Paris. I was a lone English kid who couldn't speak the language. Yet Paris had been a magnet ever since I had been there on holiday with my parents. I had seen the beautiful city and the freely available

American records. But now Paris was a hotbed of political activity.

I didn't really know what was going on except I guessed if you didn't watch out you could end up in really dangerous situations. Machine-gun-wielding police and riot cops were everywhere. There were mobile police headquarters and busloads of armed militia parked at strategic points all over the city. I arrived in Malakov, the communist area, looking for a cheap hostel. I found one near a sports field, next to a sizeable football stadium. Just up the street from the hostel was a café with a jukebox. A bunch of young French kids used to hang out there drinking Cognac and coffee. Without knowing much of the language I bridged various gaps and made close friends.

The jukebox was heavily laden with rhythm and blues records. I was in there one day eating roe and onion pâté with a glass of red wine. I walked across to the jukebox, put in a coin, pressed the button and up came 'I Gotta Woman'. A cheer went up from the French kids. I turned and smiled. 'Ray Charles, huh?' *'Oui, oui. Vive* Ray Charles!' came the cry. The sax solo came up. One of the kids stood up and imitated the solo. 'Fathead Newman,' I screamed. 'Yeah, *vive* Fathead!' So we made friends and I spent many a good night there getting pissed on cheap red wine and listening to the fantastic records. It seemed the café owner allowed the kids to bring their own records. That's why the jukebox was so heavy.

Then surprise, surprise, one afternoon I was strolling down the street and spotted a huge poster. It was an incredible drawing on a hoarding of the man himself, head thrown back, wearing those dark wrap-around glasses. Ray Charles was appearing in Paris! The rush was on. I HAD to see Ray Charles. Yet once again I missed out. The tickets were expensive. I just couldn't afford them. This was becoming a phobia – a Ray Charles phobia! Was I ever going to see him?

Back at the café that night, I was sitting over a cup of coffee, my head sunk to the floor. My French friends walked in and it seemed they couldn't afford the incredibly expensive tickets either. We were all feeling pretty down. This didn't stop us hanging around the festival site where Ray was performing, a huge auditorium in the centre of town. After the show we watched the people spilling out on to the streets. Then word came down. We couldn't believe it. Ray Charles was going to jam that night in a well-known club. Off we went. We arrived at the club. It was about 11 p.m. The place was packed. We paid a small admittance fee and made our way to the bar, and waited. I saw him arrive. He was tiny, much smaller than I thought.

His strange, animated gestures made him seem mystical ... unreal. The Raelets were there along with members of the band. Ray was helped on stage, sat down at the piano, tested the mikes and jumped into a jam, beginning with 'Rock House'.

Ray Charles was born in Albany, Georgia, USA, back around 1930. He had been blind since the age of six and orphaned as a teenager. He studied music at blind school. He was given a Baptist church upbringing which produced his gospel and soul sound, although he had jazz roots as well. His first big hit 'What'd I Say' cut in 1959 was full of that church-preaching style, with call and response. Ray was a huge influence on so many singers, particularly on the young white singers who discovered Rhythm and Blues in the early sixties.

I'll never forget the night I saw Ray Charles for the first time. The room went crazy. My French friends and I were on Cloud Nine. We couldn't believe our ears. The whole room joined in the chant when Ray kicked into 'What'd I Say'. It was indeed the most memorable night of my life. That night on the way back to Malakov on the Métro it was hot and steamy. Suddenly I felt my hair move around the back of my neck, as if blown by some hot wind that suddenly swept through the tunnels. A few seconds later – a deafening bang and everybody began to run. A terrible sense of panic overcame me as I felt I was going to be trampled underfoot. *Le Bombe Plastique.*

There was enough action going on still to make me realize it was time to leave Paris. I bade farewell to my friends.

The next time I would see them was when I was singing at the Olympia with The Animals.

Au Revoir Paris. I headed back for Newcastle.

THREE
GOOD TIMES

When I think of all the good times
That I've wasted
Having good times.

         Eric Burdon & The New Animals

The early sixties were a great time in Newcastle. But despite all the wild weekends with the girls, the music and jam sessions, there was always the pull of the smoke. London seemed as exciting as Paris to us in the north-east. I used to listen to stories from John Walters, as we sat in a dark corner of the New Orleans club in Melbourne Street. He'd tell how down in the smoke you could obtain without prescription a tiny little pill known as a purple heart. This would take you higher than anything you could experience on Newcastle Brown. And there was hashish to be had, not to mention an exciting music scene. There was something called Alexis Korner's Blues Incorporated. I knew I'd have to be on my way.

 Meanwhile, Doreen, my wonderful black girlfriend, was anxious to get engaged. I remember one night coming out of the Haymarket cinema in Newcastle, out into the cold, wet rain, when I told her of my plans. Come next college vacation I would be off to London in search of fame and fortune. Tears welled in her eyes. She grabbed hold of my arm as the bus for Shields came down the road. She begged and pleaded with me. 'For the sake of my family, Eric, for the sake of appearances if not just for me, please make a promise. Let's get engaged. Buy the ring. It doesn't have to be an expensive one.'

Her intentions were good and I was in love with her and she convinced me. Before I left, I went ahead and bought the ring. It was good to see her smile, but deep down inside of me I wasn't too sure. I knew somewhere down the line I'd have to make my choice. Her, or the road.

Danny and Pat, my two African friends, had left Newcastle to join a band in Manchester. They had extended an invitation to me, John Steel and anyone else who wanted, to come down and see the action. There were promises of plenty of big, exotic women. 'And maybe a bit of smoke, man.' Moss side, Manchester, looked like paradise. At night we cruised the illegal she-beens escorted by Danny and Pat, who introduced us to their friends. It was everything they said it would be. I remember one afternoon at their home in Moss side, watching Danny and Pat rolling up the first hash joint I'd ever seen made.

I didn't really smoke it, but my couple of puffs made it difficult, after leaving the apartment, to get from one side of the street to the other. The stripes on the zebra crossing seemed to move like a magic carpet beneath our feet, and we were aware of the people on the pavement, cracking up and laughing, as we staggered from one side of the road to the other.

Then to London, where I headed for Ealing Broadway, as Alexis Korner was playing with the harmonica genius Cyril Davies and a whole bunch of other faces who didn't mean much to me. It was March 1962. I didn't know it but history was being made. The faces I saw at Ealing would change the face of rock music and become international stars.

Around six the place began to open. I staggered in off the street and made myself invisible in a dark corner and waited for the action to begin. I recall that Dick Heckstall-Smith was the first to turn up, wearing a mackintosh, glasses and a peaked cap to conceal his balding head. Saxophone under his arm, he walked up to the bar, ordered a pint of bitter, strolled across to the stage, opened up the case, took out the sax, and began to tune up.

Then the man himself arrived, Alexis Korner. A smile on his face, he unpacked his guitar and began to prepare for the session, while the rest of the band arrived. Jack Bruce humped his huge double bass. The portly, balding figure of Cyril Davies arrived with a case full of harmonicas, a small amplifier and a pickup attached to the harps. Soon they were storming into action. It wasn't long before the place was packed and the audience was jumping.

A glass of warm beer in my hand, I squeezed my way through the crowd and made my way to the front. It was incredible to hear white Englishmen playing what sounded to me like real American Black rhythm and blues.

I had heard ska, boogie and African rhythms in Manchester but here were whites playing what I considered true American music. The wailing, harsh, shrieking harmonica sound Cyril Davies conjured up really excited me. And Alexis was the first of a long line of authentic-sounding British blues guitar players.

It seemed sitting-in was welcome. People just emerged from the audience, clambered on stage at the invitation of Alexis and leapt into three-chord, twelve-bar blues jams. These sessions featured many players who went on to form the supergroups of the sixties and seventies. Jack Bruce went on to play with Cream, as did another Ealing basement jammer, Eric Clapton. The drummer, Charlie Watts, went on to fame in The Rolling Stones and was replaced at Ealing by Ginger Baker, another Cream stalwart. Alexis helped and encouraged dozens of fine musicians during his career, and the Stones got their first big break when they 'depped' for Blues Incorporated at the Marquee. Sadly Alexis Korner died from cancer in 1984, Cyril Davies from leukaemia in 1964.

Back at the Ealing Broadway Club Alexis and Cyril pioneered, I got up enough courage during the interval to walk up to Alexis, who was leaning against the bar, and tell him I had hitch-hiked all the way down from Newcastle to see the band. He was quite pleased at this. I asked him if there was a possibility of singing with him. We discussed some songs I could try, and he put his arm around my shoulder then wandered off towards the stage to begin the second set.

I stood in the front row, clutching a beer, anxiously waiting to be beckoned on stage. Standing next to me was a tall, skinny, short-haired, full-mouthed schoolboy singing along with the music and moving in time with the rhythm. Jam-time came around. We both jumped on stage.

Alexis was diplomatic. 'How about you two singing together!' Alexis pushed his glasses back, as sweat poured down on to the rag tied around his forehead. The audience yelled and screamed. 'Come on, let's go. Get it on!' 'Do you know "I Ain't Got You"?' I asked. 'Sure,' said the buck-toothed youngster next to me on stage. 'The Billy Boy Arnold thing? Sure, I know it.'

Alexis nodded. 'By the way, meet Mick, Mick Jagger. This is Eric Burdon from Newcastle.'

The band kicked off and we went into Billy Boy Arnold's classic. We went into another blues, staying on stage because the audience wanted it that way. I had a great time and so did Mick. Rhythm and Blues was on its way. The explosion was about to begin.

I spent Sunday night sleeping in Euston station, but it was cold and the police kept moving me on. If I was going to stay in town I had to find a place. I called my girlfriend Doreen, whose brother lived in London. She gave me the address and I went round to see him. Lindy Calder was a wrestler – a middleweight champion. He was five foot seven and built like a brick wall. But he had a really pleasant face and his Irish wife made me feel at home until Wednesday night, when I took off for Soho and walked into the packed Marquee.

There was Alexis on stage, sweat rag round his head, Cyril Davies wailing away and Ronnie Jones taking the vocals. He was the first real black R&B performer I'd ever seen close up except for concerts in Newcastle and Ray Charles in Paris. They didn't count, not on this level, because they were outsiders. This was home grown, something England was pulling together. I noticed, hovering around in the wings being very appreciative and thoroughly enjoying himself, a young Rod Stewart, with his mate Long John Baldry. It was a memorable trip.

I returned to Newcastle full of enthusiasm, going from one friend's house to another, telling them they must see what was cooking in London. I made a special trip to Alan Price's place of employment, a tax office in the city centre. I told him he must go to London. But Alan was very serious about finishing his time at the tax office and making sure he was secure for life. One day, when the time was right, he too would feel the pull of the smoke.

After four years of fooling around, pulling birds and generally having a good time, in my last year of college I knuckled down to some semblance of work in an attempt to pass my final exam, the National Design Diploma, and to the surprise of all – especially my teachers – I passed – not that it did me any good. Because of my attitude I received no help from the teaching staff to secure a job. After all, wasn't it me who conducted the forum on whether students should be allowed to wear blue jeans or not? Or have hair beyond the length of their collar? And it won the support of the student body. The last day at the college, after lunch, I was walking along Clayton Road towards the college campus, and behind me came the new Head Principal, the man responsible for instigating new laws in the college – Mr Foot. He caught up with me and collared me in conversation.

'Well lad, now that you've passed your NDD, I suppose you'll be off to London to see if you can find a place in a commercial house? Or are you going to stay here in Newcastle? Maybe get into a studio up north here.'

'No, I'm off to London to become a rock'n'roll star,' I told him. He freaked. He didn't have to tell me, I knew that was it – I never would get any help from the college in securing a job. So after five years of College of Art and Industrial Design, I ended up navvying for my father on his road gang for the Electricity Board. I took the work on the promise to my father that nobody would know that his son was being employed by the NEB and working on his gang, as he didn't want to be accused of favouritism – and I agreed. It was hard work, but in a way I enjoyed it. I was fascinated by some of the stories of the men I'd run across. One such story really blew my mind. I was in a trench one day next to this skinny, wiry Geordie, and we were talking about machismo movie stars.

I was talking about the exploits of John Wayne. He leant on his shovel and spat into the ground, turned to me and said, 'John Wayne, you can stuff John Wayne. I mean look at a guy like me – you'd never think that I'd survived two atomic bomb blasts.'

'You've got to be joking,' I said.

'I'm not joking, lad.' His story was fantastic. He'd been in Singapore in the Second World War when the Japs advanced, and he'd been captured and, because he was a miner, instead of being put on the Burma Death Railway, they shipped him off to Japan where he spent the balance of the War working in a Japanese pit. With all the Japanese off fighting, they needed his skills to supervise the remaining men on the Japanese Islands, but it was mostly women he worked with. He fell in love with a Japanese woman, married, had a family. He was at the pitface when the first bomb went off over Hiroshima. They brought him to the surface a day later. Nothing but devastation everywhere. He was taken to the nearest hospital, which was in Nagasaki, and he was on the outskirts of the city when the second bomb went off there.

John Walters, who was also working on the gang at the same time, was waiting for a position after he'd left University. We were in the same gang and we used to sing Negro worksongs that we'd learned from Alan Lomax records, in the trenches. The Irish navvies thought we were crazy. John later became a top BBC Radio producer.

My father got really angry that I didn't get a post as a designer that I'd been trained for. But he was glad now to 'see me do *any* kind of work'. I did make several attempts to secure a position in a certain design house only to find that most positions were unobtainable without a letter of recommendation from the college. Even though I'd passed my NDD, I found it difficult. I was still connected to the student body.

Most of the guys in the bands that played in the New Orleans club at weekends were also connected with the colleges. So we were often approached to play college gigs. Some of the students, I'm sure, thought I was still at the college long after I'd left.

One of the students at Newcastle University was the man who would play such a key role in the future development of The Animals. He was Mike Jeffery, 'The Man in the Dark Glasses'. For good or ill 'MJ', as he was known, would loom large in my life. But he was always surrounded by mystery, right up until his death in a Spanish air crash in the late seventies. Jeffery was one of the Svengali breed of pop group entrepreneurs who put their stamp on the sixties, like Brian Epstein, Robert Stigwood and Kit Lambert. Not that Mike was anything like them personality-wise. Quite the opposite. But like them, he was the guy who always managed to be in the right place at the right time. Or if you were one of his long suffering acts, the wrong place at the wrong time.

Mike Jeffery, who eventually became The Animals' manager

and would later manage Jimi Hendrix, in partnership with Chas Chandler, was typical of the first generation of post-war Britons. He was old enough to know all about the legacy of Empire and the old order. But he had sense enough to laugh at its demise and not get hung up on old world ethics. He and others like him moved eagerly into the new age. He was so sixties. Old school but moving into the world of business like a great white shark, devouring everything in its path.

But like the great white shark, Jeffery had hundreds of admirers. Everybody looked to him. They fell for his charm. Here was a businessman who really understood the artist.

I grew to look upon him as the man who would secure my freedom. In fact he used others, less fortunate than himself, to secure his own freedom. Here was a man who could swing into action ... for himself. When the chips were down Jeffery didn't mind getting stuck in and dealing with violence. He stuck his chin out, held his head high and stood his ground. People respected him for that. Mike began his involvement with music by organizing dances at the University around 1958. He wore dark glasses, which he had on prescription, but they were dark enough to be sunglasses. He always dressed in dark colours too, usually a pin stripe suit and old school tie. Mike originally came from London and served in the army in the Middle East. Jeffery at his best was like Peter Sellers playing a spiv. In those early days, I thought he was wonderful.

When I first met Mike I used to beg and plead with him to give my current band a shot at playing support to one of the top bands he booked from London. Of course he never listened and didn't believe in us. He never did until we were actually signed with two top guys from London, Ronan O'Rahilly and Mickie Most. Then he fought, in a most devious way, against all who stood in his way, to grab hold of The Animals.

Eventually we got to play at the Downbeat and the Club A Go-Go, which he opened. And I used to go there every week to see the Rolling Stones, Long John Baldry and many more. This was how Mike Jeffery contributed to the birth of the band. He gave us a place to spawn, to play, to grow up, as The Beatles did in Hamburg, except we didn't have to leave our home town for the experience.

Mike was a dreamer, just like us. Eventually he built up a business empire stretching from England to Paris, Majorca and the Bahamas. We thought he was the ideal manager for The Animals, a guy we could rely on, who would clear the way for our creative processes. We looked on him as our Brian Epstein. In those days we were all virgins. Everything was new and there were no rules. So it was easy for the band that became The Animals to fall under his spell, even though we suspected he was crooked as hell.

He graduated with honours from Newcastle University, in languages and sociology. But he realized, after his experience promoting student hops, that there was more money to be made from the music business than in a more orthodox career. He jumped out of the system, into rock'n'roll.

Mike shut down his first Newcastle club, in Nelson Street, then opened another called the Downbeat. A third was planned, called the Marimba, which was a little more sophisticated. The Downbeat was very downbeat, although it was actually up a flight of stairs. At weekends it was absolutely wild. In 1961 I began to sing with a regular band at the Downbeat, which would eventually become world famous as The Animals.

Chas Chandler, on bass, joined us after playing with several other Newcastle groups. John Steel was on drums, Alan Price on piano and organ and Hilton Valentine was on lead guitar. The beer flowed, the chicks could be pulled and The Animals rocked the joint. Strangely enough Mike Jeffery kept himself at arm's length then. I never really knew much about him, except he ran all the clubs I used to live in.

Mike had several vicious bouncers working for him to protect his interest in the clubs. The most notorious was 'The Turk', who had two highly trained Alsatian dogs, and he was really fast with his head. The dogs were trained so that one stayed at the top of the stairs, the other at the bottom. Troublemakers at the Downbeat would find themselves imprisoned half-way up the stairs.

The Downbeat was a breeding ground for some strange relationships and stranger people. Malcolm Cecil, who played bass there with Mike and Ian Carr's jazzband on a Saturday night, later became one of Stevie Wonder's producers, living in California. There was a special club within a club downstairs, where Dave Finlay would allow musicians and their girlfriends to get strung out on uppers and Newcastle Brown Ale and orgy the night away.

There were some wild females around too. One I knew was a dental assistant. I really used to live out men's mad fantasies when I found out she had the keys to the dental practice. She was tall, blonde, brassy and had a wonderful Cockney sense of humour. She loved me because of my height. It made knee tremblers in the back alley easy. It was all up to me, wrapping my short legs around her lanky gams.

The Downbeat had quite a reputation among musicians all over the country, but Mike Jeffery had bigger plans. When he opened the Marimba it was designed to cater for Newcastle's West End late, late crowd. It was an attempt to create our own Ronnie Scott's.

It had a coffee bar and in the basement was the jazz room. It was cramped, with gas pipes and drainpipes criss-crossing the ceiling. But on Saturday nights it was packed with bodies that provided the main source of heat. So the more the merrier. Most of the music was provided by the Carr brothers. Many's the night I would spend at MJ's Marimba with a bottle of vodka in my pocket, and a cup of coffee, wearing a duffel coat which I never took off.

Then one day a strange thing happened to Marimba. It had been open about a year. It had a better reputation than The Downbeat, and didn't get raided by the police nearly so much, but perhaps because of the Latin connotation, it did less business, unless there was a guest star like Ronnie Scott. One wintry Sunday afternoon I was in The Grapes having a pint with the lads. When the last bell went I decided to take a walk through the city for some fresh air.

My route took me through the back alley which led to the Marimba. Mike Carr the organist came running round the corner, his face ashen. 'Eric, Eric, you won't believe this,' he said, huffing and puffing. 'The Marimba, it's on fire and my bloody gear's in there. Our drum kit, my vibes, everything. The whole lot's gone up in flames!' I ran to the Marimba. It was true. Smoke was pouring from the basement.

The club was engulfed in flames. Within minutes the fire brigade had their hoses the length of the back alley, trying to save the Marimba from destruction. Mike arrived. He looked as if he'd been in bed. He came up the alleyway shaking, and from behind his dark glasses, watched his club go up in flames.

There was an investigation into the fire and the newspapers said the fault lay with the electrical wiring in the basement. I read this news to my father at home one day. He was watching TV but got up, turned off the set and said: 'Listen, I'm telling you now, that guy who owns that place, Mike Jeffery, he's bent. Take it from me. I know because I installed those cables and my wiring didn't start the fire. When I do a job, I always do it right. Mark my words, there's something fishy about it.'

I took my father's words with a pinch of salt. Nevertheless, a few months passed and Mike received a huge sum from the insurance company, and he used it to open a new venue the Club A Go-Go. Funnily enough he approached me, the out of work designer, to design the club for him. I agreed as long as we could get a gig there with our band!

He looked at me from behind his dark glasses, pushed them backwards on his nose and said: 'Well I don't know. We'll see about that. Help me get the club together first. I've got a lot of money to play with. You can do almost what you like. Let's start on the drawings and plans right away. Submit them and I'll tell you what I think.'

That was it. I was on my way with my first real design job. I began work. Winston Scott and Philip Payne helped me out when things got rough. I couldn't handle all the work myself. While all this was going on there was an event of major importance. The Beatles came to town. They played the Newcastle City Hall. I drove past to see what The Beatles gig was like. They hadn't yet broken nationally. I couldn't believe my eyes. The queue was three deep, twice round the building. I knew something was going to break real soon, real big. The music I liked so much, the groups that had it in their grasp were really going places.

After what seemed like an eternity of planning and paperwork, carpentry and furnishing, the new club opened. It was one flight up on Percy Street, Newcastle. I was quite pleased with the design. There were two huge rooms, one a concert hall with bar and offices. A carpeted seating area accommodated 300 people, with a small dance floor and stage. The other half of the club was for younger members, with a soft drinks bar and larger dance floor with a capacity of 500.

On Saturday nights it was always filled. The younger set danced until midnight. The other room, catering for the older customers, served as much booze as fast as was possible. Mike booked only the best artists of the day, like John Lee Hooker, Sonny Boy Williamson, Graham Bond, The Yardbirds and The Rolling Stones. We got a chance to play there on weekends, then raced across town to play at the Downbeat as well.

We built up quite a following among local fans, and enjoyed watching, performing with and sometimes backing the other artists who came through the club, like John Lee Hooker and Sonny Boy Williamson. During one of these sessions, Graham Bond was playing at the club. He saw us playing, went back to London and reported to Ronan O'Rahilly, the guy who started off Radio Caroline, that he'd seen a great band in Newcastle and they should be investigated, with a view to management. Ronan appeared in Newcastle to watch us with Giorgio Gomelsky, manager of The Yardbirds. Ronan was responsible for taking us to London. We went down and did some exchange gigs with The Yardbirds. These were our first gigs in London. It was around this time that we sat down in a pub and agreed to call ourselves The Animals, based on the most engaging character of a local gang, called The Squatters. Animal Hog epitomized what we wanted to represent with our music. Total freedom, a little bit of anarchy, a lot of wildness and a lot of good times. We became The Animals, synonymous with the Club A Go-Go. The club became the crossroads for all the youth of Newcastle, in their basic street uniform, blue jeans, long hair and navy blue duffel coats. They would queue outside every Saturday night to join the madness.

The band was beginning to move around a lot, so we had to find a guy to take care of us and the equipment. The most engaging character I've ever known, James 'Tappy' Wright, became The Animals' road manager.

From the money we earned from all these gigs we put down payment on a blue Commer van to transport the band and its equipment. It was vital as we were about to tour the country, stepping out beyond the borders of our home town.

It seems inconceivable to me now that the early Animals' equipment and personnel were moved in their entirety in that one van. In addition to Alan Price, Hilton Valentine, John Steel, Chas Chandler, myself, roadie Alex 'The Red' Taws and tour manager Tappy Wright, it carried amplifiers, guitars, a small PA system, and our personal effects. Somehow we packed it all into our trusty blue Commer, and we were off and running.

Tappy picked up the blue Commer brand new in mint condition one Monday morning and returned it the following Thursday afternoon. The garage couldn't believe it was due for its 6,000 mile service already!

Some of the early touring was hell, especially from a road manager's point of view as there was no agency organization then. We would be booked in Newcastle, London and then Liverpool the next night, and then up to Edinburgh and back to Newcastle. They were impossible schedules to meet, but with Tappy Wright at the wheel, we seemed to pull through and it often seemed that those booking us couldn't care less as long as the money was there. Before moving to London, we did a mini-tour that gave us our first break on national radio. BBC's Saturday Club 'live' put us in front of the whole radio audience of Great Britain.

When we pulled into Liverpool with our brand new Commer van, we had no idea that when we left the next night, the paintwork would be completely obliterated with messages scrawled in various tones of red, pink and even purple lipstick, from girls, along with telephone numbers and somewhat obscene remarks.

There were times when we returned home to Newcastle, and we would be so tired we'd come off the end of the motorway, miss the snow covered island and just go right over the top, past the police patrol car in the lay-by. The next day we'd get a message from the Chief of Police through the Club A Go-Go's office. 'Hey, tell your lads the next time they return home to take it easy coming off the motorway!'

One time when leaving Newcastle to go to a gig in London, we searched around town for purple hearts to keep us awake. They couldn't be found. Newcastle didn't have the same drug scene as London. Anyway some girls provided Tappy with some pills that weren't purple in colour, they were sort of rosy-red. He was told that they were just as strong and would do the job equally well. He stayed wide awake all the way to London, got to the other end and found out that he'd been given female period pills.

The gigs were coming in hot and heavy. Some really violent, some really enjoyable, and we were about to go into the studio to cut our first single 'Baby Let Me Take You Home' with Mickie Most, who moved in as producer.

There was a shuffle for management – even to this day it's not quite clear to anybody what really happened, but Ronan O'Rahilly moved out of the picture – Mickie Most came in and we suddenly had a Ford Galaxy station wagon, Canadian built, a superb machine, for the band to cruise around in.

We went gigging in luxury and at high speed, from London to Manchester in two hours. This was cruising in comfort compared to the old Commer van. But Tappy kept on losing mirrors and headlights and the car got covered in lipstick. He was really the sixth member of the band, and we wouldn't have gone anywhere without him. A good road manager is as important as a good lead singer anyday.

It seemed Newcastle was behind us and London was the home base from then on.

Hilton Valentine, Tappy Wright and myself took up residence as close to the centre of all the action as possible, in Earls Court. Chas and Alan moved to the quieter regions of Holland Park, and Johnny Steel just hung out where it was convenient because every chance he got, he legged it back to Newcastle. First we lived in Redcliffe Square for a year, then moved on to 64, Cranleigh Gardens, which became known as The 64 Club because the front door was always open. Or the front window!

When we weren't gigging, recording, doing TV or being promoted, we hung out in the clubs. London was full of them. They were all in fierce competition, trying to pull each other's customers. Musicians in particular would be approached to put in a VIP personal appearance. The lure was free drinks, nothing to pay at the door and all the birds you could pull. What *more* could you want? The scene moved from club to club, night after night.

One of the most *in* of all the in places was The Ad Lib off Leicester Square. It was an upstairs room frequented by The Beatles and all the élite of London's new pop royalty. The club had a jiving Black cook-cum-disc jockey who would be in the kitchen one minute frying steak 'n' eggs, and next minute boogieing across the floor to the record decks. He'd spin tracks by the Stones, Beatles, Otis Redding, James Brown, Bobby Blue Band and Wilson Pickett.

Another less élitist venue was the Scene Club in Ham Yard which was one of The Animals' first London gigs and became a haunt of pill-popping Mods. Other clubs included Alexis

Korner's Rhythm'n'Blues club in Ealing; the brothers Rik and John Gunnell's Flamingo in Wardour Street, and the Bag O'Nails near Carnaby Street; the Scotch of St James, the Kilt in Soho and the Cromwellian in the Cromwell Road.

One night at the Cromwellian it was Carmen's birthday, Georgie's girl. It was wild, man. Yes, sure, Clive was there, that's Georgie Fame to you. They were all there. Eppy, Rik Gunnell, Ringo. Ringo was dressed as an Arab sheikh, perfect with his new beard. Eppy was a kind of ballet dancer-cum-clown, with one half of his face white, the other black. He was sprayed over the top with gold and wore a ballet skirt. Rik was a baby, a huge nappy round his massive body.

Paul McCartney was dressed as a Southern lieutenant from the Civil War. Very touching. Looks good with the moustache and cigar. Terrific.

I saw Giorgio. He was – guess who? Rasputin, the mad monk. He looked really menacing with the huge beard. Oh yes, it was a fantastic party. Carmen? Spanish of course. She wore a real Spanish dress, very traditional stuff, the real thing.

The food was OK too. The place was packed, but there was room enough to dance. Carmen's birthday was a night to remember. I drifted in wearing false glasses, a moustache, a business suit, collar and tie. It was perfect. Nobody recognized me. It was three floors of fire that night in the Crom.

Giorgio gazed with fiery eyes at the frivolity. Fingering his dark beard he took a drink from a pewter mug of red wine. 'Look, they're going to make fools of themselves. Lovely!' I turned to see Eppy and Rik in the middle of the dance floor, Rik like an overgrown cherub, a huge grin on his face, trying to embarrass Brian Epstein. But Eppy was dressed to the hilt and stoned too. In such merry company he wasn't going to be embarrassed, not tonight. Courageously he strode on to the floor, taking up the challenge like a prima donna. Rik grabbed for Eppy, missed and slipped on the floor. Roars of laughter from the watching crowd. Eppy danced on, nose in the air. He was having a whale of a time. Rik wasn't finished. Eppy wasn't going to get away with that. They began to roll like two big babies on the dance floor together. Before it got too disgusting I stepped in with a fire extinguisher, one of those foam ones.

Rasputin was jealous when he saw the fun I had. The crowd were ecstatic. Rik and Eppy looked like two babies playing in a bath full of foam. Rasputin stepped forward, pulling me aside and yelled in my ear over the hoots, and hollers and music: 'Burdon, if you want to play with fire, play with *real* fire. Don't put it out, start one!' He produced a lighter from his trouser pocket, walked across to the bunting and decorations hanging from the wall and set fire to them. Soon firemen were coming through the entrance wearing yellow waders and helmets, hoses at the ready. As the punters poured out into the street they either panicked or giggled. I shared an amylnitrate capsule with a friend as we made ourselves scarce.

Our first London gigs were at the Scene Club. It was tucked away in a tiny cobblestone back alley called Ham Yard, and nowadays it's a clip joint. We played there during its transitory period from being a traditional jazz stronghold, developing into a rock club.

It was frequented by US servicemen, Air Force, mostly black, so needless to say the DJ was very hip. The club had a fantastic record collection. All the latest US imports.

Incredibly vicious fights would break out in the courtyard leading to the club, often between US servicemen and Jamaicans, in dispute over a girl. You had to be on your toes, but it was exciting. Purple hearts were the buzz of the day and could easily be scored anywhere in Soho for a few pence. Now and again the sweet smell of marijuana drifted through the room when we did gigs there, adding an air of mystery to the excitement.

The dance floor area in the centre of the club was tiny and would hold maybe 200 people standing up, jam packed like sardines on a Saturday night. The comfortable night would be Tuesday when there would be about twenty to fifty people with room to dance to the great sounds. Needless to say the stage was even tinier. There really wasn't enough room to move and I often found myself performing on the floor, at the same level as the dancers, sometimes joining in with the dance. By the time the drums and the keyboards were set up there was just enough room for Hilton and Chas to find a niche on the stage – no room for me.

So I disappeared beneath the heads in the front row. The main reason for this was there was a huge white elephant of a grand piano on stage, a throwback to when the joint had been a night-club. The jazz musicians had always arranged themselves around this monster.

One night I vented all my frustrations and anxieties on the great white piano. This was probably triggered by a purple heart, I must admit, but I was feeling good and I wanted to be seen as well as heard. I was wearing thick-soled cowboy boots, so why not? I clambered on to the top of the white monster. I should mention here that its one and only function was for people to put empty glasses on, so when I climbed up and started jumping around in time to the music I was crushing drinking glasses to powder beneath my feet into the top of the grand. The audience loved it, they went berserk. I jumped so long and so hard, egged on by the boys in the band, particularly Alan Price who hated this white monster with a vengeance. It didn't ever actually play, you see, it was just a prop, but it was there and they weren't going to move it, so I had to move it for them. I continued to jump up and down, egged on by the guys – the top of the piano gave way and splintered. My boots made it through to the other side and struck what remained of the strings beneath. It made a lovely noise, especially with the microphone stuffed down there. Alan Price, a huge grin on his face, held one of the Shure microphones next to the strings as they popped and twanged. Three huge bouncers made their way towards the stage through the crowd, pushing people aside, wondering just what the hell was going on. By the time they reached me the piano was demolished with the help of most of the audience. The bouncers got there and saw what was actually happening in front of the stage, and they took it all in good fun. They too joined in the mêlée against the hated piano.

Georgie Fame was a regular face at the Flamingo. West Indians loved Georgie. He produced a black sound which in the mid-sixties appealed to the ear of the immigrant Jamaicans. They loved him, he was the king. The Flamingo Club was owned and run by two brothers, Rik and John Gunnell. They also had an agency and booked most of their acts into their own club, when they weren't booking any place else. Some of the acts that they handled and played at the Flamingo and eventually at another club of theirs, the Bag O' Nails, were Georgie Fame and the Blue Flames, Chris Farlowe and the Thunderbirds, Zoot Money's Big Roll Band, Geno Washington, Ronnie Jones and John Mayall's

Bluesbreakers. Rik and John ruled the roost with a certain kind of vicious West End flavoured humour which, depending on how you rubbed them, could manifest itself into your actual heavy games. They were loved and admired and hated by many people.

John Gunnell volunteered to be MC at the All-Nighter, a true labour of love. I am sure he could have been one of Britain's best stand-up comics. He didn't care if audiences stayed or left. But they loved his poisonous tongue. He was a star in his own club and could take on all comers from pilled-up Mods to Jamaicans, Americans or the Law.

One night there was a police raid at the Scene Club, only four blocks away. I was at the Flamingo earlier than usual, around 11.30 p.m. ready for the All-Nighter. The place was just filling up. Lionel, the Scene's manager, phoned John to warn him the police were on their way round.

John leapt on stage. Chris Farlowe's band stood with dismay on their faces. 'Hey man, not in the middle of our set, come on, we were just getting in a groove.'

John snapped back. 'The cops are on their way for a raid. Gimme a break.' He turned to the audience. 'Blow whatever you've got. The fuzz are on their way. Swallow it, drop it, flush it down the john. I don't care how, but get rid of it.'

All around me Jamaican guys stood up and began emptying their pockets, pushing nodules of black hash into their mouths, and chewing like cows. Purple hearts rained on the floor. Suddenly a guy wearing tennis shoes and blue jeans and a white sweater, jumped out of the audience on to the stage and grabbed the microphone from John's hand. He waved a warrant card and yelled at the top of his voice. 'OK, this is a police raid, nobody move.'

John grabbed the mike back and began rapping in a Jamaican accent: 'Stay cool, just blow that shit, eat it up good.' The uniformed police came pouring into the club. A sergeant, his neck red, purple veins standing out on his face shouted, 'OK you, come down from there. And you lot, off the stage.' He waved at Chris Farlowe's band. Baritone player Nicky stood with hash-glazed eyes shaking his head. 'Shit man, right in the middle of my solo. I've been waiting an hour for this. Don't you guys have any tact?'

The young undercover cop was jostled to the back of the room by irate West Indians, while police boots crushed to a fine powder the purple hearts scattered all over the club. The dust settled on their blue uniforms as they coughed, spluttered and yelled. John kept on rapping until the cops came and carried him bodily off the stage, and up the stairs to have a little chat, back at the police station.

One night Eric Clapton came by to see T-Bone Walker, one of his idols, play, and stood watching from the dressing room.

T-Bone, apart from being one of the really great technical guitar blues players, was from the old school. He had a huge telephone cord on his guitar which allowed him to move freely out into the audience, away from the band. Somebody on the stage amongst the musicians must have given T-Bone the word that Eric Clapton had come in to see him play, because during his next extensive solo T-Bone left the stage, entered the dressing room, came down the stairs and pinned Eric Clapton to the wall as he played, fingering the guitar silently but mouthing the notes to poor Eric, who was nailed to the wall with fright. Out in the audience the people had a totally different picture. They weren't quite sure what was going on. There was the back-up band playing away and T-Bone's solo could be heard blasting out of the amplifier, but T-Bone's cord just disappeared. Little did they know that he had Eric Clapton up against the wall and wouldn't let him go until he got his point across. 'I'm the original, I'm the main man, get it, get it, get it?'

Another night a blonde stripper strolled into the backstage area at the Flamingo. It was during one of Chris Farlowe's intense blues sets. Chris was out there on the stage wailing, the audience were thrilled. He held them in the palm of his hand. 'Well, baby, baby please don't go.' In the dressing room to the side behind a headful of purple hearts, vodka and Fanta, we were getting drunk and crazy. The big blonde stripper went into her thing, egged on by Rik and John.

She ended up naked – her clothes draped around the dressing-room area. She was bumping and grinding away in front of three or four men at close quarters. It was obvious from the number of slaps, pinches, kisses and remarks that her show needed more space if it was really going to get off the ground. Inevitably it overspilled on to the stage where Chris Farlowe was playing. Poor Chris, his eyes closed, sang 'Baby, please don't go' whilst behind him emerged this dotty blonde, naked except for her high heeled shoes, her pink tits bouncing as she moved across the stage waving her arms in the air, the whole band cracking up, just holding the beat together, just singing on, while the audience killed themselves laughing. Cruel joke, poor Chris. But if Farlowe had been in the back room and not on stage he would have been the first to muck in.

There were magic nights at the Flamingo, nights when the Americans and the West Indians wouldn't care about whose woman was whose or which territory belonged to which faction. One night I took Nina Simone down there. She looked at me with a frown, saying come on, Eric, you're kidding, you're going to show me some of my folks here in London? When she saw the Flamingo she agreed it was like a journey through her past. The cream of London society turned out to this underground dump to see some of the best R&B bands in Britain. I caught George Harrison a couple of nights down there on the run from Beatledom, a bit of escape to what must have seemed like reliving a bit of Hamburg. And at the end of those All-Nighters it was a truly incredible feeling to emerge from the darkness of the club. Saturday night had gone, it was cold, fresh and light outside in the garbage-strewn streets of Soho. I'd head for the first newspaper stand, pick up the first edition, go for some Indian food, go home to bed and sleep Sunday away. Flamingo weekends.

Now I had no doubts whatsoever. The band had made a move to London and I was spellbound. Although still deeply in love with Miss Caulker, I had made my choice, her or the road. I became a travelling man.

FOUR
WHEN WE WERE A GANG

The band was firmly entrenched in London, its home base. Newcastle was nothing more now than a place to visit, when we had time off. Ronan O'Rahilly had been moved out of the picture and Mike Jeffery was securely in position as manager of The Animals, wheeling and dealing his way towards a record contract for the band. The blue Commer van stitched its way the length and breadth of the United Kingdom, with Tappy Wright at the helm. Some of the gigs were easy and we were accepted. At some gigs, we were adored by the girls, hated by the guys. At others, we were hated by the girls, worshipped by the guys. Some of the gigs were like Maryport in Cumberland. You could tell it just wasn't gonna go right, from the minute we stepped through the door.

Several gangs of Teds, and leather-jacketed blue-jeaned rockers had positioned themselves in various corners throughout the hall. Tappy was setting up the equipment with the help of some of the locals. I looked out through the stage curtains, through the blue haze of smoke that filled the room. The place was filling up for a bit of Saturday night madness. One of the locals helping us with our equipment remarked 'It's quiet tonight – it's not usually this quiet.' I overheard Tappy talking to him. 'Doesn't seem quiet to me, mate, looks like we're gonna get a full house.'

'Yeah, but it's relatively quiet.' The guy went about his business. We understood what he was talking about when we started to play.

As soon as we kicked into our first number we understood. This place Maryport, they didn't hold dances, they held fights. Rival gangs, along with their girlfriends, waded into each other. It was an amazing mêlée, and yet somehow the band was encased in a vortex. We didn't get touched. We played, they fought. I guess that's the way it was for every group that appeared there. As our musical set accelerated in its excitement, so did the violence, and when we reached the peak of the set with an Isley Brothers number called 'Shout' in which the tempo accelerates to a frantic pitch, and a change of key during the chorus, it put everybody into the outer reaches. A fire axe came off the wall. Somebody in the front row started wading into a rival gang with this huge fire axe. Blood was everywhere, all over the floor. There was nothing else to do but just accept it and get on with it, so we played in accompaniment to the slaughter.

There were other towns too, like Leeds, for instance. We just couldn't seem to get a grip on the audience at Leeds. I remember standing there on the stage, several people in the audience hurling abuse. 'Go back home where you came from, you Geordie bastards.' I couldn't stand it so I jumped in from the stage. With the power of the microphone, I thought I could do no wrong. 'Go fuck yourselves, you silly cunts!' I yelled. 'If you want any trouble, we'll see you backstage.' 'Yeah, go on you Geordie pigs.' At the load out we were surrounded. There was only one thing to do. Punch your way out. There we were trying to be cool after the gig surrounding the Commer van, everybody nervous as hell. An ever increasing circle of up-tight Teds stood jeering.

We all knew it was up to us to begin this dance. Chas, the biggest of us taking a page out of The Turk's book, who he'd seen in action many times at the Club A Go-Go at Newcastle, waved a finger at one of the Teds, the most obnoxious one.

'Er, excuse me, can I have a word with you a minute?'

The guy stepped forward. Chas, as if he was about to begin a conversation, put his head to the floor then brought it suddenly back up and the guy's nose splashed all over his face in a sudden burst of red blood. We jumped into the van, the sliding door closed. Tappy gunned the engine. We took off into the night.

Some of the Teds who had a car, a Ford Cortina, jumped in and gave chase and there was a tyre-screeching pursuit through Leeds until we made our getaway.

During the tour we got the good news that we'd been signed to Decca for a year. Mickie Most had signed a production deal and we went into the recording studio and cut our first record 'Baby Let Me Take You Home'. Mike Jeffery had also secured a contract with the Harold Davidson Agency and Dick Katz in that office was personally looking after our bookings. With the power of the agency behind us and the power of our music, our first record went to 15 in the national charts. The gigs got better and so did the chicks.

We were all happy to find out that Peter Grant had been appointed personal road manager of the band and Tappy Wright's duties were moved to taking care of the equipment only. Peter Grant, what a guy! He looked like he was ten feet wide and six feet tall, but he was very gently spoken and we all loved him. An ex-wrestler, he eventually became one of the most powerful men in the music business.

The birth pains of The Animals were far from over. The closeness of travelling, crammed into the Commer van, or eventually into the Ford Galaxy; hours of travelling together, being in the same hotel room together, would cause tempers to flare over the most ridiculous things. I remember one occasion when we stopped for petrol on the motorway. The guys left the car, wandered across to the service station to pick up some magazines, newspapers and sweets. When Chas got back into the car he sat in Hilton Valentine's seat. Hilton came back. He was furious. 'What are you doing in my seat?' Chas answered, 'Whadyya mean, your seat? It's a car, it's got seats in it. You're supposed to sit in 'em. I'm not sitting in your seat.' 'That's where I left me bag, you cunt!' 'Never mind that, you bastard, just get in the car, we're late for the gig as it is.' Hilton protested by sitting down on the grass verge on the side of the M1. People passing by couldn't believe it. There we were stranded. Each of us sitting in the car, silently reading newspapers and magazines whilst Hilton sat on the grass verge beside the car.

In those early days The Rolling Stones, The Beatles, The Yardbirds, Ike and Tina Turner, The Supremes, Otis Redding, James Brown, Chuck Berry and Little Richard, Ray Charles, Bo Diddley

The Animals original band

and many more stars were out on the road together. An amazing multi-coloured pattern was woven by musical performers from both sides of the Atlantic continually touring behind hit records which they had to promote. Rock'n'roll covered the air waves across the globe.

We all ran wild in a world that was closely scrutinized and monitored by the press and the media in general. In between all this we tried our best to entertain people and generate a lot of heat from the music that men like jazz promoter Norman Granz loved to hate. If jazz was the rough diamond, then rock'n'roll was the seam of coal generating heat and flames. I proclaimed myself a rocker rather than a jazzer and was off on a never-ending road to raising hell and bringing enjoyment to the millions. Even our roadies were interviewed.

The NME newspaper, in the shape of Keith Altham, hot-shot reporter, caught up with hot-shot roadie Tappy Wright in an exclusive interview. They met at a pub in South London before a gig. Keith, with his notepad, big pen and mackintosh looked like a young Bulldog Drummond hot on the case. He took down the immortal words of Tappy Wright, road manager *extraordinaire* of The Animals, straight from the horse's mouth, and fed it hot to the rock'n'roll press. Keith was quick to point out that he had seen the equipment in the blue van outside on the street and it was ten past eight. Why hadn't Tappy unloaded the equipment at the gig for the band ready to go on stage? Tappy explained. It was his technique to arrive at the gig as late as possible, push it to the legal limit and have a concrete, watertight alibi already on his lips. The management would have some heavies help unload the equipment in an emergency. If he were on time and got there at four in the afternoon, Tappy would have to move in all the equipment himself. Tappy was pissed off to find out that, once it had been printed in the NME by Keith, he could never pull this stunt again. So we added a second road manager, Alex 'The Red' Taws.

Alex was a red-headed, bespectacled Trotskyite, a real radical and his radicalism stemmed from his love of and knowledge of black music in America which he studied in depth. It all comes down to one thing: pain imposed on others by others, on behalf of others for other brothers other than the brothers. That kind of game.

Yes, Alex was deep into it. At every opportunity he would take time out to sit down and engage in a physiological, metaphysical, political, blue-based conversation with any member of the band.

On the whole Tappy and Alex the Red were a mighty little team and they got things done for The Animals for a long time.

Tappy Wright later became witness to all The Animals' adventures and misadventures, when we experimented with every kind of narcotic and 'high'. It made Tappy realize that he, above all, had to stay straight while the band got wild. It was down to one night when he was at a hotel minding Hilton, who had begun experimenting with LSD. Somehow, Hilton's acid got into Tappy's mouth. What a mystery, we'll never know how. But he ended up in the wee hours of the morning at the Tower of London. There he was on a grassy knoll next to the Tower witnessing the Spanish Armada sailing stealthily up the Thames to capture England in the middle of the night. Hands up, England! No, no, he wouldn't stand for that, not Tappy. He fought the Spaniards single-handed and beat them. He was knighted by the Queen and then went home at six o'clock in the morning and told the girlfriend. She didn't go for it. No, thank God for us that Tappy realized that early on in the game it was up to him to get us to the gig so somebody had to stay straight – and he did.

I can recall one period that Hilton went through when he had special sunglasses made out of car reflector lenses. Two huge red plastic perforated lenses were inserted into some old granny glasses frames. Hilton had them stuck on his head for around seven or eight months. He wouldn't come out of them. It was obvious that he couldn't see where he was going – Tappy had to lead him almost everywhere. But continually stoned on acid, watching the light display coming in through the lenses, he must have been some place else for a long time. It was really bizarre. Suddenly we developed a blind member of the band, a little blind man who followed us everywhere. Hilton never took those glasses off. On stage he would be wild. The more elaborate the lights were at gigs the wilder he got as the light crashed in through his plastic reflector lenses wrapped around his skull. The fans loved the look of the spotty-faced, white-skinned young punk with his hair sticking out underneath his greasy hat, a huge grin across his face, jumping up and down, his head swirling from side to side, glasses on the end of his nose.

I remember the time the glasses came off for good. Tappy, myself and Hilton driving north from London to Newcastle for a weekend off. We had the Ford Galaxy to ourselves.

The rest of the guys were staying in London. We headed north and we had just finished a gig the night before. All three of us were really tired. Hilton was asleep in the back, or staring at the road lights flashing by in his round glasses. I had been driving and could go no further. I stopped by the wayside and tried to get Tappy, tired as he was, to drive the last few miles. It was beginning to snow. I couldn't wake him. Hilton's head popped up from the back seats, the red reflector glasses staring at me.

'I'll drive, mate.'

'No, come on, Hilton.'

'No, I'm OK, I'll drive – I'm wide awake. I've been asleep all the time.'

I couldn't quite believe what I was hearing and I really didn't trust him. It seemed like months since I'd seen his eyes. The glasses came off. He looked me straight in the face. I looked into his eyes. They did seem quite clear, even though his nose was marked red. I was so tired I couldn't argue with him.

'Here, take the wheel and I'll get in the middle seats.' I kipped down next to Tappy, 'But go easy, man, it's starting to snow.'

He made his way round to the driving seat. I climbed into the row of back seats. We took off and struck out for Newcastle.

It wasn't long before I was nodding off into a pleasant slumber. I was awakened by a sickening dull thud like a solid block of concrete was trying to burst through the floor. I stood up. I could see Hilton's head and hands staring out into the night at the end of the long American vehicle. In the headlights I could see a stretch of whiteness. Snow all around, but it was too white to be a road. It was a field. When I looked out of the window again I saw that the field had been replaced by a line of trees, then by something else. Christ, we were going round in circles. We spun slowly in the air about five times, then Tappy's head popped up from the middle seat. A huge pylon crashed through the windscreen in between Hilton's head and the steering wheel. It slid through the length of the car. Tappy ducked just in time. As if in slow motion the huge plank of wood missed his head by an inch and headed for mine. Somehow I avoided it – but it went the length of the car and came to a stop in the back. Crash! Then the car came to a stop. We must have been yards away from the nearest road, pointing in the wrong direction. The car was a total write-off. Nobody could see or hear our cries. We were stuck there for what seemed hours in the freezing cold. Hilton's plastic glasses were smashed to smithereens on the front seat. Amen.

After the wreck of the Galaxy our driving habits changed radically. Alan Price never missed his place in the front seat alongside the driver. His paranoia and fear of crashing probably saved us. He did the map reading from now on.

Eventually I got my first car, a little TR6 two seater. I got a sports car because it gave me the excuse to travel alone. But it also made me sloppy in my timing and for one show I arrived late. I remember coming through the dressing room door nonchalantly after parking the TR6 outside. The whole band looked at me with icy-cold stares. Peter Grant, the mountain, walked up towards me.

'Where the fuck dya think you've been?'

'Er, been driving to the gig, ain't I?'

'Well, you're late!'

'So, I'm late! I drove here as fast as I could.'

'Well you fucking leave earlier the next time, you cunt!'

He picked me up bodily and threw me across the room about ten feet. I hit a wall, slid down and hit the floor. I was never late again. Peter got his point across. He was what I needed. He was what we needed.

One day after a sleazy gig Peter brought us the good news. 'Here, you guys'll be pleased to know, Harold Davidson's just secured you a tour with Chuck Berry.' We stood there dumbfounded. We couldn't believe it. We were going to tour with Chuck Berry! We'd worshipped Chuck Berry since we were at school. We all sincerely believed that Chuck was America's number one poet, and probably the greatest rock'n'roll star that ever walked any stage anywhere. And we were to tour with him. Things were really accelerating at last!

Rehearsals for the Chuck Berry tour were called in a theatre in north London at three in the afternoon on a drab September day. As I arrived I could hear King Size Taylor's band kicking up, rehearsing. At the microphone in the centre of the stage was a black American with huge feet, a double cut-away red Gibson guitar slung round his neck, his long probing fingers stretched out over the frets. He was clad, somewhat inappropriately, in a white mackintosh.

'OK, let's do it again you guys. One, two, go!' He counted off the band and they stomped into action.

> I looked at my watch,
> It was quarter past seven,
> Man, I was up in a seventh heaven,
> A reelin,' a reelin' and a rockin'...

'Hold it, hold it, hold it!'

The band stopped. Chuck Berry turned to the band and glared at the drummer. 'Hey listen man, when I stomp this foot the whole *world* stops turnin'. Now let's try it again.'

Every band in Britain wanted to be on this tour. The Yardbirds, the Stones, you name it, they'd been clamouring to tour with Chuck Berry and we were lucky enough to get the gig. It was sure to draw the biggest rock'n'roll audiences in concert history up and down the country and we, The Animals, had a chance to be on that tour and get the exposure we needed. I knew deep down inside of me that every band on that tour would be trying to out-rock the great man himself, trying their level best to make a good showing against the original Mr Rock'n'Roll. They included the Swinging Blue Jeans, King Size Taylor and Carl Perkins.

But our idea was to avoid heavy, heavy, rock'n'roll. If we hit the audience with some kind of blue, melodic song to finish, we would be in a better position to leave a lasting impression than if we rocked like everybody else. We'd been playing and working up an arrangement of 'House Of The Rising Sun' for some time and I felt it was the right time to put the song to the test. The rest of the guys agreed with me. So we went ahead and put it in the show. The reaction was tremendous. When we reached Manchester, we got a call from Mickie Most, our producer, to take a train to London and take our equipment to the small four-track studio in Kingsway to cut the song.

We did just that, took the train to Euston, bribed a British Rail porter for the use of one of his push carts, put the equipment on to the cart and pushed it through the West End to the studios. We set up the equipment, did a sound check, one test take and by the second take we had it. That record sold millions and still is selling millions to this day. Later on Chas Chandler was going through the books of that tiny studio before it closed and found it cost £4 10s 0d to cut that song.

Meanwhile, back on the Chuck Berry tour I'd stand in the wings and watch him in amazement. He was just great. I talked to him one day and told him that when we reached Newcastle there would be a very special audience waiting for him. And I remember standing in the wings in Newcastle City Hall when Chuck, in the middle of his set, came duck-walking across the stage to where I was standing, looked up at me smiling and said: 'Well, you were right – this is terrific.' Then duck-walked back to face the audience, going berserk. But the last night in London, a return gig by public demand, took the cake. Teds turned out in their best drapes, their girlfriends dressed to the hilt, to acclaim their rock'n'roll idol. They went berserk. Towards the end of Chuck Berry's set they wouldn't let him go. Upstairs the kids started pounding on the lights which were positioned around the rim of the balcony. The lights broke and the girls fell to the audience below. More! More! More! they chanted. They invaded the stage, they danced around Chuck, but to their credit not one of them got in the way of his performance. I remember looking backstage and seeing the worried faces of Don Arden and Peter Grant. They were obviously calculating the amount of damage being done to the theatre and how many fines they would have to pay.

Then Chuck duck-walked his way to the edge of the stage and yelled to Peter Grant: 'Did you get the money yet?' Grant shook his head: 'No, we didn't.' So Chuck duck-walked back on to the stage again and entered into one more song. The audience were going berserk. He did the duck-walk one more time across the length of the stage – 'Did we get the money yet?' again he yelled. Peter Grant nodded his head and smiled. Chuck just kept on duck-walking, unplugged his Gibson guitar and duck-walked all the way off the stage, down the stairs and into a waiting limousine, and he was gone to the hotel, probably putting his feet up, having a cigarette and a cup of tea while the audience were still going berserk, tearing the theatre to pieces.

Chuck was a hard man to deal with in terms of promotion and management. His years in prison made him bitter and wary of agents and managers. At one gig I recall Don Arden and Peter Grant on their knees peeling off single pound notes and pushing them under the door of Chuck Berry's dressing room. Chuck demanded payment up front before the performance. Meanwhile the audience were tearing the theatre apart. It was even rumoured that a gunshot had been fired in the auditorium, which was very unusual for London. The police came charging in with batons drawn. It was a mess.

Chuck was cool, calm and collected throughout it all and when I went back to his dressing room after the last show I found him packing up his suits and guitars. I stood in the corridor and knocked on the door.

'Mr Berry...' I said. 'Chuck...'

He turned and smiled at me. 'Yes, what is it, son?'

'Well, I just want to say it's been a real pleasure working with you. You lived up to all my expectations, and I just wanted to say how much I enjoyed the music.'

'Well, I enjoyed it too. Had a real fine time. And don't worry, son, our paths will cross again.'

Which they did. Rock on, Chuck Berry.

Our commercially-minded producer, Mickie Most, never a great record producer in my estimation but who had a genius for knowing what the public liked to hear, never ever wanted 'House Of The Rising Sun' to be recorded or released as a single. The guys in the band had to fight for the right to have it recorded. But it was the use of the song and the way we displayed it on the Chuck Berry tour that convinced him that we were right. And with the help of the producers of *Ready, Steady Go!*, who also believed in the song and gave us the time and space to perform it on television, it was at number one worldwide within the space of two weeks.

Dreams were coming true. We were back out on the road again doing a gig in the West Country. We walked into the hall, the place was jam packed and the guy who managed the place walked up to us, shook us all by the hands and gave us the news that 'House Of The Rising Sun' had reached number one in the English charts. The telephone was ringing off the hook before we went on stage, people congratulating us from all over the place. And the word came from the agency that offers of an American tour had come in. We were on our way to fulfil a lifetime dream, to perform in the land that produced the music that we played and loved so much – America, the land of the blues.

That night there was an incredible feeling on stage. The people loved us, we loved them. I felt completely at home out there. When the time came to perform that song it seemed everybody's face in the whole place lit up. I walked off stage, never feeling more high in my life. There was a huge party organized for us backstage. When I got a chance I drifted away from the party, grabbed my overnight bag, climbed some stairs and went to an empty dressing room. In the holdall I had a small newspaper package and inside that was some African grass that I had been given by Graham Bond. I rolled up the joint and silently smoked it, reflecting on what we'd been through and where we were going to and I remembered what Graham had told me when he'd given me the weed.

It was actually the first grass that I had ever seen. I'd smoked hash before but this was the first time I'd smoked grass. I was half-way through the joint and feeling tremendously high and burst out laughing to myself when I recalled the words that Graham had told me. We'd been sitting there cross-legged facing each other on my living-room floor back in my apartment in London. It had taken him ages to score the good weed, he said. He opened up the package, he told me to put my fingers in it and rub it in between my forefinger and thumb and smell the residue. It was good and strong. He rolled up the spliff, handed it to me and said: 'Here, smoke it, it'll serve you well, but if you're going to live the blues and you're going to go in search of the blues, I'll tell you one thing now, the whole world's going to know your name but you'll never ever have any money.'

I burst out laughing when I recalled what he said. A record at Number One all over the world. He's got to be joking.

FIVE
AMERICAN DREAMS

Right from the beginning I had a love-hate relationship with America. First of all I was ready to join the Merchant Navy just to get there. College and rock'n'roll saved me from that, and now I had a free ride, first class all the way, thanks to music. But from the word go, our decent little band was mishandled, exploited, pushed and moulded. At least that's what they tried to do. It was a crying shame.

We had the raw energy and power to communicate, but as soon as we stepped into America our assets were stripped away. And it was all due to the greed of those around us. That's not to say we didn't have a good time!

From the moment we arrived at Kennedy Airport in New York, we found ourselves in a carnival of madness, a carnival that turned away our potential audience, while the clowns, animals, high-wire walkers, double dealers, and ring master cops with their oversized guns, made us jump through their hoops. At least between these monsters, from time to time we came across some good people.

Because of their experiences with The Beatles, Stones and Dave Clark Five, when doors and windows were smashed and graffiti scrawled, the airport authorities had decided to ban wild fan receptions for arriving British groups. Security was tight, reporters and photographers kept at bay. Even the radio and TV were asked not to mention the latest arrivals. As a result there were no fans to scream and cheer at us as we got off the Boeing 707. It was a disappointment and Alan Price said later at a press reception at the hotel: 'I think our fans were cheated. We should have been given time to wave to our fans.'

But at least MGM, our American record company, tried to put on a splash. After clearing customs we were each provided with a Mustang Ford convertible and a girl, dressed as lovable cuddly little animals in fishnet stockings and with claws on their fingers. They smiled at us from behind their masks. We were just dying to put the cat among these chickens.

Sitting with the hoods down, the wind blowing in our faces, we were frozen by the time we got to the Lincoln Bridge. But I warmed myself by holding my chick real close and feeling her exciting legs through those devastating fishnet stockings.

We tried our best to chat up the models on the way downtown, but they would have none of it. We were surrounded by police cars and motorcycles but all the way along the route, there wasn't a kid to be seen. They'd all been fooled and diverted by the security people.

Nevertheless I cuddled up close to my girl as our records and my voice blasted out over the car radio. The promotion man in the driving seat tried to get a squint in the rear view mirror of what was happening in the back seat. In the car in front I'd see Hilton Valentine's big grinning face turn around as he looked at me over his chick's shoulder, waving at me. 'Smashing here, isn't it Eric?' he yelled at the top of his voice.

There was hardly anybody on the streets except cops so it was hilarious to see our girls, each with a fixed, permanent smile waving at the non-existent crowds while we groped them heavily. By the time we reached Loews Mid Town Motor Inn in Manhattan, near the Paramount Theater in Times Square, where we were due to play, we were both frozen and elated. We were ready to take America by the balls!

The agency had booked us for a promotional stint at the Paramount before the famous theatre would close down forever. We would be part of its last show with an incredible array of rock and R&B talent. One of the stars we knew very well indeed. It was – guess who? Chuck Berry! It was quite unnerving for us to top the bill over someone we idolized, especially as not long before we had begged for the chance to support him in England!

Other artists on the show included Dionne Warwick, Dee Dee
Sharp, the Dixie Cups, and Little Richard. It was all too much. It
was even more mind blowing when we found out we were to do
three shows a day on weekdays, and *five* shows a day at weekends. This was entertainment – American style. We were also
lined up for the Ed Sullivan TV show, the highest-rated variety
show in the world. We were nervous but we knew the band could
pull it off, and we did, during our weeks at the Paramount. We
built up a loyal following in New York and earned the respect of
Chuck Berry and Little Richard. It was an uphill climb against the
popularity of The Beatles and Stones, but we did it, despite the
worst our management could do.

First came the formalities. On day one, we were whisked
straight through amazed, open mouthed people in the lobby of
our hotel, straight into waiting elevators. Just as customs were a
thing of the past, so were checking-in formalities at the hotel. We
shot up to the 122nd floor and were shown to our individual
suites. A black maid in every room dressed in pink, put the finishing touches to our bed linen.

On with the TV. A picture jumped on the screen with a fierce
crackle. It didn't take hours to warm up like it did back home.
Suddenly, there we were on the box, before I had a chance to put
my bags down. I could see myself at the airport. I looked weird. I
moved toward the set to get a closer look at myself. Alan looked
great, smiling happily. That was me – wow! I felt weird, like I was
toppling sideways, giddy and transfixed. Into a commercial
break. Knock at the door. 'Hey Eric, how are you doin'?' Sun-
tanned face, olive skin, long-nose with glasses half-way down
and a tartan jacket walking towards me. 'Welcome to America –
welcome to New York.' It was the record company man who
shook me vigorously by the hand.

'Press conference in ten minutes. No time for a shower. See you
downstairs, in ten minutes.' He held up both hands spread open
to emphasize *ten*. I took a shower anyway. It was great after
being cooped up in a plane for so long. We did have a few giggles
on the way, I reflected in the warm hissing shower. I remembered
that during the night I had looked across the centre aisle of our
Boeing to see Don Arden, Peter Grant and Mike Jeffery fast
asleep like little babes in a deep slumber, high in the open black
skies over the Arctic, lost in a dream world. But they still had their

plastic hollow tube headphones in their ears, left over from the in-flight entertainment. I couldn't resist creeping on my hands and knees to their aisle, unplugging the headphones from their armrest sockets, putting the tubes in my mouth and giving them a blast of air down their earholes. I scampered down the aisle into the rear toilet before they spotted the culprit. Boredom. It'll drive a man to anything!

I came chuckling out of the shower with a towel wrapped around my waist to find the olive skinned record company man sitting on the edge of my bed. 'Come *on*, Eric. I said ten minutes. It's been fifteen. You've got the whole press corps waiting down there. And Channel Two want to catch you for their next slot. We can't hold up the Nine O'Clock News. Let's go!'

In the conference room gum-chewing crew-cut Polyester men stood with cameras loaded and slung from their shoulders, ready to shoot the shit out of us. 'Hey, hey, hey, which one's the tiger? You the tiger?' One of them pointed at Alan Price who turned with a sharp smile. He stared the guy down then snapped, 'I'll report you to the RSPCA.' The man obviously didn't think this was funny. He kept it up. 'Hey, which one's the lion? Now growl for the cameras boys, growl like one big animal together.' Fuck, this is embarrassing, I thought.

I had to get down on my hands and knees in my new Italian suit. 'Come on you guys, just once for Papa. Get down and growl like an animal.' To my amazement, beginning with Chas, we all fell in line. We got down on our knees and growled like animals for the people. And they ask, can a white man sing the blues?

John Steel gave me back my sanity. He had a *New York Daily News* and was flipping through the entertainment section. 'Hey Eric, James Brown is at the Apollo. Wow!'

Meanwhile they had some squealing chicks lined up for our autographs. One was a 14-year-old Puerto Rican with beautiful teeth. She stood smiling. No album and no pen. How could I sign her autograph? She slowly lifted up her sweatshirt. Two beauti-ful, proud brown-black breasts stared right in my face. Sign here! She was hustled out of the room by the cops real fast. I couldn't wait to get after her, out on the streets. But for the moment, we were hemmed in by screaming fans. If one of us got up to walk across the room and showed the top of his head, there would be an immediate scream out on the street storeys below. We realized how dangerous this could be when Johnny showed his head and there was the screech of brakes. We ran to the window. Down below a girl had run across the street at the sight of John's head, narrowly missing a red convertible.

Now and then the company man would gather us together and we'd make for the underground garage which housed our Cadillac limos. We drove slowly up into the daylight with faces squashed against the windows. The game was to get as much acceleration from the ramp as possible, otherwise the kids hung on forever.

Once we left the Motor Inn with MGM executive Frank Mancini, a man with a sense of humour as cold as the Big Apple. Several kids were running alongside our limo on the sidewalk. We picked up speed. Amazingly one kid kept up the pace. We all watched him, clutching his felt tip pen and MGM record. Without seeing it, he went smack into an iron lamp post. He slid down the post and lay unconscious in the street. The Cadillac screeched to a halt. The kid didn't move. Our driver reversed back at speed. Mancini looked down at the kid from the limo's black windows. 'You all right kid?' 'Yeah ... I think so.' The stunned teenager looked at us with a glazed expression. 'He's OK, drive on,' said Frank. 'Hey kid, remember, buy the records, buy the records, buy the r-e-c-o-r-d-s!'

We didn't see much of Mike Jeffery from the moment we arrived in New York. He was totally out of his depth and that's when things began to go sadly wrong. He was doing all kinds of real small deals, like signing the group to sing for a Wrigley's Spearmint chewing-gum commercial. And we had a number one smash hit on both sides of the Atlantic! Nice work, Mike.

'What good will this do us?' I demanded.

'It's for good money,' he said, looking at the contract with pride. 'It's two or three minutes' work. All you've got to do is get this little tune off.' We weren't even allowed to write our own jingle. I was beginning to grow weary of MJ's management ideas. I'd already felt uncomfortable when he and Don Arden forced us to wear shiny suits and clean up for the American tour. I felt this was diabolical. The kids would have loved us as we were, raw, animal-like scruffs from Newcastle. It would have worked fine. Who needed cleaning up? And as for chewing-gum commercials, I knew who was going to clean up and it wasn't going to be the band. I had a terrible feeling in the pit of my stomach that we were being ripped.

Back in England our third single, the follow up to 'House Of The Rising Sun' had been released. It was a thing Alan Price and I had penned: 'I'm Crying'. It had come out there, just as we were due to start work in America. So to promote the single in England Jeffery had us jetted back home to do *Ready, Steady, Go!* and other TV shows. The idea was to get us back to the States in time for the tour. It was too chancy, too dodgy. We left New York after the Ed Sullivan show with make-up on our faces, without time for a wash. We fell asleep on the plane and woke up at the other end about to make the descent into London Airport, only to find the weather was so bad we had to be diverted north to Manchester. Then we were diverted to Glasgow. It took us two days to get down south from Glasgow. We missed *Ready, Steady, Go!* and were way behind schedule. By the time we got back to America, we'd missed two important dates on the tour.

Once back in America the agency tried to groom us and prune us. They wanted to make sure we said nothing about the Vietnam War, made no political blunders and even hired a choreographer for our stage movements. I hated it. Hated every minute and was surprised the guys in the band took it lying down. But, what the hell? In the end we went along with it, and we paid for it.

One wintry afternoon I had enough of all the boring rehearsals and business meetings, fifty floors up in an ice cool glass tower block in Manhattan. Sitting around a huge walnut table were rows of lawyers and accountants. I stood up, made an excuse, and took the elevator down to the street.

It was beginning to snow. Flakes were whirling around and it was bitterly cold. But I didn't care. Took a yellow cab to Harlem. We stopped outside the Apollo. Alas, to my chagrin it was closed. Now the sleet was falling sideways and chilling me to the bone. But I was here at last, and I wasn't going back.

I looked up at the illuminated sign full of star names. This week James Brown was top, supported by Otis Redding, B. B. King and the Shirelles. Oh my God. I stood there on the sidewalk, just gazing at the lights.

I was freezing and had to get indoors, off the street. Next door to the Apollo I noticed the Palm Bar and lounge. Inside was the warm smell of soul food, booze and perfumed women. The long bar was stocked with every kind of liquor, but was empty save for a couple of real cool dudes at the bottom end rapping. Up on a tiny stage was a cut down Hammond organ and Lesley speaker cabinet. Behind that, a drum kit and cymbals.

I ordered a large Scotch on the rocks and chose a table in front of the bandstand.

A black hand appeared behind the B3 organ. The guy was making some last minute adjustments, his head down below the wires and fuses. A switch was flicked and the Lesley whirred at a high pitch. Now the organ began to groove. It was funky. The instrument tuned properly, the black man behind it sprang up like a Jack-in-the-box, cigarette dangling from the corner of his huge mouth. A smile came over his face, ash falling on to a white raincoat. It was James Brown.

I couldn't believe it. James Brown, pumping away at a lonely keyboard. The guys at the bar twisted their bodies and cocked their ears to hear James bash away on the old house B3. A beautiful brown topless girl emerged, joined by a drummer. For the next 35 minutes I sat there supping whisky, listening to James Brown pump that B3 and watching those brown hips move like the ocean.

James had disappeared, the girl had gone, the place was filling up. I took a walk back to the hotel.

It was sheer ecstasy knowing that we'd made it, and a thrill to play the Paramount with Chuck Berry and Little Richard. 'The Animals' in huge red neon letters blazed across Times Square.

It was hard work. We'd never worked like this in England. We were in a hotel just half a block from the backstage of the theatre. There were two ways to get to work every morning. One was to make a leap for the limousine, drive some 150 yards, then battle a way out. The limos came none too cheap and were damaged every day. The only other way to get to the show was with the help of the New York City Police Department and the Brinks' Security Guards who were employed during our stay at the Paramount Theater. In a ring of cops every day, we'd battle our way from the hotel service entrance to the stage door.

One day a gang of Puerto Rican girls somehow infiltrated the security downstairs in the hotel and had made it to the 20th floor where we were housed. The band were standing in the corridor waiting for our police escort to arrive to make our way to the Paramount Theater for the first show of the day when some of the girls appeared in the corridor on the 20th floor.

Captain Burns, a huge thick-necked, wonderful character from the Brinks' Security Services, told us to get back in our rooms until he'd ordered out the girls. Minutes later when we thought it was safe, we made our way towards the elevator. We waited in anticipation. The doors opened. Inside, one of Captain Burns' sergeants, his nightstick drawn, held at bay two frantic Puerto Rican girls, one small and skinny, the other quite large and chubby. He gasped, 'We haven't quite cleared them out yet. You guys hang on here, I'll escort these two downstairs, and then I'll be back up for you. You just hold on there.' The elevator doors closed.

To our surprise, the bell rang and the door was opened again. The chubby Puerto Rican girl had the nightstick around the sergeant's neck in a choke hold. He was blue in the face as she floored him. The other, skinnier, smaller little girl jumped from the elevator, grabbed a hold of Hilton Valentine's suit, and literally tore it from his back. We took off down the corridor towards our own individual rooms before the heaviest one could get to us. Once the cop was in control of the situation, he dragged the two girls down the corridor, bundled them into the elevator and they were gone.

Bob Levine had New York and show business in his blood. He was the stage manager of the Paramount Theater. He eventually became a close friend of the band, and later our Trans-American tour manager. Bob was always standing waiting for us in the stage doorway, making sure that we all made it safely. Once we were in the theatre, we had to stay in there all day. They'd made bunks for us so that we could lie down and rest in between shows in our dressing rooms on the sixth floor.

There were always as many kids on the street outside as there were in the theatre, and the whole of the Times Square area was complete mayhem for the time that we were there. The only other English artist on the show was Elkie Brooks who'd come across from England with us. Elkie, also a black music fan, was as much in awe as we were at the galaxy of stars presented on the bill. But Chuck Berry broke the ice nicely, one Saturday night. We'd done our regular act, including our hit numbers, and worked the audience into a frenzy. The place wasn't full, as it was last show Saturday night. Most people had gone to catch the last train or bus home. So we improvised some blues. As I was standing facing the audience, clutching a microphone, my eyes closed, singing a blues at the top of my head dedicated to New York City, out of the corner of my eye I saw some movement. It was Chuck plugging into one of the amplifiers, joining us on stage for a bluesy jam. Oh, what a thrill.

At the very first gig we did at the Paramount we had no idea that the old-fashioned showband stage could automatically sink into the bowels of the earth. That's the way the old bands, in their heyday, would finish the show. They would go out playing. But it didn't work for a rock'n'roll band like The Animals, as we found out when the stage began to sink during our last number. The audience just simply went over the top from the seating area and came down on top of us. A rain of human bodies crashed on to the stage, smashing amplifiers, stealing bits of drum kit, and destroying the stage set. We learnt quickly from that one.

No more old-fashioned, big band endings. Bob Levine had a hard time holding it all together. When Little Richard joined us, he felt, and quite rightly so, that it was an insult that he had only twenty minutes to do his thing. Twenty minutes to whip up the audience into a frenzy. This was just not on for Little Richard. He'd been warned in no uncertain terms by Bob Levine that if he went over the twenty minutes allotted to him the whole show went over time. Then the City of New York would fine the theatre $10,000. But it was hard to relate this kind of a problem to somebody as crazy as Little Richard. I used to watch his show every night. He came off stage dripping in sweat, stepping into the huge elevator which transported the acts from the stage level up to their dressing rooms. He was in the corner with one of his aides who was fanning him with an open towel, cooling him down. In another corner of the elevator, a black cop stood lighting his cigarette. He'd been hanging around backstage all night watching the show, and was providing part of the security. Little Richard had just brought the house down and was feeling good. 'Great show, Richard,' I said, 'great show, man, terrific stuff, you really did it.' Just before the elevator doors closed Bob Levine stepped on board. 'Richard, I told you once, I'm not going to tell you again, you went over another ten minutes tonight, that means the whole show is going to be running twenty minutes behind time, and you're taking away the prime spot from the boys, you're taking it away from The Animals. One more time and you're fired.'

Little Richard, knowing that one of The Animals, the lead singer, was in the elevator while this was being discussed, flew into a frenzy with his high-pitched female voice. He sounded like an old woman going berserk, his wig slipping off his head sideways, and partly covering his eyes. 'Listen you mother-fucker,' he yelled at the top of his voice, 'I don't give a goddamn about your show. You can stick your feet up your ass sideways!' Bob Levine waded into him with threats. Richard struggled to get free of his aide who was now holding him back, and made a leap for Bob Levine. Suddenly the cop standing in the corner, without moving, intervened. The deep black voice rumbled from beneath the peaked New York Police cap. The cop didn't move. He just looked straight at Little Richard and said, 'Hey man, you don't shut up, I'm going to put a .38 hole right between your eyes.' Little Richard was quiet, deathly quiet, for the rest of the elevator ride up to the 16th floor to his dressing rooms.

We played the Paramount Theater for many weeks. It seemed an eternity and we became a part of Times Square, a part of the heart of downtown New York. We loved it. Great city, great people. Soul capital of America.

After we'd finished our stint at the Paramount, we stayed on and did more work in the New York area. All around me was all I'd ever dreamed of seeing and being a part of, the big sell, the hustle, the jazz, the strip joints, the shows, burlesques, queers, pimps, dime-a-dance girls, close-down sales, winos, cops cruising – the smell of it was so good.

We had moved to a cheaper hotel, the Gorham, and there we lived and worked out of New York, playing in the Boston area, Maryland and Washington South, but always driving back in the Cadillacs to New York. Many a wonderful morning would be experienced driving downstate on the turnpike towards Manhattan in time to see the rising sun, with the guys spread-eagled in the back of the limo.

We had a favourite driver, who we all began to love a lot. His name was Joe Tiger. He was Italian. One hundred per cent New York Italian. A young bouncing version of Victor Mature at his best, always neatly, sharply dressed, his white shirt buttoned down, black pin tie, silk suits, wedge shoes and when it was raining, the inevitable mac. He wheeled us around from town to town, up and down state continually, to gigs, mostly colleges, in all kinds of weather. At first we had to be somewhat stand-offish. We wanted to fire up hash pipes in the back of the limo, and we didn't quite know how he would take our offensive smoking, although none of us thought him to be a 'straight'.

We just didn't trust anybody at that time. As soon as we started motoring we would press the button which would send up the glass partition to separate the driver from his passengers in the back. But what we didn't realize was the air conditioning changed the air every fifteen minutes. This meant that the air was circulated throughout the car's system, and eventually reached the driver. We arrived in New York in the early hours. Joe's driving was a little sloppy. He was taking up four lanes and passing red lights all the way downtown. When we stopped he pulled up outside the hotel and we got out of the car. Joe was standing, arms folded looking up at the sky and laughing.

'Hey you guys,' he turned and said, flashing his movie star teeth, 'I don't know what you guys were smoking, but, man, I sure as hell would like to have some when I'm not sitting behind the wheel of a Cadillac!'

New York was full of strange rumours. The word on the street was that LSD was about. Chas still maintained that it melted your brain completely and turned you into an imbecile. Pricey said he heard it was heavy stuff. Hilton just smiled and laughed. Sure, it was about all right.

One night at Ondine's I was on the dance floor zeroing in on the chick I wanted for the night, when Hilton came up and grabbed hold of my arm. 'Hey Eric,' he said. 'You've got to help me. They are after my money. Just keep hold of my wallet for me, will you?' I guessed that he was in the throes of a trip. He gave me his wallet with $1000 cash in it. Brian Jones was there too, steaming around like a maniac from table to table, like a dervish. And Hilton was grinning his stupid grin. I was dancing with a short blonde chick, when Hilton came towards me, holding out a sugar lump. I swallowed it, and danced on, waiting for the acid to hit. The blonde seemed to be floating in front of my eyes, moving sexily, her loud laughter ringing in my ears. The band stopped playing, but I danced on, finding rhythms everywhere, in the clinking of the glasses, in the shuffle of feet.

I was tripping, grooving through the room, searching for something beautiful to look at. There was a girl with Hilton, sitting at his table. She was a black-haired beauty with sharp, stark, dark eyes, soft round shoulders and the most exaggerated, pointed, spring-loaded breasts I'd ever seen in my life. I saw Chas in a corner giving Bob Dylan an ear-bashing. Bob sat there, his face white and pale, behind dark glasses, the table lamp swinging backwards and forwards across his hollow face, the cigarette raised to his mouth in two long, spidery fingers. I danced on alone, underneath the lights. I'd lost the blonde somewhere by now. She was gone. I was alone and I didn't care, because I was over the top, but my legs couldn't last for ever, and neither could the wind of the horn players in the band. Eventually, I moved back towards Hilton's table, and the mystery girl. I sat down. He didn't bother to introduce me to her, which wasn't anything out of the ordinary. He's a Geordie, just like the rest of us. She said she danced at the Metropole.

I screamed over the music into her ear, 'The Metropole? I thought the Metropole was closed. It used to be a jazz joint. I used to go and watch Maynard Ferguson play there.'

'That's where I work, I'm a topless dancer. My name's Jerry.'

I looked over her shoulder, to get a closer look at her incredible sex pistols. 'Come on, let's dance,' I said. Through the smoky haze, I could see Bob Dylan departing. Several other figures stooped, leaving behind him. When I tried to hold Jerry during the band's musical break, she was cool enough and strong enough to deter me. 'You know I can't, I'm looking after Hilton tonight. Let's sit down.' She grabbed my hand and pulled me through the crowd towards the table where Hilton was sitting, still smiling, holding on to a Scotch and Coke. I went up to him and grabbed him by the arm. 'This is, er, some heavy stuff, Hilton ... is this what you've been talking about?' He smiled and grinned at me. Were we all on it? 'No, man, just me and you,' he said.

I took off on the hunt for action around the club. Mitch Ryder had come in. I recognized him. He was the singer with the Detroit Wheels. I walked over to him. Just as I reached his table, suddenly from my right I saw a chair fly through the air and smash up against his chest. Mitch fell backwards into a pile of other table-tops, glasses and cutlery. Two blondes were up and screaming at the tops of their voices, their arms in the air. People were running in all directions. From nowhere it seemed, two men appeared. They were smashing Mitch Ryder into pieces with chairs that they held by the legs. Mitch hit the floor, his legs going up into the air. His arms going up over his face to protect himself as best he could. In went the boot. I turned to look behind me. People ran and sped off in all directions. The bar cleared like a pack of cards falling, leaving only the two bartenders looking behind the counter, no doubt choosing weapons. They left Mitch there on the floor, cut up and bleeding. The barmen were yelling at the tops of their voices and wielding weapons, one a huge butcher's knife, the other with some sort of chain with a metal end on it. He was swirling it around his head, yelling: 'Come on, come on, you cocksuckers, I'll give you some, I'll give you some.' Not knowing whether this was reality or fantasy, I found myself feeling as if the edge of the dance floor was the beginning and end of another world. I looked over the edge into the darkness of the club. Mitch had been on the floor, but now he was gone. Maybe someone had picked him up and hauled him out, but it seemed like a split second. The place was now empty, even the barmen had left.

I couldn't understand the reason for the attack. Maybe it was a gang Ryder had offended. I never found out. I looked around the empty smoke-filled room, garbage, broken glass, table tops lay everywhere. As the cops came in I was convinced I was watching things from another level of consciousness.

The waiter tried to give me a bill for $800. 'What do you mean? What's this?'

'Well you are the only one in here, I had to try to give it to somebody, sir.' He shrugged and walked away. Eventually I got up and left to take a taxi home. At least I had survived my first acid trip in New York.

Some time later I was walking past the Metropole, the jazz club turned topless joint. I remembered that was where Hilton's girlfriend danced. I began to wonder if she was all that fantastic or whether it was the drug that had accentuated her beauty. I had to find out.

Once I was in through the doors I found a corner away from the dirty old men who were literally drooling. One man next to me held his drink with shaking hands, as the girl danced into view. She really was beautiful and to my delight in the interval she came out front to talk to me. Later I walked her home. We kissed in the doorway of her apartment. My hot hands caressed her perfect breasts. I was not her only admirer. Andy Warhol had proclaimed she had the best breasts in New York. She loved to be admired. 'Yes,' she giggled, 'Andy Warhol is gonna make me a star!'

SIX
BACK IN THE USA

It was always a gas to be in New York. We had good relationships on the streets and with the fans. They were fast but we were faster. We got very streetwise in a short time. But it was quite a strain, living in Popdom.

For instance, we didn't like to leave the hotel with Chas on our heels. He was so big he was instantly recognizable which gave us less of a chance to make it to the limousine or to a taxi and to hit the dark deep alley and get a good run away from the hotel. We would phone each other and ask, 'Hey, when are you going out? In a few minutes? I'll meet you down in the lobby.' We would get to the elevators separately and avoid each other, but inevitably stumble over each other in the lobby of the hotel. And then the first two members of the pack, be it Alan or Hilton, would spin round in the glass doorway, hit the street and take off and start running like crazy. Chas would just stand there in wonder. 'What's going on? Have I got bad breath or something?'

Uptown was always the place to escape to. We spent a lot of time in the Apollo Theatre, which for the whole band was like Mecca at the end of a long religious trek, or a pot of gold at the end of a rainbow. It was ecstatic up there, carrying my cameras around, *carte blanche* backstage, with a front house pass given to me personally by Honey Coles, the manager. Years later I discovered that Honey was not just a theatre manager. He was also America's number one tap dancer.

He wore a little derby hat perched on top of his huge frame. I was in his office one day when he smiled and gave me the nod and said: 'Any time you want to come up here, son, any time, I'll put the word out – you're to have access to everywhere, just have a good time, enjoy it.' He was a beautiful man. I didn't need a backstage pass, he gave the nod to the people that I was welcome anywhere, any time, for any show. I took a lot of photographs up there of a lot of artists. I had a great time.

One afternoon I was backstage rapping with B. B. King and Rufus Thomas, just hanging out with the two of them, listening to their rap. It was beautiful, watching B.B., in the afternoon sun, clean up and caress his guitar, Lucille. And Rufus was a wonderful old man then (he still is now), the perpetual joker, a great smile on his face. He'd do fantastic dance routines that he'd invented, like 'Walking the Dog'! He had a big hit single record which covered the world. Everybody in 1966 was 'Walking the Dog'. I went to an afternoon show. There weren't many people in the crowd, it was a pretty loose audience. But B.B. did a beautiful, perfectly played afternoon set and from the stage up there in the Apollo he personally welcomed me to the place, even though I was the only white face there. Most of the black people in the theatre when he made this announcement knew where the white face was and they all turned to look at me. I felt pretty strange but pretty much at home too. It was a fantastic place. Saturday nights at the Apollo with James Brown were unbelievable.

It was full to the brim, people standing in the aisles, people checking tickets, making sure everybody was seated in the right place. Aromas, perfumes. Up in the balconies the black girls with blonde wigs. The furs, zoot suits, the finery, it was just all too much. Well, how do you describe a James Brown act? It's been seen by many people all over the world. James has taken his show to many corners of the planet, to many different audiences. A worldwide James Brown fan club exists, active even today, twenty years later.

James could push himself through emotions of indescribable depth and width, oceans of emotions. Then he'd break down into a crying and wailing blues to the point where he was emotionally cracking up on stage. One knee would give under him and he would fall to the floor. An aide would rush to the side of the stage past the wailing horns and trumpets with a huge red robe and put it over the shoulders of the almighty R&B king, James Brown.

'James, James,' he'd yell in James's ear, 'don't do it to yourself, don't hurt yourself, ain't nobody worthy, James, listen to me, I'm your brother, James.' And James would be crying his soul out, crying his heart out, tears rolling down his black face. And just at the breaking point James would spring to his knees, the red cloak would fall back, he'd push aside the aide and grab a hold of the microphone and jump into another song, 'Please Please Please!'

'Baby, please don't go, begging, pleading, please stay, don't you go.' But this was an extra special night. Bounding on to the stage to join him in the spotlight came Otis Redding. The two heavyweight champs of R&B were slogging it out on a Saturday night on the stage of the Apollo right there in front of my very eyes. This was the stuff that I'd travelled six thousand miles to see – this was the stuff that I had dreamed of hearing for twenty years. This was the stuff that would keep me going forever, a dream fulfilled. James Brown at the Apollo on Saturday night. The theatre went wild. There were several encores until the audience was exhausted, almost as much as the performers. I looked forward to spending more time at the Apollo, the last great vaudeville in the world. But for now it was down to work. We had more touring to do.

First there were three days of rehearsals prior to the Ed Sullivan TV show. Ed Sullivan was an American enigma. He was in the very centre of this monster called television. He controlled the airwaves in terms of what could be said, what would be fashionable, what would be the 'in thing'. Even though his show featured jugglers, clowns, acrobats, and circus animals it was his show, full of the cross-section of entertainment that America looked to every Saturday night. He dictated what would exist in your world for the next few months. Even though he held this power, he was very anti-showbusiness. He didn't look or talk showbiz, and his mannerisms weren't showbusiness.

Years later I realized he reminded me of Richard Nixon. He was an old man with uplifted shoulders, a long shallow jaw, dark eyes and huge long arms that he would wave around like a traffic policeman. We soon found it was best to keep out of the way of

Mr Sullivan. He wasn't like one of your regular BBC TV producers who you could take the piss out of or push around. This was Ed Sullivan!

Our first experience of how not to rub him up the wrong way was when we wanted to change the choice of material. We wanted to come out with our new single. We had a new song in the can and we wanted to promote it. Alan and I had written 'I'm Cryin''; it sounded great and we were ready to go. But he wanted to take up valuable air time with 'House Of The Rising Sun' which we had already promoted. We couldn't understand him, he failed to understand us. We had a real bad run in, and it was either put up or shut up. Cancel the show, in other words.

It was the last day of the Ed Sullivan shoot. On the show with us were The Supremes. By the end of the show Ed Sullivan had The Supremes in tears. I couldn't believe it, three beautiful honeybrown girls all in tears. Mr Sullivan had yelled at them. What was it all about? As I passed their dressing room door I heard Sullivan yelling at the top of his voice that The Supremes would never play his show again. Old Ed really was the last of the showbiz dinosaurs.

As far as our fight with him went, about plugging the new single and not doing 'House Of The Rising Sun', he compromised by giving us an extra spot. We were to do two numbers on the show. One was 'The House' which he wanted, the other was the latest single. As it happened, after three days of preparation and rehearsal, the show turned out to be a disaster. For our appearance on the segment of the show when we did 'House Of The Rising Sun', he introduced us from stage left instead of stage right, so we all stumbled down from the wrong direction, looking like complete arseholes. Then when it came to the new single, a maniac jumped out of the audience and started yelling anti-Vietnam, anti-Lyndon Johnson slogans and had to be bodily carried out during our performance.

The TV people, because it was anti-war, decided to block out The Animals' part of the show. The only good that came out of the show was Hilton had gotten through to Dorothy and Mary Wilson of The Supremes and he told me we could go out to eat and drink with two of The Supremes. I was ready. It turned out to be a very pleasant evening. We went to one or two clubs, had something to eat, a little to drink and then all very respectable we returned them to their hotels and then we, exhausted, returned to ours around midnight.

The next day a tour bus pulled up outside the hotel. But it wasn't a band. It belonged to the world boxing champion, Muhammad Ali.

I ran into Hilton Valentine and he had another two beautiful coloured girls. These two were actually with Muhammad Ali's party.

'Hilton,' I said, 'where are you getting all these birds from? It's amazing.' I had just got over the night out with Dorothy and Mary. Now I was off for another night out with a dazzling brown female. The four of us went down to the Village.

In The Copper Rail we ran into Bob Dylan. We strolled over and said hello. Bob could not keep his eyes off the girl I was with. I felt sure he was out to pull her, and he was in the position to do so. At first Bob was regarded as nothing more than a folk singer who had written a few good songs. But then the word spread amongst the American kids. 'Hey, I think that's Bob Dylan, the guy The Beatles talk about, the guy who recorded "House Of The Rising Sun" before The Animals.'

When the fans began to mob him he could not believe it. He freaked, it terrified him. He would pile into his limousine and take off in a hurry. We didn't see him much after such mobbings.

When we did meet Bob it was briefly and socially at The Copper Rail or Ondine's in the Village. But the press back home, anxious for anything about Bob Dylan, played up reports that I knew Bob fairly well. Dylan read this before coming to Britain and took it as the truth. Obviously he took a dislike to this idea, as I was to find out later on.

The offending article was a ridiculous one in a pop paper which said: 'Me and My Best Friend Bob Dylan, by Eric Burdon.' He was silly enough to believe that I said this. So things between us became abrasive. Despite his ability to write about 'the total experience of Man in the world,' he was basically a working-class American, a very difficult group of people to put one's finger on. He was hyper-sharp and his intellectual capacity gave him a degree of silent aggression, he seemed wide-awake, somewhat paranoid. But I was a fan of his and he was everything I expected him to be. I was just having too much of a good time to really connect with him.

That night in The Copper Rail I felt it was time to make a quick retreat. I took my girl to another club, where Lightnin' Hopkins was playing. Old Lightnin's show was good, the audience receptive, but she was not. She was bored with this 'Old blues shit' as she put it, and wanted out. This put me off her and I took her back to the hotel.

As I got into the elevator to go to my room, a huge figure entered. I buried my head in an early copy of the *New York Daily News*. But I could sense the guy looking at me.

He was a massive black man, light-skinned with close cropped hair and huge meaty hands. I didn't like the look on his face.

'Hey, ain't you with that band, The Animals?' he said suddenly. 'I heard you guys were out with two of my women tonight.' I tried to get out of the elevator as it arrived at my floor.

'Excuse me, this is where I get off.'

'Listen,' he said, raising one huge hand in the air. 'This is the heavyweight champion of the world talking, Muhammad Ali. I could crush you with my right hand, boy. You and your friend was out with two of my cousins tonight. I am responsible for those girls. I gotta look after them.'

'It wasn't me,' I blurted. 'It was another guy, Chas Chandler. He's in room 1503. Thank you and goodnight.' I fled down the corridor and he didn't follow. But I put out the Do Not Disturb sign, locked the door, and told the operator to block all calls. I was trembling, but safe. Much later I found out the whole thing had been a wind up. Ali thought the whole thing was very funny.

Next day came exciting news. Bob Levine and Mike Jeffery had arranged for us to play a special guest spot at the Apollo. Mike broke the news, reading us a telegram from the Apollo as if it had come from royalty. It had. Black royalty. In fact we had been invited to play a week with The Shirelles and Chuck Jackson. Wow! What a thrill to play at the Mecca of black music. Our first show was in the afternoon, which it turned out, was also the amateur spot for newcomers! If they passed the test they carried on up the magical flight of stairs to the top of the entertainment world. But we also found out that if the audience responded in a negative sense to the act then the boat hook was brought on, a huge long pole with a hook on the end of it that was wrapped around the leg of an unsuspecting performer to drag him or her off the stage in disgrace. We stood backstage nervously playing with the guitars and the amps, trying to keep our minds off what could happen to us if things went wrong. We were all pretty nervous.

But when we hit the stage we quickly felt at home. It reminded me of the Olympia in Paris. We blitzed our way through 'I'm Crying' and 'We've Got to Get Out of This Place' but it was the third song, the Sam Cooke classic 'Bring It On Home to Me' that had the audience bopping in the aisles. We played for three successive days at the Apollo, three shows a day and every show was a laugh, a gas. In fact the afternoon shows were a little more crowded than I'd ever seen them before for other acts. I was dead chuffed and had a right to be. Even Alan Price was smiling, but then suddenly on the third day the news came down that we'd been cancelled out at the Apollo.

MJ, from behind his dark glasses, mumbled some excuse about the unions complaining about the fact that we were working two places in one town and it was conflicting with our contract, and so we didn't get to complete our week's performance. I never did find out why but I think it had something to do with police complaining about security. Young white kids followed us up town and it was causing problems in a black neighbourhood. Myself, I thought it was a gas and one of the best things we'd done.

One night in Manhattan I read there was going to be a show downtown in Radio City Music Hall with Joe Tex and Charlie and Inez Fox, two acts I had been dying to see for ages. When Charlie and Inez took the stage I heard an enthusiastic English voice behind me. I looked around and sitting three rows back was Mick Jagger. He was really grooving on the show as I was too, wide eyed and grinning. He waved back. 'Great, innit!'

Charlie and Inez finished with 'Mocking Bird' and the audience went crazy. Joe Tex followed with a funky 'See See Rider', a song which heavily influenced me. I used basically the same arrangement in the future. And Mick had come under the same spell. The next time I saw Mick perform on stage he was shimmying and shaking and flipping his hands in the air.

The combination of Joe Tex's microphone technique and Charlie Fox's fabulous dance steps became the basis of the famous Jagger strut. We met outside on the street and stood under the theatre lights. He was very high, very happy and full of the show. He had a beautiful young girl on his arm. He kept nudging me and saying: 'Don't tell Chrissy, man, don't tell

Chrissy.' He was afraid I would tell his girlfriend, Chrissy Shrimpton, that he was out with a new chick. He was understandably edgy, as photographers were following us around. We tried to hail a taxi but none would stop. Suddenly a police car pulled up and out strode a cop, armed with a nightstick. 'Trouble,' said Mick, looking worried.

'Hey, you guys, come on,' said the cop, reaching into his back pocket. I thought he was going for his gun. Instead he produced an autograph book. 'Quick, you guys, sign here. If I let you two get away, my wife will kill me.' Mick and I obliged. 'Thanks a lot,' said the cop, getting back into his patrol car, and driving off.

'Well, he could have given us a lift to the Village, the ****,' swore Jagger.

It was around this period that I first got to experience the magic of jazzman Roland Kirk, while he was doing a two-week stint at Birdland. I'd been an avid collector of his records and wanted to see the man in the flesh. He was something else live. His sense of timing was unreal. Kirk was blind and played three instruments. He also sang with all the power of a gospel choir, was a superb percussionist and possessed an extraordinary breathing technique which meant he could play non-stop solos without pausing for breath. He was a true black American guru.

When I first saw him on stage, he looked like a ragged Samurai warrior, festooned with gleaming silver and brass instruments that looked like swords. He was also covered in wires, pick-ups, and miniature tape machines, all plugged into amplifiers and echo units. He was, as he called himself, a 'sound tree'.

A black newsman from *Life* magazine looked me up at the Gorham hotel. He'd heard it around town that a white band had played at the Apollo. He was interested in why I was interested. It was a groove. He said he could get me into Daddy Grace's church in Harlem, which was like backstage at the Apollo. It had been in existence since as far back as the twenties and was one of the biggest black churches in the nation. Daddy Grace had an incredible reputation.

He had never cut his hair or his finger nails and had once demanded that his congregation step right out of the window and crash on to the pavement below to prove their love for him. Not many white people get to look into a place like that he told me. I believed him. But he could get me a backstage pass. 'So let's go,' I said. The church hall was massive, holding maybe some 1500 people and as we stepped through the main doors over the threshold into the place I had a feeling as if I was going back in time some fifty years. The congregation was mostly women, children and old men. We took our seats, some twenty rows back from the front. On the podium in the front of the congregation there was this old black preacher going at it hammer and tongs.

Three young girls stood in front of him, two of them were obviously pregnant, the third was being accused of being pregnant by the wailing preacher. 'Your wicked ways, your evil ways, your wayward sinful ways will lead you to nothing less than death,' he was screaming at these three terrified young girls. One of the girls' eyes went straight up into her skull. She fell over backwards and hit the floor, and I could hear her skull bouncing off the floor like a cabbage. And then she began to writhe on the floor, screaming and yelling in a strange foreign tongue. It infected the rest of the front row. The other two girls began losing control completely, the preacher towering over them and pounding at them with all kinds of words. Behind the preacher, to his right, sitting beside the huge church organ, I saw another white man.

He was old and had long white hair and a long white beard, and had a black child in his lap. The black child played with his white beard, his eyes looked up in pure admiration and love for the brother who was wailing to his congregation about fire, hell and brimstone.

Several women with headscarves and flowered skirts with small children stood around a stove, tending food, handing out bowls of soup to people in the congregation. Smells of the cooking greens drifted through the church and made it seem even more strange that this should be in the centre of New York.

Walking the floor at the back of the room were several private detectives, armed cops who were there to prevent anybody from really freaking out. It was just all too bizarre, the church with its own kitchen going, its own police force and at the front the preacher working, working, working up the audience, making them aware that the devil was everywhere. I was fascinated by him, the reaction to him and how much power he had. I realized the roots of popular music stemmed from this kind of high energy fire and brimstone preaching. This was where the feeling came from and this was the way you delivered it. Preach it, preach it, preach it.

It was late when my reporter friend dropped me back at the hotel. Graffiti scrawled on one of the walls outside the hotel read in huge white letters, 'Eric Burdon is a nigger lover'. Yes, I thought, I guess I am. I turned to my black reporter friend. We both cracked up. I shook his hand and thanked him a lot.

MJ and Peter Grant lined up some gigs in the south and out west. Joe Tiger took us to the airport to catch a plane to the Carolinas, to begin the northern leg of the tour. I felt apprehensive. We would have to deal with rednecks and cops who had been recently beating up the black people who had been protesting at the ridiculously antiquated race laws.

We were also travelling with a young black roadie from New York who had been added to the crew. We had run into Sonny backstage at the Apollo. Bob Levine knew him well and had suggested he come along to help us out. The crew was getting bigger all the time. Sonny was very welcome, but I wondered if he knew what was in store for him, a black guy in the south, with a bunch of white English guys? Or had he been down south before, with some black bands? Well, I didn't know. I got myself together, ready for our first trip south.

SEVEN
JOURNEY THROUGH THE PAST

Goin' back to Memphis
That's where I wanna be
I heard it in a song
When I was very young
Memphis Tennessee

'Memphis Tennessee'
(Eric Burdon/Steve Grant)

We flew south for our first full American tour in the long hot summer of 1965. It would be a trip filled with excitement, tensions and surprises. The entourage included Bob Levine and his girlfriend, Kathy. Bob had formed our New York fan club and we'd met during our season at the Paramount. With a pointed nose just like Bob Hope's, he was an excellent road manager. His girlfriend was a squeaky-clean Manhattan version of my Hollywood dream girl. She was cute and good with tea and sympathy. She needed a lot of both, as she was the only girl on the tour.

Assisting Bob was Sonny, the black guy we'd met at the Apollo. Sonny replaced Tappy Wright who had business in England. I would miss the laughs with Tappy, but Sonny had his own sense of humour. At the helm was MJ still in his dark glasses, celebrating our American success with the purchase of a gold watch. There were the boys in the band and to make sure nobody got out of line, Peter Grant. It was wonderful to watch Peter adapt to the American scene. But I discovered he was no stranger to the States. He had been there three years before with Gene Vincent when he was filming *The Girl Can't Help It* in Hollywood. He had some horrendous stories to tell about Gene and the way he was ripped off.

Peter was a born music man, although he'd started out his career as a wrestler and later a bit part actor. He was on his way, in his late twenties, to becoming one of the best booking agents in the business, and later he achieved fame as the mastermind behind the success of Led Zeppelin.

We all had a lot of respect for Peter. With his enormous size, you had to!

We flew in our own chartered plane, as most of the stops were too far apart to cover by road. Our own plane! We were convinced this meant we had real fame and fortune. The pilot, Bobby Mack, was a Second World War 'flying leatherneck' and a drunkard. Not an alcoholic, but a drunk of the staggering kind. Nevertheless, when he got behind the controls, somehow he straightened up and flew right. I didn't mind Bobby Mack at all. He didn't make me nervous. I related to his staggering around then straightening up on the job. That's exactly what I was doing in my own way. Anyway, he was always ready with a great war story when he was pissed. He usually had a bottle of vodka stashed somewhere and was good for a hit of oxygen in the morning, a great way to start the day.

The plane we used was a twin-engined Martin, a real old tub, and a bit like a DC3 Dakota, sitting angled on the runway. When it took off it levelled out and everything was upright and outa sight! Pilot and plane were perfect together. Up in the cabin, just outside the pilot's door, several rows of seats had been removed to make way for a gaming table. Fierce card games raged all through the hours aloft. They began in a casual way with Mike Jeffery, Chas Chandler and Peter Grant. Later on the tour Herman's Hermits joined us, and Peter Noone, their gap-toothed singer, joined the gamblers. The stakes went up to some 7000 dollars. Peter Noone got hopelessly beaten time and again, but he was always game. Chas would walk away from the table, all rosy faced, and smiling, with a wad of notes in his trouser pocket. 'Right, let's crack open a bottle of Jack D,' he'd say with a grin.

Two rows down Hilton would be feverishly working away at some Columbian weed we'd scored for the band. He'd tear apart the block, get rid of most of the seeds, and I'd be across the aisle with a stack of papers, rolling up joints, and firing them.

Alan Price usually looked out of the window, in awe of the vast country below. Behind him were amps, guitars and organs. Hilton often slept on top of the amps. Sonny was usually in the toilet doing the laundry, and hanging wet clothes from a line stretched across the amps. Sonny was proving to be almost as funny as Tappy.

When we arrived at Memphis Airport we found a little cotton patch right there on the runway, just to prove we were in the Dear Old Southland. A little signpost explained that the cotton patch was put there by the Airport Authority to give visitors their first look at a real cotton plant. Cute.

As we were off-loading the gear Sonny jumped into a Confederate States flag, the stars and stripes, which had been given us by some fans. Chas and I took an end each and slung it over our shoulders, with Sonny reclining in the middle, as if it were a hammock. We paraded round the cotton patch, singing 'Are you from Dixie? Yes, I'm from Dixie, well I'm from Dixie too', to the amazement of airport officials and fans. The press turned their camera lenses away from this spectacle. Two jackass white boys and a crazy nigger, reclining in the ole Southern Cross and waving and smiling. I should explain that at this time President Johnson hadn't pushed through his Bill for Racial Equality, and the race laws still had to be changed. Well, we felt we had to put a brave face on things.

Memphis, Tennessee. Elvis Presley's home town. What a gas. Elvis's spirit moved through the band and all during our stay his songs ran through our minds. We walked up and down the hotel corridors singing 'Blue Moon Of Kentucky, Just Keep on Shinin' Bright...' It was infectious, that white southern thing. Now we were right down in it.

The audiences were terrific. Many of them were reserved little schoolgirls until we kicked up the music and then they turned into whirling dervishes, assaulting the stage. They threw their bras, their knickers, braces from their teeth, jelly babies, which they'd learnt to throw at Beatles' concerts, animal crackers, which they were throwing especially for us, hairbrushes, address books – all kinds of shit. And backstage after every show, was the inevitable cake. 'We brought you a cake' the band would sing out in unison as the girls entered the dressing room. 'If I knew you were comin' I'd a baked a cake...' we sang. Or Alan Price would chortle: 'Hey, good lookin', what you got cookin', how's about cookin' something up for me?'

It was Sonny's first night in the Deep South. 'Why don't we see if he's really got a sense of humour?' I suggested. Chas got the idea and slipped a pillowcase off its pillow and put it over my head. 'Yeah, let's do it man. I'll get Pricey, we gotta look like a crowd.' Using a steak knife off the dinner tray, we cut eyeholes in the pillow cases and took off for Sonny's room. The plastic curtains were drawn and the TV was on. The door was locked. We slipped the hoods over our heads. We could see our reflections in a glass panel. What with the burning gas torches that surrounded the hotel swimming pool, we freaked ourselves out. We looked ghastly.

I rapped on the door with my knuckles. 'Excuse me, sir, room service,' I said in my best southern drawl. Silence from within. 'Excuse me sir, your hamburger and milk.' A voice mumbled from within. 'I didn't order no goddamn hamburger and milk.'

I rapped again. Silence. This time I hit harder and two eyes came to the window, looked out and saw the hooded Klansmen in the night, holding torches, burning bright. Sonny freaked and almost jumped six feet in the air in fright. The curtains drew back. 'Get the fuck away from me, man, I'm calling the police right now.'

Next morning I saw Sonny loading the bags into the car. Nothing was said, but he looked at me sideways and mumbled something. It sounded like 'motherfuckers'.

We travelled further south to a state which had best remain nameless. There we penetrated the Governor's mansion. What the Governor told us in confidence would probably get us all into trouble, even today, twenty years later.

The Governor, it seemed, was a music fan. Country and Western, of course. Nevertheless he was aware of what rock'n'roll meant and what power it had over young voters. We met at the

Governor's mansion, the White House on the hill. 'Now this is a dry state, you know,' said the Governor, cigar in the corner of his mouth. 'Alcohol is against the law, but if my cops can't get you the best moonshine in the county then I'm damned if nobody can.'

The Governor was true to his word. Late in the afternoon on our day of arrival, two police cars pulled up outside our motel. Four burly cops got out shouldering huge jugs of moonshine liquor, sour mash white lightning. Yihah! Those old boys were magnificent.

We were all rapping away in our various English dialects. Neither understood a word the other said, but we all agreed and nodded furiously, as one of the cops got down on his haunches, and with the squeaking of holster leather and the smell of grease around him, popped a cork on the white lightning. He produced, sanitized for our comfort, four fresh wrapped plastic glasses. The next thing I recalled was staggering across the courtyard of the motel and walking into the swimming pool, fully clothed, before the sun went down. Later that evening, still heavily under the influence Chas and I went to an after-hours club where you could get set-ups. This meant you were a member of the club and had your own key to your own liquor locker. The bar would provide you with a Coke or 7-Up with ice on the side, and you used your locker key to fill up with liquor. That was the only way we could get a drink. The cops had arranged lockers and keys for us. They were good guys.

Next day we had a gig at Memphis Coliseum. But we had a few hours free before the sound check and we were invited to an Otis Redding record session. We drove across Memphis. Everything was Anglo Saxon and white. Suddenly everything was black. Black cops, black people, black business, black music. A friendly DJ took us to the famous Stax Volt recording studio, an old converted cinema in the heart of the black section. Within the halls of the old cinema it was a different story. This was what I was longing to see, the new south, the new America. Black men and white men working together to produce soul music. As we passed through the main studio where the band were sitting in a circle around the microphones, we stepped across snaking cables and between drum kits and pianos. The house band included Al Jackson on drums and Steve Cropper on guitar. Behind the control board was producer Jim Stewart, another white boy, who owned the Stax and Volt labels which were distributed by Atlantic. The big star of the label was Otis Redding who had a string of soul hits. We were all keyed up to meet him when word came. He wasn't coming. I was just about to feel disappointed when into the studio walked Sam Moore and Dave Prater, the hot new vocal duo, Sam and Dave. This was a Sam and Dave session which had been switched around. Otis was across town working on a new album. I would meet him later. But here in the studio came two little packets of dynamite. The music roared. About an hour later it was take 19 of 'Hold On I'm Comin'' which would be one of their greatest hits. A classic in the making.

Producer Stewart leaned over his talkback mike. 'OK, you guys, ready for one more take? How does it feel to you?'

'OK, well, just give me one more take. This is going some place. Sam, Dave, you ready in there?' A stony silence from the speakers. Then two black heads popped up from behind the vocal booth. Both of them simultaneously went down quickly for a taste of the 'real thing', both heads smiling looking towards the control booth, 'OK, roll it, we're ready.' Take 20.

One, two, three-a-four. 'If you ever feel sad, call me when times get bad.' We staggered out from the air-conditioned darkness of the studio into the hot sunlight. I wasn't ready to go to the sound check yet. It was only a few blocks to the Holiday Inn where Otis was staying. Years later, I recognized the place in photographs. It was where Martin Luther King was gunned down by James Earl Ray who escaped to London. But here I was, in another point in time, for a historic meeting with the great Otis Redding.

The bedroom door was slightly ajar, the air conditioning turned up full blast, the TV on. Otis lay back on his bed, strumming a guitar which was hooked up to an amp. Lyric sheets were spread all over the bed, and the air was filled with smoke.

'Come on in, y'all. Make yourself comfortable. Sit down.' He was big and muscular, a middleweight boxer. No wonder he and James Brown looked so magnificent together on stage. They were both ex-boxers, both with a boxer's timing and delivery. POW!

I can't recall much of the conversation. I didn't stay too long. I couldn't. I just know this guy left as much of an impression off stage as he did on. He sat there strumming the guitar, running through a song he was soon to record. It was The Beatles 'Day

Tripper'. It was obvious his mind was open to more than just the immediate soul circle. He would be reaching out to other areas in future. He invited us to a recording session if we were going to be around the next day. I invited him to our gig. 'I don't know if I can make it, but y'all have a good time, and come back to Memphis,' he smiled. Otis had a smash hit that summer of 1965 with 'I've Been Loving You Too Long' and he had many others, like 'Try A Little Tenderness', 'Mr Pitiful', 'Respect' and 'Satisfaction'. Otis died on 10 December 1967, just a couple of years after we met, in a plane crash in Lake Monona, Wisconsin.

What I had seen in the afternoon had made me truly happy. This was the new South working together. Then suddenly, as we drove to the Coliseum, over the brow of the hill we saw them. Standing gathered under an oak tree, their silken robes glistening in the early evening light, the poison belching from a burning cross, the Ku Klux Klan. A ring of light-blue police shirts stood on the outer perimeter of a sea of pointed heads, as our car slowed for a police road block. We discovered later this was just a way to get everybody to slow down, while the Klansmen handed out their literature to passers-by.

Peter Grant was riding up front, the band in the back. I hadn't noticed Peter's reaction to the scene so far. I was too taken aback myself. But as we went through this checkpoint I grabbed at the proffered sheet of paper, more to get a souvenir of the South than for any other reason. Peter Grant absolutely burst at the seams with rage.

'You racist motherfuckers, you bastards!' His window went down and he was yelling, red-faced, straight at the Klansmen. 'Go wipe your asses on it, you shitheads!' He was hollering and screaming. Of course, I sat there and mentally slapped the side of my head. Peter was Jewish. I was only just waking up to what racial prejudice was really all about, and what it meant and how little we really knew about such things. Otherwise, would we really have made a joke the other night with the pillowcases over our heads outside Sonny's room? I think not. The memory left me cold. But by the time I got to the gig I was hot, and angry. The mood was decidedly grim.

When we reached the Coliseum, whilst waiting to go on stage, for the first time I found myself looking with real resentment at the authoritarian figure of a policeman. Within this society he would perform any function his government required, without question, even if it meant enforcing a law that made one citizen second to another. I wanted one of the 'Colored Only' bathroom signs that were dotted about real bad. I couldn't get a screwdriver to take one down, so I satisfied myself taking a photograph of the cops underneath one of those 'Colored Only' signs. I would get my own back. I knew how as well.

The night after the show we'd been invited to a prominent local politician's place for dinner. I took my tiny Japanese tape machine. When some juicy conversation popped up, I'd tape it secretly, take the evidence back to New York and play it to my black friends. I'd prove they were still racists down south. It became my mission for the evening.

The show went well. The audience were enthusiastic and to our surprise the blacker the slant we put on our music, the better it went down. What a paradox. Black music gets you there, and when you get there, you can't go no place, if you're black. But if you're white and you play black, you can go anywhere you want. Strange. Somehow I couldn't grasp it. Never have, and never really wanted to. Now I know what the real root is and it can't be denied. It's black.

The well known local politician gave me all the evidence I needed to haul back to New York. 'Yeah, me and my wife's going huntin' tomorrow morning. You boys are welcome to come along. I'm sure I can borrow some more guns for you. We can all go on a pheasant shoot. How does that grab you?' Laughter, enthusiasm. We loved it. The dinner was excellent, the wine good and then we started on the white lightning.

And then the magic word popped up somewhere along the line in the conversation. 'Nigger'. It was as if the electric hare had suddenly entered the stadium and the greyhounds were off in pursuit. 'You see that big old Browning over-and-under that I got? A magnificent gun, magnificent. I could kill ten niggers with one blast from that goddamn shotgun. You're talking about hunting, boy. Huntin' shit.'

Underneath the table resting on my knees the tape machine was on, and I was getting it, all good stuff. As we laced into the white lightning, I looked over my shoulder at the cops out on the lawn who were on guard, and I hated every one of them. I was having a good old time though. It was terrific. I loved every moment of it, knowing that one day the South would turn around, a change would come and that America's real new-found strength would then emerge.

At another gig, in another state further down the line on the same tour, we ran into it face to face, blow for blow, for the first time. When we checked in at a Holiday Inn in Mississippi, the guy at the desk refused Sonny admittance to the hotel on discovering he was one of our group. Bob Levine, our tour manager, went into him with his gloves off. 'Now listen, we use your hotels a lot, mister. We spend a lot of money and a lot of time in your rooms up and down this country, and you're refusing that man there a place to sleep for the night? Do you want the world to know that one of the world's top musical groups from England has been refused admission to one of your hotels? One black guy and one New York Jew refused entrance into your hotel – you fuckin' schmuck!' He went at the guy like a tiger. Kathy, his girlfriend, stood in the entranceway, her head held high. She was proud of her old man, and so she should be.

When Peter Grant arrived, he almost blocked out the sun with his presence in the doorway, and in his real East End accent he said, ''Ere, what's the trouble, Bob? Gotta problem?' The guy soon changed his mind. We broke down the doors. We actually integrated the first motel in Mississippi, probably in the whole of the South, before the laws had been changed.

We celebrated that night. We felt proud, especially of Bob Levine, but our celebrations were short-lived. The Coliseum was empty and the gig had to be cancelled. We sat on the twentieth floor of the hotel that night with Mike Jeffery, Chas Chandler and Dick Clark, the TV host. We looked out of Dick's window down below at the black shanty town which was just a few blocks from the hotel in embarrassed silence while Dick Clark defended everything that was American and apple pie, even the race laws, as they were. Although he didn't agree with them, he had to live with them. He pointed out that we knew little of the problem in England as we had no great black populations then. He was right, of course. Reality is altogether something else. The reality of the situation was that although we had won the battle, and had succeeded in getting Sonny a room at the hotel, it was only in an annexe off the main building. Our gig was cancelled, and everybody lost money on the deal. Sonny wasn't admitted into the restaurant or the bar, as it was owned as a private club, separate from the hotel, and could enforce a different set of rules.

We sat all night cussing poor Dick as a racialist and damning the American system, while Sonny slipped across town to where his black brothers were, picked up a couple of black sisters, came back to the motel annexe and got pissed out of his brain and fucked to death. He had a rare old time.

The load-out at the airport was watched by three State Troopers from behind their sunglasses. I had nothing to do so I was giving Sonny a hand. The rest of the band were having a late breakfast in the airport restaurant.

As we loaded the last amplifier one of the cops yelled: 'Hey, don't y'all forget to come back and see us again someday, y'hear?' I turned and smiled and said 'Thanks, man.' And Sonny's simple reaction was to wave his hand and say 'Thanks, man.' One of the cops yelled back. 'Not you, you motherfuckin' black-assed bastard. You stay back up there in New York where you belong, if you know what's good for your ass!'

We flew out of there relieved to get away. Now we were headed for New Orleans, the Land of Dreams, our next stop.

EIGHT
NEW ORLEANS

There was a torrential downpour as we entered the city, it was monsoon time: hot, sticky and raining. We arrived at our hotel early morning travelling in limousines from the airport. We had dozens of radio interviews lined up all morning long. I'd hoped to get a chance to look round the city; I'd longed to see it since childhood. I was impatient because the little we could see on the way into town was blowing my mind. It was everything I'd seen in jazz history books. The Martinique, our hotel in the French Quarter, was magnificent.

Bob Dylan's song 'House Of The Rising Sun' had obvious associations with New Orleans, and because of our then current hit version of it we were particularly welcome in the city. We felt warmth from the DJs, and the newspaper and record promotion people we met. As I was finishing off the last radio interview of the day the DJ asked me a question on the air.

'Tell us, sir, there is a house in New Orleans they call The Rising Sun. Are you really gonna try and look for that fatal house here in this city tonight?'

'I'm always looking for it,' I said. He broke up with laughter and slapped me on the back. 'Good to see you – welcome to New Orleans. Hey, you guys, have a nice show tonight. I hope that stadium's packed for y'all.'

For the show that evening the promoters had taken the football coliseum. The stage was built on the in-field and the audience was in the remaining half of the stadium. It was a good, healthy, wild crowd, and underneath the spotlamps our two limousines slid across the green grass toward the stage. The response from the audience was wild. Our first song 'Baby Let Me Take You Home' created a great furore. Hilton, our lead guitarist, was driving the girls crazy tossing his head wildly, his hair tracing a high arc underneath the stage lamps as he jumped to and fro playing his guitar solos.

When we played the opening chords of 'House Of The Rising Sun', the place completely erupted, the crowd went crazy. It was a wonderful show before a great audience. We performed an encore, a version of 'Talking About You,' that seemed to put everybody on the moon.

I couldn't wait to hit the streets. The show had finished early, so we were lucky, we had a whole evening in front of us.

Safely back at the Martinique, I stood at the window of my room. I looked across the city as I prepared to go out. Taking a deep breath I filled my head and lungs with the various aromas of New Orleans, and I vowed that some day I'd spend a longer period of time there, maybe six months, maybe a year. It's still an unfulfilled ambition, but one of these days I swear I will achieve it. I promise myself over and over again . . . aaah, New Orleans – the city of dreams.

Hilton asked me to go down to his room. I took a walk down and knocked on his door. The latch went off, the safety chain clattered, and he opened the door peeking left and right with a big smile on his face.

'Come on in, man,' he said urgently, 'quick!' Then he closed the door.

I was curious. On top of the TV set were two sugar cubes on a saucer which I took to be impregnated with LSD. We took our acid and made off into the psychedelic New Orleans night, all systems go. It was about 10.45 p.m. and we were heading for Bourbon Street.

Streets of fire! The town was alive. We passed by many blues joints, the music rolling out of the windows and doorways on to the main thoroughfare. We could have stopped at any one of them, staggered in and found ourselves a table and never moved, but something kept us walking. Walking – our mouths ajar and eyes wide open just letting the music take us along on a magic carpet ride. Where it would come to rest we didn't quite know for sure. I kept on expecting to feel something from the acid that we'd taken, but no, nothing yet. I checked with Hilton. He came back with some words of wisdom.

'Don't search, man, don't look for it, y'know? This trip's different, y'know, just take it as it comes, you'll never find it if you search for it.'

We wandered on from joint to joint. We put our nose into Fats Domino's club. No Fats Domino, but there was a good rocking band. We went in, stood at the bar and watched the band in amazement. They were terrific. A black bass player and drummer who worked eye to eye, locked into each other, making a sound like jungle telegraph. A raggy-assed kid was singing his messages across the heads of the audience. He danced around, rock and rolled and swayed with the music.

New Orleans was filled with young, fresh musicians, virtually straight from the 'bush' of Louisiana. They had come into the city to make it. They would play for a pittance and what they could drink from the bar, perhaps a few tips besides, but none of them got paid much. But they were eager for the break, just for the chance of playing music itself. They came into the city and flooded it with talent and music, such as I've never seen since.

Oh God, I was so high! Then reality hit me like a cold wind. I could hear angry voices coming from around the corner – high-pitched, screaming, frantic voices. I was drawn to them as though by a magnet. Three whites were leaning heavily into a black dude. The black had a strange glazed look in his eye, belying the fact that he was completely aware of every move made by the three white bulls that were threatening him. Hands on their hips, they were smoking cigars, eager to enjoy beating up a poor black. Saturday night's right for fighting.

When I realized it was serious I tried to pull myself away, but I couldn't. I simply stood there rigidly watching it all come down. The black guy was standing his ground, his neck seemed to be swelling as he breathed slowly, controlled, deeply. Their debate was a distant and distorted gargle, but I managed to surmise that the three whites were bouncers. They were telling the black guy that if he didn't move they would call the cops who would haul his ass off. I was amazed that this could happen in New Orleans, the place where jazz was born. Even on that hallowed, almost sacred ground, people had to face that shit, that Southern scourge: racial prejudice. My feelings were so intense, it was actually beginning to hurt me.

The black man was now in a state of disarray standing on the corner. He was talking to himself, looking first at the ground, and then at the sky. He started to walk. I was listening to his insane, solitary conversation. It seemed that he was beside himself with anger at what had happened to him. I thought how strange the place was, as I tripped along beside him on the street. Black musicians had been playing on the stage, white audiences filled the town where jazz was born, and they wouldn't let a black man into a bar? Race prejudice goes against all human logic when you see the true face of it. The man became aware of me walking along beside him as he mumbled under his breath. He turned and gave me a sideways glance. I felt a twinge of shame running through me simply for being a white man. I finally broke my silence and started to spill out my commiserations.

'Listen, man, I agree with you, man, it's terrible, it shouldn't ought to be, you know, I mean it's fucking awful, man, it's just not on. I'm a stranger here myself, I'm from England. It's just bizarre, but you have my sympathy, man, you really do.'

'I'm in the military,' he babbled back at me. 'I'm in the special forces, man. I done Vietnam for them, a year back here, and I dunno. Just trying to have myself a good time, y'know? Come back, man, feeling like a man, you come back and they treat you like a goddam kid.' I felt I had to help make the peace.

'Well,' I said, 'if we can get into some place I'll buy you a drink, man, come on.'

Professor Longhair's was cool. We found a place at the bar, a hot band was on stage and although I didn't see Professor Longhair himself, I was well satisfied with the music I heard. It seemed to make the soldier feel better as well. By the expression on his face I could see that he had warmed up a little. But goddamn! Those eyes of his, those glazed fucking eyes – strange. A table full of people from across the bar were looking at me. I was beginning to feel paranoid. I remembered we'd done a concert earlier and there had been some 17,000 people there. Some of them might have been at the show. It was that now familiar look of recognition that I saw on their faces. Although they didn't approach me, which was a good thing, I knew that they had me pegged. After a second drink the band took a break. I was approached by one of the band. He asked me if I'd like to sing a song as somebody in the house had recognized me. I said I would. He asked me to hang around, and said that maybe we could jam together later.

I turned to look at my black companion. He just grinned and nodded his head.

'Well, all right, so you're a singer, huh?' I nodded as the black soldier continued bitterly, 'Me? Well, I'd trade you places any time. I signed up for three years. I'm with the Green Berets, man. They told me at base not to wear my uniform in town. Town's mean. Mean edge to it, man. First time I've been in the South, the real South. All my folks are from Greenborough.' I knew that was a little further north, so we were both getting our first taste of the Deep South.

The band began a second set and the music was hot and exciting. The audience really warmed to the band and my sadness became consumed in a great feeling of simply having made it out that night. A great trip, even without that acid. A huge slice of my boyhood fantasies were being lived out right then. The music caught me, took my mind and put me in another place. The people at the bar were beginning to move around and break into dance. Everybody began throwing their glasses into the air and taking deep swigs on their rum and Coke with shots of enthusiasm – some of them screamed in wild abandon and jumped from table to table throughout the room.

Half-way through the set I remembered that I'd been asked to sing and yet nobody had approached me. What the hell? I hung in. I'd almost completely forgotten about it when, at the end of the set, the black soldier reminded me that I still hadn't been called. Strange. The set finished. It felt weird.

'Shall we have another drink or do you want to go someplace else?' asked my companion. I was nonplussed.

'Er, yeah, I think we'd better go,' I replied. I put my drink down and asked for the tab, the barman brought it and I paid. Just as we were about to leave someone grabbed me by the shoulder.

'Hey listen, pal, I wanna explain to you why you weren't called, man. I mean the guys in the band would love you to play, but we forgot to take into consideration there's a city ordinance in New Orleans that forbids white men to play or sing on the same microphone as black men, you know what I mean? It's tough, man, but ... shit, what can I say?' I stood there, mouth open. I couldn't believe what I was hearing.

'What did you say?' I asked incredulously.

'You heard me, man, I hate to repeat it. Black dudes can't use the same microphone as white dudes and that's the bottom line.' I suddenly felt myself half complaining – half commiserating with the black super trooper. I had experienced a different shade of hurt – pain created by the same prejudices that had affected him. I thought I was really seeing the real thing in Mississippi when I had seen the segregated toilets for coloured and white folks but now, I saw what he had really been through. The soldier had a thought.

'Hey, you feel like going to Algiers? That's where most of the brothers told me to hang out, want to check it out?'

'Yeah, sure.' I realized I was hungry too. I thought that maybe we could find one of those great Southern kitchens that I kept hearing about. At least we could get a good meal. We hopped into a cab to look for Gumbo.

Just like the Bourbon Street area Algiers was noisy, open to the street, and had lots of action. Music everywhere. It amazed me to think that this wasn't a special tourist area, it was just the normal atmosphere of the black section of Algiers in New Orleans. We picked the place that had the best jukebox. They had a good menu too.

'Hey,' the soldier said grabbing the menu, 'allow me. I do know something about Southern food – let me order for you.' After trying my best to eat a huge plateful of spare ribs, green and black-eyed peas, I found myself hanging on to the music machine. The jukebox was amazing, and filled with musical gems. Then two other soldiers walked into the restaurant. Immaculately dressed, badges and eyes gleaming, they too had the strange look of my friend. They were black and proud and well turned out, but decisively cool towards me. Even though the two of them were in uniform and my friend was not, he was already beginning to become again the proud black soldier, reminded of his role by the presence of his buddies. They all three laughed and joked and slapped each other around. I walked up to the table, sat down, and picked up my drink. I nodded my head and said hello. The three bald heads shined brightly, gleaming underneath the lights as they moved backwards and forwards, grabbing at cigarettes, lighting up, rapping real fast, hip, Army talk that I couldn't comprehend. The black trooper had left me, gone back into his own world. I took a taxi across town, towards the French Quarter. I was amazed it was only 1.10 a.m. The boys in the band had arranged to meet in the quarter around 2 a.m. The avenues were wonderful, each one lit by ancient gaslight with shade trees in between the lamp-posts casting all kinds of dancing shadows across the wet cobblestoned streets. I easily spotted them dressed in their identical suits and their longish hair. They were standing on the corner of Bourbon Street, looking up at a third-floor window, where a woman was doing a dance, the like of which I'd never seen before. The female form cut a clean, crisp shape, and because of the distorted shadow thrown on the screen, the legs, the arms and the breasts all looked three or four times larger than they actually were. She combed her long hair. Three windows down from where she danced hung a solitary, shining red bulb. Never taking my eyes from this vision, I fumbled for my wallet.

'I've got 50 bucks,' I said.

'Alan's been in already,' said Chas. 'It's gonna cost you $300 for an all nighter and we've only got $185 between us, but we've got to go for it, I mean just look at it.' We all looked up at the undulating silhouette.

'Let's pull straws and whoever gets the $185 will have to try a bit of blag, it might work, let's take a chance.'

Johnny took two cigarettes from a packet of Camel. He snapped one short, and stuck them both behind his fingers, holding them with his thumb.

'Right, Chas, come on, which one?'

'Which one's the short one? Long one, oh fuck,' Chas cussed.

'Come on, Alan, come on, which one's the short one?'

'Shit, long one.'

'Hilton, come on.'

Hilton, not saying a word, his face still beaming in a huge smile, turned and nonchalantly picked ... the long one. Even he cracked up, the rigid smile dissolving into a slightly down-faced look when he found he hadn't pulled the right straw. My turn came. *Short one, come on, short one.* I picked it. The short one.

'Okay,' I said with a smirk. 'Hand over your bread.'

I reached the ornate wrought iron gates and stood there in the entrance. A beautiful garden lay before me full of palm trees and magnolias, arching as high as the street lights. They reflected an incredible splashing array of colours and shadows before me on the ground. The psychedelics had begun to pump through my system.

I heard Earl Bostick's throaty sax playing in my ear. He played 'Flamingo', almost taking flight. A small, plump, round faced black lady stood in the doorway.

'Evenin', how y'all doin'?' 'I gotta little money I want to spend, and wondered if I could spend it in your establishment?'

'Well, little money will get you precious little, but come on, try your luck, step right up. I can provide you with the ultimate dream,' she said.

'I've already seen it,' I said, smiling and nodding towards the upstairs.

'Be careful, son, all is not what it seems, just be careful.'

I thrust my hands into my pockets, spread my legs, and spoke again. 'Madame, I haven't got time to be careful, there's plenty of time later for that. Right now, I know what I want.' 'Yeah, for a price,' she retorted, 'there's always a price.' I stuffed $150 into her hand. 'Here,' I winked, 'that's just for you. It's OK?'

'It's OK,' she nodded.

I proceeded towards the foot of the spiral staircase that would elevate me further into a dream. In the distance I could hear a blues guitar wailing its way across the Louisiana night.

Then, there she was, three floors up, standing in the doorway silhouetted against a warm backlight. She continually combed the strands of her long black hair that fell all the way down to her tiny waist. She had olive skin, and a green silk dress, and the large heels of her golden slippers accentuated the shape of her beautiful, muscular limbs. She looked up as I entered the hallway. She was the first to speak.

'Long time or short time? It must be straightened out. That's how I make my living.'

She smiled at me, huge green eyes almost luminous in the dark. A perfect set of pearly white teeth gleamed as she gave me a businesslike smile.

'Well, I gave three hundred to Madame,' I lied again, 'and she just said to go ahead, so I guessed it was OK. Call if you want to check it out.'

It seemed to work. She turned and motioned me to follow. As she walked she left a trail of erotic perfume. I was so jacked up I could hardly walk. We climbed a tiny wrought iron spiral stair-case which led us even higher into the attic.

'Give me a sample of what you have in your book of little tricks,' I said.

She laughed. The things she said in my ear set me on fire. With the back of her hand she stroked my cheek, then her hands fell down to my chest, to my belt, tearing it open professionally with one jerk, her hands skated over the top of my pants, her head moved in again towards mine, I could smell the sweetness of her breath.

'Long time, short time.' She repeated, then she grabbed me in the crutch. 'Short time indeed,' she said, 'you've blown it, you've come.' Indeed I had, I couldn't hold back any longer, there was a wet patch soaking through my pants. I stood there embarrassed.

'Well, the rules are when you come, you go. That's it, whatever you paid has now been wasted.'

'Oh, no, you can't do that to me,' I stammered and pleaded, 'please, don't say that – I'm just a little over-excited, I've never been with a woman like you.'

'What a pity,' she cooed. 'I sympathize, I really do, but rules are rules.'

'Look,' I said, 'please believe me, you've got to believe me. I didn't come here just for myself – I came here for all men. You are the ultimate female. You're it, baby, and you're going to throw me out? No, you can't do this to me.' I convinced her.

'For a short time,' she said.

She turned around, unzipped the silk dress and stepped out of it. She moved towards the French windows, and leaned against the doorpost. I was soon beside her, my socks and shoes thrown on the floor and my pants down. I grabbed hold of her hair and shoulders and pulled myself towards her, her legs were apart, her hands gripping the doorpost – I mounted her like a stallion and my feet were soon off the floor, my whole weight resting on her hips.

We made love in the morning light as the sun rose on the hor-izon. At first, all that could be heard was her breathing. Then, carrying across the skyscrapers in the early hours of the morning,

House Of The Rising Sun

I could hear the sound of sirens wailing. Not one, but many, a strange backdrop of sound to accompany our lovemaking.

'What a lovely way to start a day,' she said, then nudged me: 'Hey, look, what's that over there?'

Now on the horizon, we could see, to our amazement, a building engulfed in flames. The sirens continued. Helicopters were encircling the building in downtown New Orleans. The clack clack sporadic sounds of rifle and machine-gun fire could be heard in the distance.

'Oh, no!' she said, 'why do they have to spoil such a moment. What the hell's going on?'

I leant against her and looked out across the city. The gun ships were whirling around the pall of black and blue smoke which went up into the ice-cold blue sky above it all.

'Oh, God, forget it, baby,' I said, as I kissed her thighs, encircled her breasts and chewed on her brown nipples.

In the background the city was on fire. I thought quickly before launching into her body again. Maybe the black trooper and his buddies had gone over the top; maybe a bit of Vietnam had come to downtown New Orleans. And as the helicopters whirled and the guns spat out their lead, the lightning flashed and the thunder crashed, we made love one more time, not giving a damn.

I woke up in the back of the station wagon with a hellish hangover. I was wrapped in a blanket in the back, my personal stuff piled high next to me. I could hear the rest of the guys talking in the front seats through the baggage that was piled high.

'Morning,' I grunted.

'Morning,' they yelled back. 'Hey, what happened to you last night?'

'Fuck knows, man, it was just too much.'

'Well, in an hour and a quarter we'll be on our way to Denver – we've got a gig tonight in Denver Coliseum.'

'A gig tonight – oh, yes.' I felt drained, cold and hungry, and fell asleep again.

I was awakened as the station wagon pulled into a truck stop. There was the usual row of newspapers. The headlines screamed out: TERROR GUNMEN IN NEW ORLEANS STALK CITIZENS – POLICE USE ARMY GUNSHIPS TO ROUST ATTACKERS FROM HOTEL ROOF – PICTURES INSIDE.

According to the papers, in the wee hours of the morning commuters on their way to work in the city of New Orleans were stopped dead in their tracks by a volley of gunfire from the roof of a downtown hotel. My first thoughts had been, as I was reading, had the black trooper and his two buddies gone over the top? Chas said he'd heard that three black men were seen on the roof of the hotel and that police had said the men were experts in military tactics. The police had been forced to use Army helicopter gunships to move them.

'The strange thing is, Chas,' I said, 'I've got a feeling I met these guys last night.' He turned and looked at me, eyes bulging out of his head, half a hamburger in his mouth, the rest stuck in his throat.

'You'll be telling us next that you discovered the "House Of The Rising Sun" last night.' He laughed.

NINE
THE PROMISED LAND

'Where's Hilton?' I enquired.

'Asleep in the car. Come on, we've got to hit the road soon. Let's go – Denver awaits!'

At the Denver hotel we were checking in when MJ in dark glasses, dark suit, red shirt and tie, strolled into the lounge to greet us. 'How was New Orleans – how did it go?'

'Fantastic, Mike. The show was great. We had a great time in town. You must go there some time.'

'Yes, sorry I missed it. Business in New York. We should have a meeting now, bring you up to date. Has everybody eaten? Maybe we can meet in the dressing room before the show.'

The show went well. Denver was a good audience, and the city still had the smell of the Wild West. But then we were told the attendance had been down, although we didn't see it from the stage. All we knew was the kids were as wild and frantic as anywhere else. At the meeting with MJ it was explained to us that the West was our weakest area. In New York we had built up a strong following and in the South, too, our record was faultless. But out West it was gonna be tough.

MJ had been busy in New York with record producer Mickie Most doing a deal involving The Animals, Herman's Hermits and girl group Goldie and the Gingerbreads from New York.

Mike wanted to sign the girls and break them in England as they had no chance of success in the States. He also decided to invite Herman's Hermits, who had had a number one hit, to join us on our Western dates. We didn't mind if it helped bring in more kids.

MJ also brought news of a tax relief scheme for The Animals being set up in New York and London, so the tax man wouldn't get his greedy hands on all our money.

Since the start of the tour we'd each been given a wage of $200 a week. The rest of the money was being banked in New York and would be held there until the tour was over. It would be stupid to take the money from there back to England where it would be heavily taxed, so another plan of action had to be investigated.

It would cost us twenty-five grand to get into the scheme, a lot of money then. The tax shelter was to be controlled by a knighted English businessman. Our company, along with several others, would have its financial holdings in Nassau, in the Bahamas.

The money would be safe and sound away from British taxes and kept with interest until we needed it. We would probably just squander the money anyway. Yes, Mike was doing us a great favour. Good management, Mike. He would, he said, be speaking to his Lordship in the near future and inform him the five stockholders in The Animals Corporation would be flying down to the Bahamas to spend a couple of weeks to get to know him and his operation. The deal was done quickly (and I didn't like it). Cash was handed over to the lawyer who represented the firm in London. MJ had come up with the company name, Yamita. 'Animals backwards,' he joked.

'But for now,' said MJ taking out a white handkerchief and blowing his nose, 'it's back to the mundane busines of getting this American tour over with. The other news that's probably closest to your hearts, lads, is we have signed Chuck Berry to join us on the tours as well as Herman, and he will be joining us after Albuquerque, New Mexico. We'll be meeting him at the airport and he'll fly with us to San Francisco.'

All of the guys agreed it would be great to see Chuck again. After our gig in Denver that night, we had three days off. He suggested we keep a couple of the station wagons and drive south to the next gig and take in a little of the real West. How did that sound?

He had us just like a scout master. He was in his element administering the pain and the pleasure. We took the candy. We'd head for Albuquerque, New Mexico, via Laramie, Wyoming and stay at a dude logging camp. The two station wagons made their way south through the silver of the night, lit by a full moon. I sat in the back of the station wagon wide awake, playing with my Nikon camera, wishing the film was fast enough to photograph in such an incredible light. We were on the edge of desert country and could smell it. It was beautiful.

Hilton was at the wheel and we were switching, taking turns. I couldn't sleep anyway, I was wide awake. The sign said Laramie, Wyoming. We were there at last, the dusty streets, the store fronts, the four-wheel drives, the rifles with telescopic sights on the back, the high mountains in the distance, the clear blue sky, the heat of the morning. Downtown, the sheep men, cattle men, gamekeepers, hunters, sheriffs, old cowboys, straw hats, Western stores, buck knives, rifles, saddles, saddlebags, cowboy boots. Wow! I was an idiot for guns.

I bought a replica Colt. It had a beautiful red leather holster. But when I ran into Chas and found he had bought a neat little .22 I traded in my replica for a similar target gun.

Even the most unlikely, non-violent member of the band had to fork out money to buy one. Hilton Valentine with a pistol, I couldn't believe it. There he was. Bang, bang, ricochet!

When MJ saw us with the guns and holsters he freaked. He lined us up military fashion for a lecture. 'OK, I want this understood, lads. Don't fire in the air or on the premises. No one should have more than five rounds at one time. Please keep your weapons pointed away from you. Always check the gun is empty after you've been firing. Don't everybody fire at once...' He rattled away as we headed for the woods. He was still mumbling as we reached the trees.

'You've got to understand that weapon in your hands can kill. You *must* be careful.' His voice was drowned in a roar of gunfire. Blue smoke drifted through the sunlight shining through the trees. A rabbit – I saw a rabbit!

I took off after him down the trail. Luckily for him I had no idea what I was doing. Trying to run and empty a .22 pistol into a bopping rabbit is impossible.

The evening meal was barbecued steak, beans and maize, corn

on the cob, served on a tin plate with coffee in tin mugs, real Western style. It was terrific stuff.

John Steel and I were up to a bit of mischief. 'Do you fancy we piss off and leave the rest of the guys and go downtown and have a drink? We could see what we could get into. You never know, it might be exciting!'

We 'borrowed' a truck, which we promptly reversed into a lake. We were ignominiously rescued by two hard hats with a harvester. We headed into town as the guys behind us jeered. 'Don't get lost you two, have a nice honeymoon.' We took our guns with us, hidden in our jacket pockets.

The bar room was warm, friendly and Western style. The juke-box played the latest country hits. Ruddy-faced hunters, con-struction workers and cowboys hung around in the smoke-filled room playing pool, drinking, smoking and talking. We headed for the bar. 'Two large whiskies, please. Easy on the ice,' said Johnny. 'I wonder if they've got any rock'n'roll on the jukebox,' he muttered to me.

Johnny walked across to the jukebox. He stood there looking at it. The guy next to me was craggy faced, sporting Levis, cowboy boots and a blanket jacket. I turned as he touched me on the shoulder. 'Hey, hope you don't mind me asking, stranger, but is that a weapon you've got in your jacket there?'

'A weapon?' I said, 'Oh, you mean the pistol?'

'Yeh, pistol, that's a weapon. Well, look here, son, don't want to be seeming like I'm coming down on you. Everybody's got the right to own a pistol, but it is against the law to conceal a weapon. You can have a weapon on your person but you must not conceal it. I'm part-time gamekeeper and sheriff round here, you've got to take my word for it. You want to be sporting that gun, you've got to check it in behind the bar here or you've got to wear it.'

I was taken aback by his seriousness and would have laughed. But he pushed his authority just one step further when he asked me to call Johnny over to the bar. I explained the situation.

Johnny's face flushed. This guy had made us look like a couple of tourists, when we were trying to be so cool. The two of us stood there, English idiots under the professional scrutiny of several gunmen in the room, as we uncoiled our gunbelts. The sheriff was having a good laugh. We bought him a drink and explained we were English musicians.

'Nice one! Welcome to Wyoming.'

After he'd downed his Jack Daniels he asked us with a serious look, 'Do you really want to have some fun? Well, I am a part-time gamekeeper, like I told you. Come on, I've got a truck out-side.'

We went outside into the inky blackness of the night. There stood an old police four-wheel-drive flatbed truck. Underneath the seat in the front was a .38 revolver and a Colt woodsman .22. In the back a twelve bore shotgun. We were off into the night, down the moonlit wide roads in search of prey.

Jack, the deputy, took the wheel of the jeep. Johnny and I were in the back, standing legs astride, a pistol in each hand, fully loaded, waiting for the prey. A spotlight operated from inside the cab by Jack darted backwards and forwards across the inky edge of the wide white highway. If the rabbits showed themselves in the moonlight we would surely see enough to get a good shot at them. Jack's head popped out of the cab, 'Go on, give it a try,' he said, 'see if you can hit them with the .22. It's impossible.'

We were soon to find he was dead right. To the right! We opened fire. Crazily we emptied our revolvers at a rabbit. He was gone. Another one, to the left, look, over there. The truck squealed to a stop, covered in dust, the sound of the .22 ringing in our ears. We were high as kites. Jack got out, opened up the bottle of whisky we'd brought. 'Here, take a slug. You'll never hit them with that. Try this.' The shotgun from the front of the cab. The monster. Now the poor rabbits would be facing the flying artillery. We were all wound up and crazy. Jesus, what a lethal mixture, alcohol and guns. No wonder the Americans once had a police force especially put together to control the use of alcohol, firearms and tobacco. Either element alone is enough to hurt you. Mix them together and it's lethal.

We closed in on three rabbits. Johnny let fly with a salvo from his shotgun. He hit two and injured one with a full-on blast. The truck screeched to a stop and we were covered in dust. I finished off the injured rabbit with the .22. Blood lust. We were insane with laughter, high as kites, swigging away at whisky, whooping and hollering. We went in search of more mischief, circling the valley. It was getting bitterly cold. We turned a corner and in front of the truck stalked the majestic sight of a huge multi-horned stag, a full grown female and a family of young bucks. It was a magnificent sight. We had been behaving like crazy killers. Now we lowered our guns in respect. Jack sat in the cab as the engine ticked over. The creatures crossed in our headlights, slowly at first, then they suddenly bolted, darting out of sight into the darkness.

Jack popped his head out of the cab. 'Hey guys, see that? A whole family, man, a whole family. Wonderful.'

On the way back to the dude ranch we took out two more rabbits. Jack dropped us back at the ranch just before sun up. Johnny and I, feeling tired but elated, climbed the stairs to bed. We decorated the beds of the other Animals with five rabbit carcasses. We fell into our bunks giggling and laughing like two high-school girls.

Johnny and I were proud of the spectacle we presented at the airport next morning. Blood from the dead animals was splashed over our dusty, filthy clothing. We felt like a couple of *real* hunters. Next stop Arizona!

The flight over the desert to Arizona from New Mexico was one I'll never forget. The intense heat on the desert floor, the uplift of the desert wind and flying at low altitude made the small Martin bop around like a cork in the water.

The show was mayhem. There is a certain kind of female that populates the Arizona area. They are usually brown-skinned, blue-eyed, blonde, healthy-looking girls, all apple pie and American flag. Excitable and very desirable, but when they are 15,000 strong and fifteen years of age, as the braces on the teeth flash, and wet knickers and jelly babies begin to fall on the stage, they can be a dangerous breed. We survived.

During one of the last encores, 'Talking About You', we had this arrangement where the whole band would be steaming along playing all together and I'd be screaming at the top of my voice: 'Every day, every day, on Monday, I'm talking about you; on Tuesday I'm talking about you; on Wednesday', then it all dropped away, leaving Johnny Steel to hammer out the drum beat. When this happened I was usually facing the audience, jumping about, screaming at the top of my voice. This particular night when the drum break was supposed to arrive, I couldn't hear any drums. Nothing happened. I turned around to look over my shoulder and to my surprise I saw a huge shaggy gorilla lifting

Johnny Steel effortlessly under one arm off his drum kit. Johnny was waving his arms in the air, his drumsticks still in his hands, his legs kicking wildly out. The gorilla disappeared with Johnny off the side of the stage. We couldn't believe it, a bloody gorilla, at the height of our act! We ran the length of the corridor, heading for the dressing rooms. There was John yelling and screaming until the veins were standing out on his neck, at a guy in a gorilla suit. The guy had the gorilla's head under one arm and was standing there in a state of tears, his eyes one minute looking at Johnny and then looking down at his gorilla feet in shame. Johnny was giving him a mouthful, 'You twit, don't ever do that again, man, this is a bloody performance. You came on stage in the middle of my solo, never mind anything else, you bloody fool!'

After the show we sped down the road with a police escort. We'd had nothing to eat all day except hamburgers in the afternoon and I was getting quite hungry.

We pulled off the freeway. A huge neon sign flashed 'Ivan's. Burgers. Ribs. Sundaes.' Yeah, yeah, this place would do. The police jeep that had been escorting us disappeared into the distance.

We breezed into Ivan's. Ivan stood there in his white apron, beside his huge ovens, ready to serve us. 'One pizza, please, with everything except the anchovies, those little fishy things. Er – a giant submarine, please, with everything on it. Gents, what shall we get to drink? Hey, let's get some orange now. We can mix it with the vodka we've got in the limo.' Ivan's place was suddenly very busy. He took the orders, labouring away to understand our accents and eyeing us suspiciously, a gang of young longhairs, leaping all over his restaurant. Strange. We were even dressed identically.

The seats were instantly filled up by the band waiting for their takeaways. Big Chas Chandler parked his carcass on the top of the main serving counter and turned his back to Ivan. John Steel was sitting facing him, his legs dangling over the edge of a yellow chair. Johnny casually lifted his left leg and broke wind, surprisingly enough, because it wasn't usual for Johnny to do this sort of thing. It ripped through the room like a bull elephant on the rampage. Ivan freaked, although he had gotten it all wrong. He thought Chas had farted on the top of his serving hatch. 'You dirty young bastards,' he screamed at the top of his voice. Oh no, not again, I thought. Chas turned around to face the huge, open, gaping barrel of a Winchester pump. 'I have had it with you teenagers, do you hear me. I have had it! Get the hell out of here!' He was screaming at the top of his voice in a foreign accent.

Chas spluttered: 'Take it easy, it wasn't me!' Hilton and Pricey were out of the door, Johnny slid out after them and they fled. Ivan pointed the monster in Chas's face, then motioned the barrel towards the door. 'Get out of here. I have had enough of you kids.'

Chas made an undignified exit, leaving me to face Ivan. For some reason I felt innocent. I hadn't farted and the guy who had been accused of farting wasn't the guy who farted anyway. It was all too confusing. It seemed so ridiculous, pulling a gun on a guy for breaking wind.

'Look Ivan, we're from England, we're not local kids...'

'I too am a foreigner,' he said. 'I am a White Russian and I am proud of it. But everybody round here takes the piss outa Ivan. They think I am a communist. They're crazy.'

'Tvarich, we mean no harm.'

The muzzle lowered slightly. The one Russian word I knew had broken the ice. I persevered. 'Now don't be silly. We are hungry, we haven't eaten all day.'

'Yes and the pizzas are still cooking. Nobody here to pay for them!'

'I'll pay for them.' Just then a jeep drew up and Hal the Arizona cop assigned to our protection arrived, pistol drawn, two hands clasping the butt. Professional like.

'OK, everybody freeze.' I had just got Ivan to put down his gun and this guy comes in packing a pistol. 'Wait a minute,' I yelled. 'I've just got him to put his gun away.'

'I don't care,' said Hal. 'I heard he pulled a gun on you. I'm gonna make an arrest.' Carefully I explained it was all a misunderstanding. 'Yeah, yeah, it was a mistake,' said Ivan.

'Anyway, Old Betsy, she ain't loaded.' He put away the shotgun. 'But this is.' His hand went beneath the counter and he pulled out a well oiled .38 revolver. The cop freaked. 'Are you threatening an officer? Eric, this guy has got to be busted.'

Just then Dave, our driver came running into the pizza place. 'Hal, Hal, quick, your jeep!'

The jeep was rolling backwards down a slope, picking up

speed. 'Jesus Christ!' He holstered his gun and we all ran out into the street. It took six of us to stop the runaway before it crashed into the traffic. Hal jumped in, snatched on the handbrake, whipped off his helmet and threw it on the ground. He was out of breath and totally fucked.

'That's enough for me. I'm taking a holiday.' But what about Ivan? 'Let him go fuck himself. I've had enough. I'm gonna get you guys back to the motel and that's it.' We followed in our car while he led the way, siren wailing.

Later a nasty thought crossed my mind. What if we had been carrying our own guns during that incident at Ivan's? So much for the right to bear arms.

Peter Grant and MJ looked worried when we got back. They had heard conflicting stories about us being involved in some kind of crazy shoot out. 'Are we gonna survive this trip?' I asked Mike as we headed for his room for a debriefing. 'Well, life is full of ups and downs,' smiled MJ.

We met up with Chuck Berry in St Louis at the airport. He was due to play with us on the West Coast leg of the tour. He was the rock'n'roll loner, guitar under his arm, making it from one gig to the next, all on his own. I later realized Chuck wasn't travelling light for the romance. He was stacking up dollars in the bank to make up for the years he was ignored by the American public. Due to the English invasion, he was now enjoying a great revival.

I touched him on the arm. 'Well, well, The Animals. How are you guys doing? We're playing San Francisco right? It's gonna be a blast.' It was an honour to be in the presence of America's number one poet. I sat next to him on the plane and in between eyeballing the pretty stewardess, he wrote an incredible song on a napkin called 'The Promised Land'. Travelling the world, laying his lyrics on people, armed with his trusty Gibson Chuck gave people everything. If they didn't like it, screw 'em. That was his attitude. It was to become mine.

He was my mentor, and although Chuck had a reputation for being a hard man, I found him nothing less than a gentleman. In Sacramento he took me out to dinner, alone. He gave me stern fatherly warnings about the dangers of alcohol and drugs. 'Don't let it do to you what it did to me, son,' he said.

That night in my hotel room I felt a sense of pride in what we were doing, when I read in the local San Francisco paper about our arrival. It read: 'Another surprising catalyst has been the British invasion in general. The Animals, in particular, have made us aware of our own musical potential. Although there is a great deal of talent coming out of England, face it, they are repeating what has been the mainstay of American music for hundreds of years, that is Negro Blues and the breakdown of Southern Mountain Folk. It's the old story of an outsider showing you what a good thing is right under your own nose and in that respect we thank you Beatles, Rolling Stones and Animals.' This was San Francisco prior to the psychedelic explosion. This was the 'Frisco of Kerouac and John Steinbeck.

The concert was more like a festival. A huge bill of rock'n'rollers, with Chuck Berry and The Animals headlining. But it was typical of The Animals lifestyle and typical of MJ's promotions to find out that when we reached the huge hall, with an audience of 20,000 kids, there was no road crew. We had to go on stage and set up our own equipment because nobody else knew how to do the job. We had to walk on stage dressed in baseball caps and huge ill-fitting overalls, disguised as workers, to set up our PA system and backline. If any one of those 20,000 kids had recognized us, it would have all been over. And as we minced around the stage trying our best not to be recognized we knew that we were in a dangerous situation, which was borne out after the show. The stretched-out limousine that was supposed to take us back to our hotel, downtown, was suddenly lost in a sea of swirling bodies. As we left the stage door area, two San Francisco cops climbed on top of the limousine to join the fight, dragging kids by the scruff of their necks, their hair, or whatever they could grab at and throwing them to the floor, only to be assaulted by another onslaught of kids who would clamber on to the car roof. We were terrified. The roof began to bend and buckle and the door-wells began to swell and get pushed out of shape. We knew the roof was coming in. It was a frightening situation. Somehow we got from that car and were manhandled into another and within a few minutes we were on the freeway, heading back downtown, watching a full moon over the San Francisco bay.

Sacramento was next, then Fresno, California. It was a slack gig, Fresno being hot, dusty and deserted. I wondered if there was any population left to come to the show. But that evening, in the hot night air, they emerged. Here I saw for the first time a different Chuck Berry. This was the Chuck who, if the audience didn't show their appreciation, didn't care what he put out. 'Reeling and Rocking' was changed into very blue, dirty, double-meanings, which went far above the heads of the young kids. He winked and smiled at us as he poured out dirty underground lyrics. He came towards the side of the stage to adjust his amplifier. I was able to grab him by the arm and ask him a favour. 'Hey Chuck.' 'What's that?' He wiped the sweat from his brow. 'Strange audience tonight, huh?' 'You tellin' me, son.' 'Listen, can I ask you a favour? Seein' as the audience is not on tonight why don't you sing me the blues, man?'

'Ah, come on,' he said, 'I'm not a blues singer, that's for Muddy Waters. I'm just a rock'n'roll singer.' 'Chuck, come on, do me a favour,' I persisted, as he turned to walk towards the microphone and begin the show again. 'Listen man, just once, man, I won't ask you again. Sing "The Wee Wee Hours", man.' He walked up to the microphone, mumbled something about a change in the programme, turned towards the back-up band and broke into the sweetest, tenderest blues I had ever heard. 'In the wee wee hours, that's when I think of you, I wonder if you still remember all the things we used to do, in the wee wee hours.'

From Sacramento we travelled south by road to Los Angeles, California. My first look at Los Angeles, the city of angels, and my first glimpses of Hollywood. I knew that one day I'd come here and spend a lot of time. It fascinated me. With its background of film making, this small town, seven suburbs in search of a city, held a lot of excitement for me, a lot of visions and a lot of beautiful women. Celluloid attracts women like oil attracts dollars.

One day I was out in one of the better restaurants in town with a girlfriend of mine, and spotted James Garner, the well-known movie star, sitting in another booth across from us. Garner kept looking across at our table. I thought he was eyeballing the good-looking woman I was with, but as he picked up his bill and prepared to leave he swung by the table and asked me if I was with The Animals. He said he didn't dare go home unless he went home with my autograph. He put me on the moon. I couldn't believe it. We in the rock'n'roll game could give the movie people a run for their money in popularity. It was an amazing revelation to me.

We were booked into one of the worst venues The Animals ever had to play, a theatre in the round, where the stage goes in a slow circular motion so that every part of the audience can get a good look at you. It was a terrific idea in theory, but when you have a revolving band, you have revolving sound and you end up with a churn of noise where neither the audience is satisfied, nor the act. When you are revolving, you only get to play to a fraction of the audience for a few seconds at a time. Ridiculous. There was no way we could get from the dressing rooms to the stage. The only way was to surround ourselves with policemen and make a dash. Well, all's fair in love and war, as they say, so I would point towards Chas and yell at the audience, 'go for him, go for the big one!'

Of course, we were all going to get it anyway. That night, both Hilton and I got it in fact. We had done our job. As usual, we had worked the audience up into a frenzy, they were wetting their knickers, throwing boxes of animal crackers, the usual. When it came to our final song 'Talking About You', a gospel whip-up, the audience went berserk.

The security people had made some kind of arrangements to get us out, although I couldn't see it coming off. The idea was for them to get a signal from Peter Grant when our final numbers were in progress. Then they would crowd around the front of the stage, surround us and just baton charge to the back of the hall. One of the cops turned to me and yelled, 'OK, we're getting ready to go, now just hold on to my gun belt. OK, let's go...' We pushed, elbowed, scratched and charged our way up the length of the hall, to the dressing rooms. Chas in front of me looked like a mountain. To my left Hilton was a jogging blur, his hair leaping up and down on his head, his paranoid eyes to the left and to the right. Me, head down next to him, charging forward, trying my best to merge with the cop in front. It was impossible.

I figured, well, these cops have done this before, surely they know what they are doing. I tried to follow instructions. I held on to his gun belt for dear life. Some of the fans got in from behind, went for my legs and floored me. It was time to let go of the gun belt, but it was too late. They pushed from behind. I went forward, into the policeman's equipment. The butt of his pistol caught me in the mouth as I slid down his legs, a jarring pain shot right across the front of my mouth and I felt pieces of teeth in between my lips.

I returned to the dressing room to find Hilton in even worse condition. His light-grey stage uniform was torn and splashed in blood and he sat in the corner on a couch holding his head in his hands looking really down at the mouth, angry and pissed off.

We had to get ourselves organized. 'No more theatres in the round, Mike, please.' It was a disaster. Then the argument got deeper that night in the hotel. 'Why the hell were we playing out in the San Fernando Valley anyway?' I didn't get to play the Hollywood Bowl until several years later with my own band, The New Animals.

TEN
THE RAVERS

We were the Ravers, little lords of a new privileged class in our royal castles, the In-Clubs of the rock cities. We had our women lined up for us, we got fat and wasted.

In Los Angeles we tasted a glossy lifestyle that in the end became boring. Interviews, television, lawyers, fan clubs, record deals ... money. What were we gonna do with it? What was it gonna do to us?

John Steel walked through glass doors. Hilton Valentine practised hypnosis by getting whisky drinkers to drink vodka. Chas and Alan turned into pool hall sharks. Tappy and I spent most of our time on the phone, figuring out ways to get new girls up to the house.

But eventually we returned to reality. We went home to Newcastle. Soon we'd all be back in a Tyneside pub. When The Beatles returned home to Liverpool after triumph in America they were snubbed by the population. We wondered if this would happen to us. We didn't expect much better treatment. But as our train pulled into Newcastle Central station at 8 p.m. we heard a strange noise. A high pitched whine. 'What's that, Chas? What do ya think that is, a new diesel train or something?' Chas cocked his ears: 'No, that's no diesel train, it's kids.' We couldn't believe it. We were veterans of enough encounters with massed rioters not to be stupid enough to put our heads out of the window. Thousands of kids had turned up at the station for a huge, spontaneous reception. The train slowed as we neared the barriers. We saw a frightening sight. Kids writhing, just going simply crazy. Cops on horseback and on foot couldn't keep them under control. They were behind the barriers. At least they didn't get on to the tracks. Hilton and I turned around and made for the back of the train. It was every man for himself and we both lived at the other end of this local line. With our overnight bags, we did a U-turn across the tracks, behind the back of the train and down to a local connection we hoped we could catch, towards the coast, away from the seething mass.

We were lucky, we hadn't been noticed. We could hear the commotion in the distance. Our hearts beating, we made the local connection, just as it was leaving, to Whitley Bay. My home stop was along the way to the coast. Hilton would travel on all the way down to the end of the line. It was a strange feeling. In a matter of ten minutes I was in my home station, down in the suburban English streets. My overnight bag over my back, I walked from the station, home, through the streets, people gawping at me.

I kicked open the front door and yelled up the stairs. 'Hello, is anybody home, it's me, the prodigal.' I dumped the overnight bag at the foot of the stairs and climbed up. My mother greeted me: 'Ee,' she emitted, as she usually did when surprised or moved. Her face beamed behind huge glasses which made her eyes seem larger. My father appeared: 'Eric? Welcome home, son.'

Back home in Newcastle. Wall to wall tea and scones. God . . . the telephone never stopped ringing. 'It's on television, you're on the news, it's on now!' The phone rang again and there was knocking on the front door. 'Who is it?' 'It's a schoolgirl, she wants an autograph.'

It was unbelievable madness and my parents were actually enjoying it. I had to get out. I had arrived home just after 8 p.m. By 10.30 p.m. I was back in town hanging out with the fellas. I was out on the street looking for excitement. I was hooked on rock'n'roll and hooked on the search for experience.

From Newcastle we moved back to London. It was our working base. MJ and Alan and Chas took a place in Holland Park.

Tappy and Hilton stayed in Earls Court and I moved to Dalmeney Court, 6, Duke Street, in the heart of the West End. We made
ourselves right at home.

I loved living in St James's. The entrance way to my apartment
had an elegant cut-glass crystal chandelier and a shaky old elevator, which I rarely used. It was so slow I worked out a great
system. If I had a visitor that I wanted to impress, I would put
them in the elevator first, press the button, send them up to the
third floor, run up the stairs, open the apartment and clear up any
mess, before they entered. 'Come in, you're welcome. Glass of
Beaujolais or a bottle of Newcastle Brown Ale?' I was always
ready to impress the birds, the Beaujolais being obtained from
one of the world's biggest liquor importers and distillers right
downstairs in my own front street in St James's. The brown ale
was shipped in by hand by Tappy Wright in the blue Commer van
all the way from Newcastle. Yeah, St James's, W.1. had everything a young lad needed. A lock-up garage for my Corvette
across the street, an Italian restaurant downstairs who were good
enough to serve me at my bedside if I was ever ill, a nice little pub
on the corner, leading through a mysterious, Dickensian, cobblestoned backyard and a series of alleyways which led to the club,
The Scotch of St James'. This was the nightclub owned by Louis
Brown and managed by Joe Van Dykes, the guy who secured the
pad for me. You see, Joe liked to live above his work, but his
growing family had forced him out of the bachelor-sized apartment. For me, it was perfect. The bands, musicians and person-
alities that I'd looked to from afar, or collected their records,
were now becoming regular in-person experiences. Whether I
was working or not, I would fit in a visit to one of the local clubs
as a part of my regular weekly timetable.

Out of this line-up of characters was formed a small society
known as The Ravers. To 'rave' was to give yourself completely,
physically and mentally, one hundred per cent to having nothing
less than a good time, every minute of the day. When you were
raving, you loved the world, you had no enemies.

Zoot Money's place in Fulham was really a trip. I'd been an
avid fan of the Big Roll Band since I saw them on a weekend in
London some years earlier when Zoot first moved with his band
up from the south coast. Several of his band members lived
together with him in his pad in Fulham. In the basement was

guitar player Andy Summers. Zoot and his old lady, Ronnie, had the main floor. Above them their drummer, Colin Allen. Their place was a crossroads for musicians coming in and out of London. I'd go over there to visit them briefly and end up staying for hours, running into all kinds of interesting people, getting into incredible raps on every subject under the sun. We talked of our enthusiasm for dreams; how to create them, the need to pursue them, the belief that there was a chance to create a new world and forget the old values.

For a city of its size there was very little in the way of narcotics and there were probably only five hundred registered junkies in the whole of the metropolis. We had good clean fun. That's what raving was all about. Anyone who found a method of ridding ravers of the curse of wasted hours in bed would be hailed as a saviour. The Ravers was a Hell Fire club for musicians. Perhaps the only difference was we had no permanent headquarters. We were continually on the move, from one club to the next. Club owners, when they heard that the scene was moving towards their club, would be filled with a mixture of joy and horror as they knew an influx of influential people was about to descend upon their place. But they also knew they would end up having to re-decorate before they'd left, possibly several times over.

The Ravers also allowed outsiders in, non-musicians, in the form of Keith Altham and Richard Green, a couple of journalists who were responsible for reporting the early sixties British wave from its beginnings. A commentary written by Green in one of his columns ran:

> Into London poured the Ravers and the undisputed kings of lunacy were The Animals. Wherever the lads from Newcastle went with their tough accents and their warm friendly faces, they'd leave behind them a trail of tottering revellers. The Animals, amongst the groups, have set the standard for raving and anyone else is just an honorary second. Undoubtedly, in the all night drinking stakes, The Animals are outright winners. George Bruno Money, leader of the legendary Big Roll Band, and Eric Burdon are brothers in booze, while their cohort is Brian Auger.

I really do believe Zoot and I were the original Blues Brothers. The main purpose of raving was to trip round London and follow the latest house bands, cheer them on and maybe sit in from time to time. The Ravers loved Brian Auger's Steam Packet incorporating Rod Stewart, Julie Driscoll and Long John Baldry. Ah yeah, beautiful Julie Driscoll, we all remembered her. When people like this got down to a club like the Cromwellian and jammed they were guaranteed full houses every night, and there were never any punters, no outsiders beyond the inner circle of musos and their friends. The Cromwellian club was one of the best places, and Joe Van Dykes, my buddy who found me the apartment in Duke Street, was often working on the door as a bouncer.

Surprisingly, the music would not drown the wild conversation that went on around the huge table in the main room downstairs. It was really medieval down there. Food got thrown around as much as it got eaten, the wine went down our throats by the gallon, but Scotch and Coke and Methedrine were favourite and at the table people would be jaw-wagging all night until jaws locked and they could talk no more. Then they would stagger out into the cold morning light, frothing at the mouth like sick dogs as the band played on. Some nights there'd be shock commando raids by teams of guitarists who'd take over the place and wouldn't allow any other instrument to be played.

One such crack unit was the SLAGS – the Society of Looning Alcoholic Guitarists. Its founder member was Eric Clapton, Chief of Slags was Andy Summers, guitar player from Zoot Money's Big Roll Band, Rosko Roskams of the Mark Leeman Five, John McLaughlin, Jeff Beck, Pete Townshend, and in his absence Hilton Valentine. Stevie Winwood who also played lead guitar as well as piano, was allowed into the clan.

Word got out around town about the wild and wonderful guitar jams at the Cromwellian one night, so in answer, another unit of shock troop musicians stormed into the club and took over the place. This time it was the drummers. They started by storming straight downstairs to the main room, ignoring the bar upstairs and whipped out drumsticks and practice pads from their pockets. Knives and forks were used by outsiders allowed in on the bash. They started to pound and play away complex polyrhythms on top of the huge Crom dining table. No one found out who the group was until the cleaner found their calling card on top of the chipped and splintered table. It had been the Thinking Union of Rolling Drummers, or TURDS, consisting of Micky

Waller, Mitch Mitchell, Brian Davidson, Ginger Baker, Colin Allen and Viv Prince.

Another favourite haunt was the Scotch of St James'. Although unsuited to live music it saw a lot of action. We returned to attack the place in October 1965. Club owner Louis Brown had been tipped off we were coming and was ready at the door. 'Good evening, lads, we've missed you.' Louis was acting strangely. I couldn't put my finger on it. Perhaps he was miffed we had been away. The Ravers filled the upstairs bar and free Scotch and Coke flowed. The tiny bar was filled with lunatics like Brian Auger and Long John Baldry.

Louis was sober as a judge, totally removed from the action. I couldn't understand his reserve. I decided to explore downstairs. The place was empty. Well sort of. Soft middle of the road disco music was being played and there were several couples hiding in the shadows. Then a couple began to jive in the soft lighting. I sat down at the corner table reserved for The Animals. It even had a brass name plate for us. I surveyed the room.

Then I recognized the dancers. They were Princess Margaret and Antony Armstrong-Jones. 'Wonderful,' I thought. 'They are out to check out the local disco! After all, they only live down the street at the palace!'

Then I understood the worried look on Louis' face. Sure, he had to be worried. How could he handle this? The new rock royalty might clash with the real thing. Eventually more people drifted downstairs. Amongst the crowd I could see bespectacled John Lennon. By now, the word was out. We had royalty present and the young couple were having a good time. But there was a strange urge to do or die. Somebody would have to say something. It had to be John Lennon. Johnny guitar had to go for it. He waltzed across the room, a foolish clown-like look upon his face, glasses perched upon the end of his nose. Naughty Mr Punch side-stepped up to the bopping couple of Royals on the dance floor and whispered a welcome in Margaret's ear. Her Highness smiled. She had become one of The Ravers.

When summer came, Clubland extended all the way to Palma, Majorca, where MJ was beginning to expand, opening three clubs using The Animals' name. We did a gig for him there. So did Hendrix. I think MJ only managed The Animals to use them to expand his interests. We were the currency he used to buy his way into the local politics of the City of Palma. We did an appearance, an open air festival, in the streets, promoted by the local government. A beautiful 50-foot sailing yacht was placed at our disposal in the marina near the centre of Palma.

On that first visit, Terry the Pill, an old trusted friend and colleague from London, was there to greet me. He was now working at Mike Jeffery's new club. The Pill was looking quite dapper in white summer jeans, white plimsolls and a striped T-shirt. We drove through the narrow streets and past the main plaza towards the beach at Haima. He filled me in on what was going on in the world of 'MJ Majorca Branch'.

'Oh aye,' he said in his Liverpudlian accent, 'I'm having a great time down here. MJ has got nowt for me to do, but guess what, John Bloom's coming in in his yacht and he needs somebody to look after it. He's gonna leave it down here, so I'm the Captain,' he laughed. I laughed with him, slapping him on the knee. 'Is that why you're dressed like a sailor?'

'Yeah, you've got it, buy me a drink?' he said, putting on a false woofter voice. I stepped through the front door of Mike's penthouse suite on the beach. A pall of hash smoke filled the air, Otis Redding was on the box, the room was filled with faces, some of whom I recognized. I seemed to be the only one who cared as I stood on bodies, staggering through the room in the semi-darkness. Eventually The Pill led me by the arm to the balcony, which overlooked the white beach and blue Mediterranean beyond. I hadn't recognized him at first. The last time I had seen him he had a moustache and before that for years he had a beard. Now he was clean-shaven and chinless, but sun-tanned, brown as a berry. It was midnight and the dark glasses were on. The table on the balcony was covered with diving gear; tanks, flippers, mask and knife. Jeffery was in heaven. His favourite pastime was amassing gadgets. Obviously he was only here for the diving. Diving and gadgets were all part of MJ's Secret Service image. In New York, he was always in the radio stores buying the latest bugging devices, receivers and transmitters. He was the first man to have a mobile phone, that I knew about. So it was not unusual to find him here, sober and sane, whilst everyone else in the place was obviously stoned, preparing for a dive next morning. He looked up from the table – 'Hello Eric. Just got in? Pill see you OK? You're gonna have a great time in this place. Er, I'd show you around but it's a little dark at the moment. Maybe in the morning for that, eh?' He turned to look at me, at least I think he was looking at me – you never knew behind those dark glasses. 'I suppose you'll be partying all night like the rest of them, but I shall be down on the beach at the crack of dawn, out for a dive – it's wonderful. I'll show you how to use the tanks, would you like that?'

'I'd love it,' I said genuinely.

'Oh, by the way,' he said, 'don't be surprised in the morning if you see a line of great big battleships out there. You see those lights?' He pointed out towards the horizon. I could indeed see lights in the inky night. 'Well, the Americans came in – that's the Seventh Fleet out there, son. When the sun comes up in the morning you'll see them in all their glory.'

'What are they doing here?' I inquired.

'Oh, then you don't know about the two atomic bombs,' continued The Pill.

'Two atomic bombs? What two atomic bombs?' I almost laughed. Jeffery turned to me.

'It's true, the American navy have lost two atomic bombs off the coast of Spain, somewhere on the ocean floor. They're here to retrieve them and, er, people don't like it. They're really upset, the Spaniards. Anyway, Palma's crawling with the US fleet. Every night you can't move for sailors. I wouldn't bother going into town. That's why everybody's here getting stoned. They've taken over all the clubs, everywhere, it's murder. Anyway, lads, I bid you goodnight, I'm off to bed. The Pill will show you where to sleep, won't you, Pill? Goodnight lads.' Then he was off. I staggered off into the kitchen to raid the fridge before joining the not-too-well-defined circle of hash smokers.

The sun woke me up the next morning. The beach was already filling up. The October sun was warming up and people were already out enjoying the water, skiing, snorkelling, and high-powered boats were moving to and fro across the wide, beautiful bay. I stepped barefoot into the hot sun, a little shaken from the night before. Amazingly, I saw MJ coming towards me from the water, wetsuit on, flippers in his hand and tanks slung over his back, still wearing his dark glasses. How did he get away with it, I thought. I couldn't figure that one out.

'I've been up since 6 o'clock. The water's nice and clear, it's lovely,' he said. I could see the huge grey ships of the Seventh Fleet. 'Amazing sight, isn't it?' he said. I made myself comfortable applying sun oil, eyeing Jeffery's wonderful tan. He looked like he'd been there for a whole year. He was almost black. As he dumped the oxygen tanks, he said, 'You want a drink? Just stick your hand up in the air and the waiter will come across from the bar.'

'Hey, terrific,' I said, 'who could ask for anything more? Vodka and orange, please.' Mike refused a drink and promised he had something interesting to show me. His actions were rather suspect.

He picked up a black box from the beach towel at his feet. 'What's that?' I inquired. 'Oh, just another of my little gadgets. I picked this one up in Switzerland just recently. Now let me see if I can do this properly.' His head turned towards the skyline. He crouched down about five feet away from me, the little black box in both his hands, connecting wires running towards a small battery. 'Right,' he said, scanning the horizon, 'I just have to wait for the right moment.'

'Right moment? What you got up your sleeve?' I asked.

'I'll have to fill you in. You see those markers? There's a net there under the water that divides the swimming area from the boat area, so it's a no-go area for craft. Now I was out there this morning at the crack of dawn. Wait a minute, the time's right,' he said. He turned a handle on the little black box. Boom, boom, boom!

A succession of violent explosions roared out from the water, leaving a column of smoke and spray. People ran in a state of panic. My mouth fell open in surprise. 'What the fuck!' I said. MJ quickly covered up the black box with the beach towel, got to his feet, a grin upon his face. I too stood up in amazement and looked at bathers who were a few seconds earlier swimming peacefully, fleeing the sea. I turned to look at Mike. He was trying to contain himself. His stomach muscles rippled uncontrollably. He picked up my towel and dropped it over the flippers, facemask and snorkel, then gathered them up and hurried off towards his apartment, the two of us killing ourselves laughing. When we reached the bar we could hear wild speculation. 'Is it the Americans?' 'What's going on?' 'Are they going to blow up the A bombs?' 'Let's get out of here!' There was confusion at the bar, and on the beach thanks to MJ's peculiar sense of humour.

Big Peter Grant sent a message over the wires to Palma. Mike and I should return at once. He'd pulled off a showbiz coup. He was ecstatic. Little Richard had been booked to do the first ever 'live' *Ready, Steady, Go!* But it seemed Little Richard and Don Arden, the head of the agency, had had some last minute dispute. They needed somebody else to fill the bill and who better than The Animals, the band that had been campaigning for live TV. It wasn't for any artistic reason, other than the fact that Eric Burdon could not lip-sync.

But I was not alone in this shortcoming. Many of the bands preferred to perform live. Lip-syncing was a chore and looked unconvincing as we mimed to our hits. The people at *Ready, Steady, Go!* sensed this. Director Michael Lindsay-Hogg instigated the change, realizing that it meant harder work for the whole crew, but the end result would be outstanding. Probably some of the best rock television ever produced came out of the live *Ready, Steady, Go!* shows. There were great live performances by the James Brown Band, Otis Redding, Nina Simone, The Rolling Stones, The Yardbirds, Pretty Things, the Manfred Mann band, and The Who. They became regulars on *Ready, Steady, Go!* because they could really play, not because they could manufacture a hit in a recording studio. All of the bands concerned were proud at having won this little victory.

But first, in London, we had some recording work to polish off. We needed a B side. It was 2 o'clock in the morning and we'd been working pretty hard. Mickie Most behind the desk, looking like a fresh-faced high-school kid, wasn't ready to give up. As long as the band wanted to record, he'd be there, pencil in the mouth, sitting in the producer's chair, feet up on the console, relaxed. Over the intercom, into the main room, he spoke. It was the voice of God, the producer. 'OK, if you guys feel you've got something else to come up with, we need a B side for the new single. Have you got anything?' In the middle of the room AP sat behind the red topped Vox Continental, his feet nervously tapping out a fast gospel-type rhythm, his fingers skating up and down the keyboard surrounded by baffling and studio blankets.

He was playing fast, uptempo, hot and nasty gospel. I was in the isolation booth, headphones clamped on my head. Pricey opened, swirling through the changes. The door swung open.

Chas and Johnny appeared with armloads of manilla bags filled with goodies. During our 2 a.m. lunch break we guzzled on lager, and ate sandwiches as the song was emerging. Soon, Big Chas put on the bass guitar, Hilton got behind the lead guitar, Johnny on the drums, Pricey on the Vox Continental. We kicked into 'I'm Crying'.

'I want to hear you knock upon my door,
I don't get your loving any more,
I'm crying, I'm crying, Baby, I'm crying, I'm crying.

We left the studio at sun up, after putting yet another hot track in the can. Always a good feeling, leaving the studios in the wee hours of the morning, the sun on the rise, the straight world on its way to work, to be locked up in offices for another eight hours whilst we slept, the sound of our music still ringing in our heads.

Soon after came a shattering event that would hit the headlines, the first crack in The Animals' unity.

The danger signals came when we were out on the road doing some college gigs down south. They were warm-ups before a European tour. We arrived in Oxford to play at the University. There we were, half a dozen scruffs from Newcastle drowning in a sea of academics. Oh, they were all very nice and they all wanted to get into the music and all that, but we felt totally out of place. Maybe this was what caused Alan Price to start acting strangely.

But no, it started well before we got to Oxford, in the car on the way to the gig. We'd left London late in our flashy Ford Galaxy and as fast as Tappy drove, we were still way behind time. So we made a pact, often done on a rush trip. When we came to make a gas stop we wouldn't get out to eat in the roadside café. We would just fill up with fuel and take off. Agreed? Yeah, OK. So we stopped for gas.

People piled out of the car and into the cold night air, wandering around the service station to stock up with chewing-gum, nuts, soft drinks and whatever they could find to bring back to the car. Tappy was on the fuel pump. The huge Galaxy sucked in gallons of petrol. Hood up, oil and radiator checked. 'OK, let's go.' We piled back into the car. Tappy turned to make a swift head count. 'Wait a minute ... where's ... ?'

The instant we realized someone was missing we all looked out of the Galaxy window and peered into the restaurant. There we could see AP in the process of committing a cardinal sin. He was actually eating. 'What the fuck?' snarled Chas. 'He knows he's not supposed to do that,' snapped Hilton. Tappy scowled, his face unshaven, a black leather cap on his head. He looked like a New York taxi driver. 'Well, somebody better go and get him, I don't pull enough rank.' Chas volunteered. 'I'll get the fucker.' Johnny followed. I opened the car door and stood there and watched it happen. John Steel and Chas Chandler thundered into the cafeteria. Pricey was into his sausage and chips and before he could burn his lips a second time, they were on him. They grabbed him by the arms from behind and frog marched him past the bemused faces of the truckers. 'If there's no more delays we MIGHT make it,' growled Tappy, throwing the car into gear. We arrived late at the Oxford Union. The audience and the organizers let us know it. There we were, manhandling our own equipment, setting it up in a sea of chins, trying to get on with the job of entertaining, while they hassled us about being late.

'They all look and sound like penguins,' complained Tappy. The backstage dressing area wasn't a proper dressing room at all. It was part of a large kitchen where some of the staff prepared food. There was a tea urn, some scones and sausage rolls, but that was about it. The toilet was shared by the artists with two thousand members of the public in the adjacent dance hall. I'd been in there taking a leak and was about to leave when I noticed AP.

He was coming through the door towards me. He was drinking vodka and orange juice, Carl Perkins style. That is you take a bottle of vodka, a bottle of orange juice, put both in your mouth at once and take a hit. It looked like it was going to be an interesting evening. After much silliness, we eventually made it to the stage, except there was nobody on the Vox organ. 'Where the bloody hell is Alan?' demanded Chas, drawing on a cigarette, stubbing it out on the floor and screwing it with his foot. 'Come on man, we're ready to go.' Johnny looked distastefully from behind his drums and shrugged his shoulders. 'Tappy!' I yelled. 'Where's Alan?'

Nobody knew. No sign of AP. I could feel it in my bones, he was gonna pull a moody. I knew he'd been acting strange lately. The incident in the café wasn't like him, more like Hilton. And then the other night at a party he had got the DTs. 'I don't know, man, I gotta bad feeling,' said Tappy, as he went off in search of Alan. He returned with a worried look on his face. The sea of penguins and their mates began to squawk. They wanted fish. Tappy ran across to me and Chas. 'Er, sorry lads.' 'What's happened?' we chorused. 'It's Alan. He's passed out, pissed, in one of the toilets. He's lying on the floor face down with his head next to the bowl. The vodka bottle is almost empty and there's not much left of the orange juice.'

'Christ,' said Chas. 'Fucking hell,' said I. 'That's it.' Yes, that was indeed it. I believe that was the last time I saw Alan Price for a long time. I heard from him on the telephone, but the next time I saw him was in the Bob Dylan movie *Don't Look Back*, where he was backstage in Newcastle with Bobby and they were discussing whatever happened to The Animals. Alan was still drinking vodka and orange Carl Perkins style.

Somehow we managed to scrape through the gigs without him. In Sweden we appeared with young Micky Gallagher, a replacement keyboard man from Newcastle. Poor Micky, he'd never been on stage before in his life and his first appearance, his first ever gig, was in front of 12,000 in Copenhagen's famous Tivoli Garden. We fulfilled contracts as best we could until a decent, competent, lookalike replacement for Alan was found. Dave Rowberry came to us from the Mike Cotton Sound. Dave was indeed competent and gave the band new colour. From the commercial point of view he even looked a lot like Alan Price with the same sculptured features, same hair colouring, and he was physically the same size. So it worked out perfectly and although I must admit the spark was gone, as far as recording went, Dave Rowberry delivered, and The Animals held their own once again in the pop record market, as we moved on, with the second generation of Animals.

I recall a phone call from Alan Price somewhere along the line. 'Hey, nice of you to call.'

The voice crackled back at me. 'Yeah, I'm out on the road with Bob Dylan like. I thought it would be good for me head. The band was screwing me up, all the drinking and travelling. I couldn't stand it. I hope you understand.'

'Oh, sure I understand,' I said. 'Sure.' I just felt embarrassed. I didn't know what to say. He had little more to add. I guess he just

wanted to impress me that he was still swimming in the best musical circles.

'Yeah, well give my regards to Bob Dylan. What are you doing,
hanging out or touring with him, or what?'

'Yeah. I think I'll just go round with him for a while. You know
what I mean?' He didn't let much go. He never did.

One morning back in my London flat I was cooking breakfast
just wearing my socks, when my new black girlfriend Selina slid
up behind me. During the night she had hit me with something,
but I couldn't quite figure it out. I didn't want to lose my cool by
asking her! I knew I'd eventually find out what it was that caused
my heart to race and my blood to rush to my head. She always did
me in. Now she was about to hit me again.

From behind, she slid her hand around me and cracked an
amylnitrate capsule under my nose. She was a real devil. Not
knowing quite what to do, the fumes found their way up my
nostrils into my brain. I just stood there naked, arms in the air,
wigging out. She in turn, with one swift movement, picked a fresh
egg from the small corrugated cardboard carton on top of the
table next to the cooker, thrust her hand forward and crushed the
egg into the pit of my belly. The yellow and white ran down my
belly and all over my cock, which instantly volunteered itself to
be serviced. Another Jamaican trick. Oh God, the effect of the
drug and raw egg together made me feel like the whole world had
just come at once.

I was never one for divulging my sexual acts with another
person, but I couldn't resist telling my mate Terry the Pill what
had transpired between Selina and myself.

'What a scene,' he said. 'With a fucking egg!' That's when I got
my nickname 'Eggs'. It would stick with me for a long time. Quite
a few people thought E for B meant Eggs for Breakfast. The
Eggman cometh.

I lost sight of Selina but years later in the seventies I bumped
into her in Mayfair on the street. 'How ya doin' baby,' she said,
from behind huge dark glasses. 'Ain't seen ya for ages.'

'Hey Selina.' I grabbed hold of her and kissed her on the cheek.
Her huge soft red lips wrapped around my mouth. She wanted to
know what I was doing in town.

'Oh, a little business. Looking for pleasure,' I said.

'Oh yeah, where are you staying?'

'Could be the Hilton up the street.'

We decided to make an afternoon of it. I'd forgotten over the years, that the egg business had begun with this woman. We strolled up the street to the Hilton and took a room. It blew my mind, and the bellhop's mind too when he arrived freshfaced at the door looking like a Philip Morris commercial. She was in the doorway, half-naked, her long lithe legs encased in nylon stockings, tits like bowls of brown Windsor soup spilling all over the place.

'Here,' she said, handing the guy a five-pound-note tip, 'have these clothes pressed.' She turned to look at me with her big brown eyes. 'I may as well if I'm staying here all afternoon, Eric, then I'll be ready for this evening.'

'Er, wonderful,' I said, 'please, go right ahead.'

'Yes, I'll have these pressed,' she continued, looking at the bellhop, not doing much to shield her naked body from the kid, 'and bring us a bottle of Moët, a bucket of ice and, er, a dozen raw eggs.' I nearly fell through the twenty-three floors below us. It all came flooding back, or should I say it all came running back. Anyway, we had a great afternoon. Hardly got round to the eggs. We spent the rest of the afternoon on the balcony, drunk, throwing them at the workers on the Wimpey site across the street from us. Didn't hit a thing, but we laughed a lot.

Sex orgies were plentiful and if for no more than childish curiosity, I wanted to find out, I wanted to know. So when this huge-titted blonde monster with a mad look in her eye grabbed me one night at the bar of the Scotch of St James' and winked, 'There's a bit of a party at my place later.' I said 'I'll be along.' It was all nod nod, wink wink, nudge nudge, otherwise one could slip into the abyss of the *News of the World*. A murky place for anyone to end up, but that was a large part of the game, the danger, you see.

I must admit, the first one is kind of like having your cherry broken again. It's the fear when you first walk in. It's that same fear that you sense as a virgin, before you know what it'll really be like. You may not have enjoyed yourself the first time, but you won't admit it to anyone and you get over the fear eventually and begin to either enjoy sex or despise it. It didn't take much, just one or two orgies were enough to make me understand that I really didn't need to see human beings on such a level. But I had to find out, it was like a magnet dragging me towards the challenge of actually playing a part in a Sunday newspaper serial. You never knew who you were gonna run across, it was amazing.

Within the Mayfair flat, the light from the grainy 16mm projector grinding away gave the room a strobic light effect. The film was a total bore, it looked like it had been shot in the thirties. The women were ugly and everyone was masked. I lay on the shag white carpet with my head in my hands, more interested in looking at the people in the room than the film. I found it strange that people had gathered with an unspoken word, they all knew for what purpose they had gathered and yet they all preferred to sit there and stare at the wall. The blonde next to me on the armchair had beautiful legs. My hand went out and grabbed her round the ankle. I pulled myself across the floor and slid my hand up her legs. She looked down at me, smiled and moaned, then she pushed my hands away and cracked up laughing. 'Oh no,' she said, pushing me away, 'I've got the biggest one in the room.' In her hands was a large rubber object. She got up and walked away. I lay back down on the floor. Another head crossed the projector, casting a giant shadow on the wall. A familiar face. Click. I knew him. 'Hey, how ya doing, Johnny boy?' The bright white illuminated face of an unshaven John Lennon in a pin-striped suit ducked underneath the beam of light, across the room, out of the door behind the blonde.

The ice-cold blonde with the huge tits, dressed in fishnet stockings and high heels walked across towards me. 'Oh, you got here at last,' she said, a big smile across her face, not even the slightest hint of being anything less than completely at ease. 'It's my birthday,' she said. 'I've been given lots of presents, they're in the bedroom, would you like to take a look?'

'Of course, this is a birthday party,' I said stupidly. 'Yes, come this way, I'll show you everything.' I sat upon the bed. She stood in front of me. 'Do you like these?' she said, running her hand across her legs, emphasizing the fact that she was wearing fishnet stockings. I began to undress as she talked. I still didn't see any birthday presents, but nevertheless she produced a small white cane. It went thwack as she hit the palm of her hand. 'Would you like some of this?' she said, a crazy look in her eyes. I wasn't quite sure what she meant by 'some of this'. I'd seen books that I'd bought whilst I'd been on trips to Amsterdam that had strange bizarre acts in them, but I had no idea what this was leading to.

'Stand up,' she said. Without thinking, I followed her orders and stood up. 'Turn around.' Somehow, she got me to do it and I turned. 'Now then, some of this.' Whack, the pain was incredible. I jumped across the room howling. 'Owwwww,' and sprung back at her without thinking. I jumped upon her, grabbed the cane and savagely attacked her in the corner of the room. She loved it.

An oriental girl stood next to a blonde Patti Harrison looka-like. They posed either side of the sink, casually talking to each other, half-naked. It was then that I hit them both with an amyl-nitrate 'popper'. They greedily went for it, sucking it up into their nostrils. It was then I hit them with the eggs, one each. Both shrieked in surprise and then moaned with pleasure as I moved in on the pair on my knees. The refrigerator door opened, shedding its cold light on this bizarre duo. Behind us in the half-light, Johnny stood in the doorway, his National Health glasses perched on the end of his hooklike nose. 'Go on, go get it, Eggman. Go for it. I've been there already, it's nice. I'm off. I'll see ya.' Passing ships in the night.

Brian Epstein's place in Belgravia became the rock'n'roll palace. It would be unthinkable now for a man in such a vulnerable pos-ition to keep such an open house but we could all call by any time, and Brian would make us welcome. He was obviously a man in deep pain, but when his boys were happy and people were party-ing at his expense, the pain lessened. Eppy was the first rich and lonely person I'd ever met. When he could play the role of pro-ducer he had something to do with his life, he could be a nice fellow. When he was bored he fell into a state of homosexual silli-ness. However, Eppy made another contribution to rock in the form of an eyedropper bottle, a magic potion imported from Switzerland. This little bottle, I feel sure, was at least partly re-sponsible for the creation of The Beatles' new psychedelic wave, which included the monumental album 'Sergeant Pepper's Lonely Hearts Club Band.'

During the sober hours we had fascinating conversations, par-ticularly about The Beatles' experiences in America. He loved the Apollo Theatre, but because of their fame The Beatles had never been able to visit the citadel of black music.

Brian now had a burning desire to open a London equivalent. I thought this an exciting, admirable idea. The Saville Theatre in Shaftesbury Avenue was to be his Apollo in London. Eppy had secured a liquor licence and the opening act would be Little Richard. 'Would you like to compère the show?' he asked. 'Come on, Eric, it's a great scheme, you must agree.' Yes, it would be a great honour, or so I thought.

Opening night arrived, with Little Richard topping the bill – 'And your compère for this evening, ladies and gentlemen, from The Animals, Eric Burdon!' Lord, what had I got myself into as I was announced and the garbage started to hit the floor. The audience were one wild seething mass of Welsh Teds. They just didn't listen to rock'n'roll music, they lived it, it was a religion and Little Richard was one of their gods. The Animals, The Stones, The Beatles were shit.

It was great to see Richard again, I hadn't seen him since New York. Richard is always described by himself and others as wild, flamboyant and the Georgia Preach. Sometimes he's a preacher, but most times he's probably one of the best rock'n'roll stars of all time and one of the few originals to survive and still be sane today. Little Richard fascinated me from the first time that I saw him on film in the movie *The Girl Can't Help It*. Both he and Chuck Berry had that wonderful glazed look in their eye. They were some place else. It was where I wanted to be. Now, here I was, sharing the stage with Little Richard again.

Nobody could beat Little Richard. But why had I agreed to this mad scheme? I could see why Brian was such a good manager. 'It's all right,' he soothed. 'It's gonna be a great night, Eric. I'm so glad you could do it. You're rock'n'roll, everything will be fine.'

I went to take a look. On the way past Richard's dressing room I had to squeeze past sneering Teds who pushed me up against the wall. I had an even bigger shock when I peeked through the curtains. The audience was a raging sea of greasy heads and beehive hairdos that crashed against the barriers. Even the balconies were draped with legs and arms, bodies ready to fall on to the crowd below. What was I gonna do? I needed protection. I phoned a mate called The Hawk. 'Get a cab and get round to my place,' I snapped. 'Chris Farlowe just gave me a US World War II gunners' helmet. Fetch it round quick and anything else you can find to protect me from this mad audience. They're absolutely wild. The Welsh have poured over the border in busloads!'

Welsh Teds weren't just rock fans. For them it was a way of life. Eppy had put me in the firing line, the bastard. Backstage a voice called: 'Fifteen minutes to show time!'

Chants began. 'We want Richard, we want Richard!' But Little Richard was still in his dressing room psyching himself up for the show. Still no sign of my mate. Then the stage lights went up and the houselights down. I walked on stage. 'Yaroo!' The crowd screamed abuse and hurled a rain of missiles. I made it to the mike. 'The Saville Theatre proudly presents...' then the sound went off. Someone had yanked out the wires. The crowd loved it. The house PA was wrecked.

I made a hasty retreat. At the side of the stage a door burst open and crashing through, leaving a taxi with its meter ticking over, was The Hawk. He was armed with the US helmet, netting and camouflage, a dustbin lid for a shield, and a portable loudhailer with battery pack. 'Hawk, you're a genius,' I said. He smiled, clicked his heels and did a Nazi salute. 'Here we go, this is it!' I said, grabbing the armour. The dustbin lid in front of me, the helmet over my ears, and the speaker system strapped in place, I marched back on stage. 'All right you fuckers, you asked for it, so you're gonna get it. Here's Little fuckin' Richard!'

The place went berserk as Richard opened up. 'A wop bop a loo bop a wop bam boom!' It was a wild night. I felt satisfied. At least I had done my bit and fulfilled my promise to Brian. I was proud of my part in his attempt to bring the Apollo to London. It was fun while it lasted.

Chris Farlowe was everyone's favourite singer. He was admired by The Stones and The Beatles for his cockney soul voice and he had his own great little band, The Thunderbirds, which was like a nursery for a lot of good players, like Carl Palmer, Albert Lee and Dave Greenslade. Eventually he had a big hit with 'Out Of Time' in the summer of 1966. He was signed to the Gunnells for management and recording, but it seemed everybody had a hand in his management from time to time, and Rik and John were loose enough to let it happen. Everybody wanted to do things for Chris because he was reckoned to be one of the hottest singers in town. All he needed was a break.

One day he phoned me at my Duke Street pad. 'Hey Eric, how ya doin', it's Chris Farlowe here,' he said in his hoarse voice. I asked how he was getting on. 'Oh, I'm OK. 'Ere listen, you'll never guess what happened. Paul McCartney – you know Paul out of The Beatles?' Yes, I had heard of him. 'Well he came round to our house in the middle of the night. I was out doing a show, but me mum was in and he left her a demo disc for me to listen to.'

This was wonderful news. When was Chris going into the studio to cut this gift from the gods? 'Ah,' he growled. 'I don't like it. It's not for me. It's too soft. I need a good rocker, you know, a shuffle or something.'

'Yeah, but Chris,' I said. 'Anything to give you a start, man, I mean even if it's a ballad, you should go ahead and record it.'

'No, I don't like it,' he insisted. 'Too soft.'

'So what are you gonna do with the song?'

'Well, I sent it back, didn't I?'

'What was the title of the song?'

'"Yesterday",' he retorted.

It was around this time The Animals did *Ready, Steady, Go!* live instead of Little Richard who couldn't make the show.

The gig proved very important for our prestige and reputation showing we really were a great live rock'n'roll band. RSG, as it was affectionately known, was a vital ingredient in 'breaking' The Animals as a pop attraction as well.

On one RSG show I sang with Chris Farlowe and Otis Redding, all three of us jamming together. When they booked Nina Simone on the show, some time later, the production team thought she was a very cagey individual, very anti-white and hard to handle. The Animals had a big hit with a cover version of her song 'Don't Let Me Be Misunderstood' in January 1965, and I had subsequently met Nina. Michael Lindsay-Hogg called me up to be a special envoy and translator of sorts between himself, the RSG crowd and Nina.

I'll never forget when I first met Nina Simone. It happened during a tour of America when 'Don't Let Me Be Misunderstood' was still high in the charts and constantly on the radio.

We went to see her perform at the Hunter College Campus theatre.

I was wondering what her attitude was towards The Animals – and me. I had heard she was a heavy lady. Backstage passes had been arranged by a photographer friend of ours, Linda Eastman (McCartney). She held the young audience spellbound. Ballads of pain and love poured out, like 'Slave And Martha', 'Visions Of Freedom', and 'The Damnation Of The White Race'. Like a fire-brand preacher, her musical onslaught was unmerciful and re-lentless, but not a soul in the two thousand strong audience was against her. They all understood and seemed to share the pain and agonies which this beautiful black woman harboured inside her. She was wonderful. When she announced 'Don't Let Me Be Misunderstood', I knew what was coming. She said coldly that it was in the charts by a popular rock'n'roll band. I could feel her eyes boring into me. She recognized that stocky little fellow from The Animals who dared to sing Nina's song. The audience turned round to glare at me. Screw 'em, I came here to see her and not worry about what they think.

But, by the time Nina had finished singing her version of the song, I was in total sympathy with them. I hated myself. I hated the band for playing the tune too goddamn fast. We always did it too fast. 'She's magnificent, but she's tearing herself apart,' I thought.

After several encores, and bouquets of flowers, Nina left the stage and the audience began to leave the theatre. Linda Eastman made sure that we didn't bolt. She sat on us and made sure, as much as I wanted to escape, that we would wait and go backstage and meet Miss Simone face to face. The backstage dressing rooms were packed with well-wishers. We hung on for fifteen minutes and I was about ready to go. Then I was told that Nina was ready to receive us. We entered a large dressing room, which was empty of people, apart from a short, stocky, very busy gentleman, who I found out later was Nina's husband/manager – an ex-New York City policeman. Nina sat in a corner. 'So you're the little honky who's been stealing my songs, making gains out of Nina's music, out of my music. You got some nerve coming back here, boy.' He folded his arms, stood his ground and backed up his woman. 'That is the worst rendition of that song I ever heard, mister,' Nina said turning round to look into the mirror. I stood there stunned for a moment, trying to gather my thoughts, feelings, and get my brain to function in a way I could defend myself. 'I make no apology for what I've done,' I said. She spun around in the seat to face me again. 'Make no apology? Make no apology? Why you . . .' I interrupted her. 'Just a minute, I'll make an apology, I'll make an apology sure, if you'll apologize to the poor bastards that you're ripping off, who are still serving time down there in the Mississippi State Penitentiary. If you'll go down there and apologize to those guys, if you'll make sure that when you come to record those songs that you've got those prisoners' names and numbers on the label. [Miss Simone had recently recorded an LP which included work songs originally recorded by producer Alan Lomax, in-the-field on location, Mississippi and Alabama state pens.] Because that's their song not yours and I'd like to remind you that since the Animals recorded "Don't Let Me Be Misunderstood" the name of Nina Simone has got bigger in the eyes of the English record-buying public. They are waiting over there for you now, waiting to hear your voice, and your great songs, waiting to buy you, Miss Simone.' I turned to leave. She got up and grabbed me by the arm, then her hand extended into mine. She cracked a smile and said, 'Call me Nina. What's your name, boy? Sit down.'

It was fortunate for us that one of our first public appearances, after the departure of Alan Price in May 1965, was The Animals Big Band at the Richmond Festival that August. Dave Rowberry, our replacement for Alan Price, had come to us direct from the Mike Cotton Sound who were formerly the Mike Cotton Jazzmen, so Dave was particularly at home with Our Big Band experiment. After three days' rehearsals at the Marquee it sounded like we had been together for three years. We just let go, had fun and did our favourite R&B songs from the fifties, like 'Outskirts Of Town', 'Let The Good Times Roll', 'Roll 'Em Pete', 'Two Years Of Torture', and 'I Believe To My Soul'. It was a mix of Ray Charles meets Count Basie.

In between rehearsals I dropped by at MJ's office in Gerrard Street. His secretary handed me a message. It was from Brian Epstein's office. It said: 'Good luck with the Big Band at the weekend. Regards. The Beatles. A band.'

I began to prepare myself for the gig, then drove down to Richmond.

The audience had built up steadily. It was Sunday and the weather had been kind to us. Above the audience a mass of blue smoke drifted towards the blue sky. During the afternoon there was trad jazz. Before we were due to go on with the Big Band, there was a set by Jimmy James and The Vagabonds. Around dusk I saw two Austin Princesses making their way slowly through the dust and crowd. The Beatles had arrived. My belief that great changes were in the wind was confirmed. This was the first time I saw The Beatles in what you could call psychedelic dress. John was wearing, for the first time in public, the famous Granny glasses, perched on his nose, together with a colourful quilted jacket, bottle green velvet pants and open sandals. Paul was dressed the same. Colourful, wild, psychedelic. George looked dapper, a leather pouch strung around his neck. They tried their best to mingle in the beer tent, like normal people, but it wasn't working. The music business folk began acting like groupies. John Steel walked towards Donovan's caravan in disgust. He sat down on the steps and looked across at the milling crowd. 'Ah damn,' said Johnny. 'I feel sorry for The Beatles, man. Ya know, from now on it looks like they're never gonna be able to appear in public without being hassled. It's a drag.'

Yeah, it was true. Even in a hip crowd backstage, everyone wanted to touch them, everybody wanted a piece, so The Beatles left.

'OK lads, ten minutes to kick off.' Tappy came into the tent where the horn players and The Animals were changing into stage gear. It was a wonderful new feeling for me, being in a dressing room full of horn players, tuning up, cleaning and polishing their instruments. Then we heard the announcement.

'Ladies and gentlemen, the Richmond Festival presents The Animals Big Band!'

We were off and into it. The sound of the horns engulfed me and carried me away like wild surf. It was wonderful. A terrific feeling, one you could never get from guitars and amplifiers. It had a soft strength to it. I could feel the brass tickle my ear with melodic power. The same feeling communicated to the audience. They were carried away on a ship that could take us anywhere.

The set went down well and the guys played their hearts out.

The jazzmen were straining at the leash to get to their soul-partners and express themselves to a new-found audience. It was a great experiment that worked.

I knew we had covered the loss of Alan Price. Alan had done so much, but he was gone and so was the first phase of The Animals. Now the second phase was under way.

ELEVEN
THE WEDDING

Angela King, that was her name. She was Anglo-Indian and that was a buzz in itself for me, as I'd made a promise at the tender age of fifteen, that one of the first things I would do would be to have a deep, meaningful, long lasting, memorable, erotic affair with at least one member of every ethnic racial group. There certainly was a difference between the girls who gathered backstage at a theatre and squealed and would force their way into your bedroom or bathroom, or the front door at your mother's house. There was a difference between them and the group of girls that the bands in London hung out with and got to know as friends, and saw every night on a social level, and, of course, enjoyed each other every night on a sexual level. I'm talking about girls like Hendrix's friend Cathy Etchingham. I'd met her before Jimi and we were close friends. I could see instantly when she fell in love with Jimi. Then over in New York there was Linda Keith. She was such a great free floating spirit. I remember talking to her one night yelling in my ear over the roar of the club in New York: 'Groupie, sure I'm a fucking groupie. I've been a groupie for John Lee Hooker since I was eight years of age!' This was the girl who found Hendrix in New York, and begged Chas Chandler to go and listen to him. That's who *really* discovered Jimi. Yeah, Angie was one of these girls.

One of the ladies of the bands, well loved and respected. Angie was always there, it seemed, at every party and event worth being at.

The first time I saw Angela's breasts my heart stood still. She was on a staircase in a cinema in the West End at the opening night of The Animals' movie which we'd produced in Poland. Mike Jeffery had done his best to organize a swish little *bona fide* première, and there were several notable faces there including Julie Christie. Sitting on the stairs was Angela. She had a low-cut T-shirt on and from where I stood above her on the staircase, as she leant forward with her head in her hands, I could see her shapely breasts.

This is going to save me going all the way to India, I thought, if I can cop this bird. I had to have her. I'd seen her around before. There had been giggles in the back of a car on the way home from the Flamingo in the early hours. But that's when I decided I wanted her to move in with me. She had a nice face. It's funny how the vision of an exposed breast can suck you right in and every other consideration goes right out the window. She'd been living with Andy Summers in the basement of Zoot's pad over in Fulham and this must have been the end of the line with Andy. We started holding hands and all that. Before she moved in, and I committed myself to the mad act of marriage, I went through the period of trying out somebody else first. But she'd always find me, no matter where I was. I'd wind up in an orgy, and be in bed with someone else, stare across the room and there'd be her eyes burning at me.

Then she revealed a threat. A rich old man was going to whisk her off to the South of France. There was no future for her in London leading this crazy life with all these drugs. She was going to go to the blue Mediterranean and live among the palm trees with her rich old man. Well, whoever it was told her to say that, it worked, because I went to the airport to stop her and brought her back. Popped the question. I remember the group had a gig in Edinburgh. Angie and I took the train together to Scotland. We spent the weekend in a very conservative Scottish hotel, with clean white sheets, brown body, glassy eyes, special underwear she'd bought in London. I was in heaven. This was it. Marriage. Great stuff.

So after that weekend in Edinburgh we planned to make it

official. Angie just giggled and smiled from that point on and never said much about anything. For the first few months, I was in paradise. My apartment was small and we knew we had to move, but I didn't want to relinquish my rights to the pad where I'd had so many wild love affairs. Its situation right above the Scotch of St James' made it so convenient. I'd planned on keeping it as my weekend, in-town getaway. But we would move into a town house, further away from the city centre.

Everything was hunky dory. I kept getting hit records, and there was lots of TV work. I knew Angie two years before I married her. We lived with each other for six months and it was over. There was a lot of acid going about and my world was one of visions and hallucinations. I lived from day to day, on an hourly basis, not knowing what was going to happen next. I was having a good old time. I was doing regular LSD sessions. Serious ones at a mutual friend's house. During most of the acid sessions, taken either as a group or separately, we exchanged ideas. With The Dodger, The Pill, Brian Epstein, Zoot Money, and Hilton Valentine. We'd all purposefully drop, stay home, meditate and then exchange opinions and ideas about what we had encountered.

There was this heavy session going on in The Dodger's house one night. In attendance was Barry Jenkins, The Dodger, Andy, his Indian mate and myself. Andy was creating a mural on seven panels which explained the birth of the world as taught by Krishna. In the end-panel amongst the trees and foliage, was a Princess who was Kali, goddess of death and destruction. One night, after staring at this woman emerging out of the foliage in the last panel, under the influence of the drug, I began to have visions of an idyllic female. Of course Angie, who was Anglo-Indian, was moving through my life daily, or at least three times weekly. After staring at the goddess in the mural I fell into a deep coma on the floor and was surrounded by the rest of the people in the room. We all reached, under the influence of the hallucinogenic, the same level. We could all talk and describe where we were and discuss the place we arrived at. Andy's voice said 'Can anybody see the staircase?' He told me to climb up it. I was thrust into a sky, filled with bright shining stars, which turned into eyes, trillions of eyes. 'Go for one,' Andy instructed. I sought out one eye, and moved right into it. Then I came face to face with Kali. I was covered in a void. Darkness, darkness. Then a voice asked what right I had to come there and disturb Kali. 'I'm just a man,' I said. 'And what makes you think that you're man enough to disturb me while I'm making love?' 'My ego tells me that if I have a chance to change the world, I have the power to make that change.' 'Ah, so you need answers,' said Kali. 'If you want that information you have to make me a gift.'

I didn't know which world I was in. My own was left behind me. 'I can't see you. You've already taken my sight. What more do you want?' She laughed a wicked, cruel laugh in the darkness. 'How much more are you willing to give?' 'My life.' I said. My life was sucked out of me. I was Gonzo. Melted into the floor. Dead.

When I came to, I found myself staring into the eyes of Angela. She was the most beautiful thing I'd ever seen. 'Let's get married,' I said. That was it. Kali was Angela, the goddess of death and destruction, who I was about to marry!

My bachelor party started the day before a final drink up at the Cromwellian. The celebrations were planned to start much earlier, by myself and The Pill. I was in a bar with The Pill having a pint of reality, talking over the prospects of me getting married and being the first of the raving lunatics to fall victim. So it needed discussing in depth. But The Pill liked Angie a lot, and vice versa. The Pill was generally a good judge of character which was why I confided in him. The consensus view was 'I wish you luck. She's a good lass. Get on with it. Here's to you.' We clashed our beer mugs together, hunched over the bar in the Ship, up the road from the Marquee. We made our plans. The reception of course had to be in the Speakeasy, so it could accommodate all the faces. We wouldn't announce it to the public. It would be a very private affair, we agreed. Terry went along with my plans. Totally informal dress would be the order of the day. But he had to wear top hat and tails. We had a good laugh over it. The Pill was my closest friend now that the first group had fallen apart and the second group was coming into my life. But The Pill hadn't changed his loyalties. We were still good mates. I made him swear that if I went through with the marriage, and before meeting the guys for the bachelor party, around 11.30 p.m., he would help me line up the best of all the girls I'd known in London, and make sure it was telephone co-ordinated, and that I could get from one to the other, fast enough to meet the guys around midnight.

'Sure, you're on,' he said. There was one condition. He wanted to clock me during an egg session with Sylvia. 'You're on,' I said. A big smile cracked over his face and he rubbed his hands together. The Pill was about to prove that he was best road manager in the business. He always wanted the job with The Animals but Tappy Wright held that position and was one of the gang, so The Pill could never quite muscle in on the job, although he would have been capable of doing as good a job as Tappy.

He had a tight schedule made up for me, and he would handle all the telephone calls and taxis to be at various places, on condition he could watch an egg session. I told him it would probably be the last egg session – ever.

'Here's your schedule. You start in Mayfair, at noon tomorrow. You've got Pam, the girl you met from *Ready, Steady, Go!* to meet in the bar at the Hilton. Where you take her is your affair, but you've got to remember noon is the middle of the night for most of the girls on this list.'

Next came Shana in Fulham in the afternoon, and then at 7 p.m. in Mayfair with Sylvia. 'That one is the egg job,' said The Pill. 'Don't worry about me. I'll be in the cupboard, ready to clock.' We both laughed. At 9.30 p.m. was Jeane from New York over at Jimi's pad. 10 p.m. was 'Ziggy'. 'You've only got 45 minutes with her, and you know how she likes to talk. Next comes Sue. She'll meet you at her place in Mayfair. Then at midnight, Eva at her place, again in Mayfair. Then at 1 a.m. I had to meet all the boys in the bar at the Cromwellian (not the Speak). 'Any questions. Ready to rock?' 'Yessir, stand by!' I said. I can't really remember much about that afternoon or that night. Bits come back to me in splodges. Splodges was the right word. Pam, my first date, was black and beautiful. I met her at the Hilton bar. 'Morning,' she said sarcastically as I walked in. 'Do you realize I've never met a guy at 2 p.m. in my life,' she said. She got down off her stool hugging me and squealing, and making a terrible din with everyone looking at us. It was embarrassing. But she was wonderful. 'You're just a big kid. You're never going to grow up. Life's just one big party for you,' she said. 'Do you want a drink? And by the way, have you got us a room upstairs? Is that what you've got me here for?' She laughed in her East End cockney accent. 'Why, sure it is. Pam, I couldn't go without one more of your blow jobs, it wouldn't be right. What would you like to drink? I'm buying.'

'Oh good, then I'll have a large Scotch and Coke,' she smiled. The next thing we were high on the 23rd floor in a suite booked by The Pill.

We rounded off the afternoon love session and I kissed Pam goodbye. I was still tying my shoelaces as my taxi sped towards Fulham. Shana was at Zoot's place. The door was open and the house was empty. I climbed the stairs. It was dark at the top. Then came a shaft of light. It was Shana. We groped on the staircase. We talked about getting married. She was gonna marry. We talked and kissed. I said: 'I have another appointment.' She said, 'I'm sure you have. Bye.'

Back at Mayfair I met Sylvia. Automatic buzzer. Door opens. Up the stairs. The Pill was already there in one of the cupboards, playing one of his games. Anyway, it was Eggs for Breakfast while The Pill watched.

We sat there and had a beer later, all three of us. We had a good laugh. It was farewell Sylvia. At nine I went on to Jeane's place in Soho. The excuse was, I wanted her to play on my latest record. She liked a joke anyway. 9.30. Cathy's over at Jimi's place. It was more talk, a kiss and see you tomorrow at the wedding. 10 o'clock. Ziggy. She was on the roof as usual staring into outer space, looking for flying saucers. It took me ages to get her downstairs, and when I did, I had to do her on the floor, on the lino. It was cold, uncomfortable, but I made it.

Come 10.45 p.m. I went to Sue's. She wasn't in as promised. I had to climb in the window up a drainpipe. I found her underwear lying on the bed. She came in nursing a bottle of champagne ready for my last lusty session. 'How are you doing, what *are* you doing? How did you get in here? You don't have my key, do you? The window again, Burdon! You are terrible. Listen, does your wife know about you and ladies' clothes?' 'No, but she's about to find out,' I said. 'What are you doing in my wardrobe? Get out of there!' she said, hitting me sideways with a rolled up ladies' corset which had spilled from her magic box of tricks. 'Oh no, not more champagne,' I said.

'Where have you been before you came here?' She had me sussed. I had to spill the beans, and tell her the whole story. She found it quite funny. She was about to break my balls and she knew it. She lay on the floor naked, clutching the bottle of champagne. 'Come and get it, honey, let's see what's left in you.'

Herculean trips and experiences are hard work and really never much pleasure. I was now beginning to tire, I had to admit. But by the time she finished with me it was wonderful. I staggered from her place at 12 o'clock. The last destination was to meet Eva, back again in Mayfair. The taxi was waiting for me at the street corner. I was about to burn out. Eva was German, and had beautiful dark features.

She was devastatingly beautiful and she was a maniac. Just my kind of girl. We enjoyed many experiences together later in Los Angeles when I got to know her better. But back in those days we were just feeling each other out. In her own circles, Eva was a star. So it was no surprise to me that when the elevator reached her floor this disgruntled black guy, who I knew from the clubs in London, was leaving, cursing under his breath. He walked by me scowling, leaving Eva's door open. I could hear her screaming at the top of her voice. 'And shut the fucking door.' I put my head round the door, expecting something to hit me. 'Eva, it's Eric.' 'Oh yeah, come on in.' I pushed open the bedroom door. Inside there was a candle burning and in the light I could see two girls on the bed – Eva and a blonde. Wait a minute. It was two blondes. Eva was wearing a blonde wig. In the candlelight, because of her dark features, she looked spectacular, as did her lady friend. What can I say? It was about all that anybody could take.

By the time I reached The Cromwellian at 1 a.m. I must have had that look in my eye, it brought a round of applause from the gentlemen at the bar, all with beaming faces. I could hear old fashioned songs like 'I'm Getting Married In The Morning'. 'Do me a favour, gimme a drink,' I said. 'Coming right up.' It was more champagne. Oh no!

I ran into all kinds of faces, Chris Farlowe, Jeff Beck, and Keith Moon. It was 'Have a drink on me' until I could drink no more.

The Pill and I sat alone in the empty, quiet, darkened club. Upstairs they were cashing up. Just me and The Pill now. 'Well, almost sun up, and you are getting married in a few hours.' The Pill stood up. 'Good luck.' He shuffled off into the darkness. It was time to go. I walked home, and rode the lift to the third floor. The room next to mine, William Burroughs' place, was silent as usual. I stepped inside. This would be the last time I'd be alone here. I laid out a new pair of jeans and a spectacular bright blue and gold embroidered Afghan jacket I'd picked out the weekend before. It was gonna be a real casual affair.

The next thing I remember is walking through St James's Park heading towards Petty France in the early morning, checking my watch to make sure I was on time. I didn't want to leave her standing out there. So I kept a steady pace, trying to fight back all the alcohol swimming around my system from the night before. I saw statues of some huge lions, sculpted stone symbols of Britain's strength and historic past. Pride, integrity, marriage, the family unit. Magnificent!

I felt much better as my head cleared from the walk, but it was further than I anticipated. Then suddenly round the next corner, I saw them, their headscarves waving in the wind, hundreds of women with prams and babes in arms being controlled by several overworked boys from The Met. I had to face it. There couldn't be any other reason for these wild women's presence. It was just because I was getting married. 'Pill, you bastard,' I said to myself, 'you promised me a quiet affair.' I had to blame it on someone. There wasn't anybody else I could think of. I couldn't stop now. My feet carried me towards the registry office.

The crowds were out of this world. There was The Pill at the top of the staircase in a very smart top hat. It made him look tall and dignified. He was the only one normal and formal. Everyone else was totally freaked out. Even I looked relatively straight. It was a wild, beautiful bunch of hippies, and among them I could see my father looking very handsome, conservative, cool and re-laxed and having a helluva good time with a broad grin on his face. Next to him, beaming like a Cheshire cat, my Mum, her eyes looking even bigger through her new spectacles. The crowd looked like a giant bouquet of flowers, and they were all there, but her.

She was nowhere to be seen. 'Anybody seen Angie?' I asked casually. The most bizarre look comes over a woman's face when she has to explain something like this to a man. A half-way mark between love and hate, pain and ecstasy, when they tell you some-thing they know they have nothing in their power to stop. They are deeply sympathetic but at the same time they are laughing at you. It was explained to me. 'No, she hasn't arrived yet. She's a little late. Don't worry.' I sat on the staircase inside the ante-chamber, leading to the main room where the deed would be done, trying to keep a distance from the press. Now a BBC TV crew arrived. It was getting wild and I was getting worried. I could see many familiar faces giving me sympathetic looks and thumbs up signs. Among them, Jeff Beck and The Hollies.

Then she arrived. She looked beautiful, stepping out of the limousine in the morning sun, dressed in a bright orange sari, a white carnation in her hair. It was quite a buzz. I was happy, and in love. I was blinded by love.

I was about to experience a young, hot, doomed-from-the-start marriage. Oh, so easy to slip into, and oh, so hard to get out of. Ring on the finger, ring in the nose. Tough. We had a good re-lationship. Until we got married. All hell was about to happen. But for the moment my eyes could see nobody but her. Looking back at an old photograph, I have to laugh. It was a giggle, and after all when I look at the line-up in the now-fading picture I can see what in the straight world were called bridesmaids. I never thought of it that way before, until I looked at the picture, but there they were, smiling! Pam, Shana, Sylvia, 'Ziggy', Jeane, and Sue, and Eva, outa sight! Angela's mother and my mother smil-ing, trying to put on a brave face, my old man content, arm in arm with hippie friends. The Pill, Zoot Money, Andy Summers, an endless list of friends and acquaintances. 'Ee, we had a right old time!

Then we staggered back for a few pints after the ceremony, the local in this case being the Speakeasy. I felt a sense of relief at being away from the ceremonials in the dark cool Speakeasy with everyone huddled around the bar. The ladies formed a crowd in one part of the room, the men in the other. More famous faces came pouring through the door, including the guys from The Ani-mals and from my new band. I noticed a strange, blond guy, an obvious speed freak in a flying jacket, with a rather distinguished face and jutting jaw. He had a 35mm Nikon slung around his neck, and a Pentax in his hand. He was continually chewing gum. Occasionally he would shoot photographs of me, but I noticed he was paying far too much attention to Angela. The seeds of jea-lousy were sown.

The reception finished. Just a few faces were left. Angela and I leaned against the bar in the empty Speakeasy. Beneath the sari her body was rigid, quivering. She was ready. It was time to go home. We climbed the staircase. It must have been 9 o'clock. There were no taxis to be had. I realized that in my pocket I had the keys to the van belonging to The Animals. There it stood in Margaret Street, where it could usually be found, covered in lipstick, messages from frantic fans.

'Come on, we'll take the gig wagon home.' Inside there was so much equipment that Angie, in her elegant sari, had to lie sideways across a row of Vox amplifiers. As the van slid, rocked and rolled under the weight of the heavy equipment, I drove Angie home. The bride in the gig wagon. I thought it was hilarious.

She didn't think it was very funny at all.

TWELVE
GOIN' TO CALIFORNIA

The new band with Dave Rowberry, Barry Jenkins, Chas, Hilton and myself went back to America in 1966. We all hoped it would be a success and the gigs would be good. But the way things were going it couldn't last, and I began to feel disillusioned with the whole saga.

MJ went to the Bahamas to set up the tax avoidance scheme which we had finally agreed upon before leaving London. Mike assured us we would meet the British businessman who was running it for us. We were invited to stay on his yacht. Meanwhile we had been promised some more US TV. We had been booked for a Christmas special with Liza Minnelli as Little Red Riding Hood. We would play the wolves. Big deal! Was this rock'n'roll? This kind of stuff really disturbed me, yet the band seriously considered it. I wanted to go out jamming instead in the New York clubs, but I was warned off by the American musicians' union. Mike ticked me off for doing it, as it jeopardized our whole US tour.

I felt imprisoned, and wanted to escape. I hated the long boring hours in the TV studio shooting the Christmas special. I hated The Animals playing the five little wolves with false ears and hair stuck on our faces. The make-up took three hours to apply every morning. MJ was still trying to push a raw blues band into being a pop group. I didn't like this one little bit. I was beginning to resent everyone around me. It didn't seem to bother anybody else. They just got on with it. Chas was seen out with Liza Minnelli. That kept him happy. When the TV shoot was over it was back to rock 'n' roll. We had some gigs upstate NY. Feelings strung between panic and couldn't care less crept over me again. Something had to give and it was me.

It felt claustrophobic. I had to get out. Without saying goodbye I left and headed for Central Park. I wanted to see my favourite animal, the tiger. The magnificent Indian tiger paced around his cage, backwards and forwards. People paid to see him perform, this symbol of open space, freedom and savagery. He was just like me and the band. And he was probably insane, imprisoned all his life. He symbolized everything that was right and wrong in my life.

I don't know how long I stood there, staring into his hypnotic eyes. Soon it was getting dark and the zoo was shutting down. I knew I had blown an important gig. I was due to fly to upstate New York that night, and I'd missed the plane.

Next day MJ read the riot act to me. Somehow the guys had struggled through the gig without me. In the cold light of day I saw how badly I'd let them down. I promised I would fulfil my obligations for the rest of the tour. MJ was relieved, so were the band. They welcomed me back and we were off on the road once more. But the whole tour was a touch bizarre. Dave Rowberry began to wonder what he had got himself into.

He soon found out for sure when we arrived in the Bahamas to stay on the yacht and meet the tax experts. It was here that The Animals finally came to an end. We had suffered too many personnel changes. Alan and Johnny Steel gone. Although I liked and got on well with the newcomers, the magic had gone. We had endured the strain of heavy touring and not seen much return for all our hard work. Incredibly we were still on a wage of £200 a week. It might have seemed a lot for those days but it was nothing compared to what had been generated.

MJ told us the bulk of the money was going straight from our accounts into the tax shelter. So that's why we were living on the yacht, recording with a mobile studio. With a new producer Tom Wilson at the helm, we seemed to be making good commercial records like 'Don't Bring Me Down'. Looking on the bright side we had completed successful tours of the US and new territories like Poland. But I still felt that being 'commercial' meant selling out. Seeking the magic was most important to me, and if it wasn't there, I wanted out.

Sure it was great being down in the Bahamas, living on a yacht that had once been used by a royal family. I could have spent forever down there, but I just knew in the pit of my stomach that we'd never ever see the fruits of our labour or the living. I climbed out of my bunk one morning, a hangover from the night before. I recalled a ferocious fight on the deck between road manager Tappy and Chas. They called it quits and we'd all climbed into the sack. I made my way to the galley, Tappy was in there already cooking breakfast for all of us.

It seemed the fight from the night before was not yet finished. Tappy was standing in the galley over a cutting board with a sharp knife cutting up small pieces of fresh steak and throwing them through the porthole window into the Caribbean, where outside Chas was having his early morning swim. Tappy was hoping to attract sharks, knowing that they might finish off what he couldn't last night. Shit, it was all too much. This was the last straw. I wanted out. We had a meeting in the poop deck with MJ and the rest of the band in the afternoon sun.

I told them I could go no further. I needed a breath of fresh air, something new. 'I think I'll go and live in Los Angeles,' I said. 'I want to put a new band together. I want to struggle for more psychedelic, innovative sounds. We've become stale.' I walked away, leaving them shaking their heads. It was a hard decision to make, but I had to follow my gut feelings.

A girlfriend wrote to me. I'd met her on the first Animals' tour in Sacramento. She was now living in San Francisco. 'You won't believe what's goin' on here,' she wrote. 'Come down and see the action before it's too late. Love Judi Wong.'

I jumped on the next plane to San Francisco. The last time I'd been there it was still a land of beatniks and cool jazz. When I touched down I could sense the changes. Even at the airport kids were sporting multi-coloured shirts, and open sandals, Indian headbands, long hair and painted faces.

I climbed into a yellow cab, handing the slip of paper to the young long-haired freak at the wheel. Looking at the address as he drove, he spoke to me, turning to face me, looking over his shoulder. 'Where've you just come in from?' 'London,' I said, 'via the Bahamas.'

'You in the music business?' he said. 'You pegged me,' I said. 'You playing in town?' he inquired. 'No, just looking around. Came in for a quick holiday. My girlfriend said there's a lot going on in town.' 'Well she didn't give you a bum steer, there is a lot going on, there's a lot of good home-grown music coming out of SF at the moment, you'll enjoy it. In fact if you're into some good blues and boogie, I'd stop by Bill Graham's place at the Fillmore, that's down in the old Haight Ashbury area. I hear they're gonna kick out the jams there tonight. Big Brother and the Holding Company, Country Joe and the Fish, they're all gonna be down there tonight. Take my advice – check it out.'

'Oh, I'm sure my girlfriend's got it all lined up for me,' I replied, 'I'm looking forward to it.' Soon we were zipping past Candlestick Park and an immense cluster of New World pueblo buildings. The freeway ended suddenly and dropped us in downtown San Francisco.

The yellow cab pulled up at the address on the piece of paper, a small house down by the docks. Judi was living with a friend, Chris Brooks, a well hung, bright-eyed, round-faced, sharp-nosed, jovial woman who had two children by her former marriage to a jazz musician. Judi was small, oriental, always smiling, a very warm personality.

I awoke to find an empty house. I walked the length of the building wondering where the girls were. Well, they'd be back soon. I had a few dollars so I thought I'd take a walk. I knew the waterfront wasn't far. On Fisherman's Wharf I found an English pub which sold Guinness and draught Bass. I couldn't resist it. I stood at the bar and ordered an over-priced half pint of draught Guinness. It was delicious. Across the room at the other side of the bar, a long-white-haired individual with an Indian headband was munching away from a paper full of fish and chips and drinking a half pint of Bass. His eyes darted back and forth to me and then to the bag of chips. After he'd finished he came strolling towards me, wiping his greasy fingers on his jeans. He laid his half pint on the table next to me, then said, 'You're Eric, aren't ya?' 'Yeah I am, er, sometimes I am anyway.' 'I'm Eric too,' he said. 'I'm English as well.' I could detect a northern accent. I laughed. It was quite a coincidence. The first person I met in San Francisco would have to be English and have the same name. 'I'm known locally as "Eric the Head",' he said, shaking hands. I could still feel traces of the greasy chips. 'Excuse the muck,' he said. 'Oh it's all right, I'm used to it. Where there's muck there's brass an' all that.' 'You're not Eric Burdon of The Animals, are ya? I heard you broke up. Inevitable, inevitable,' he said, looking at his feet. He had a huge nose, big blue eyes, an uncrackable smile. He was smaller than me, with long white hair and beard, a leather pouch hung around his waist, from a large brass-buckled belt. 'I've been here since 1948,' he said. 'I jumped ship, couldn't stand it no more, been here ever since, love the place. It's like a little bit of England within America.' 'It really does have a European feel to it, I must admit,' I said. 'I'm staying with friends up the street. I'm staying with a girl called Chris Brooks.' 'Chrissie? Oh everybody knows Chrissie. Big girl. Aye they'll take care of ya. Can I buy you a drink?' 'Sure, I'll have another half of Guinness.' He ordered the drinks.

'Good luck, Eric,' said Eric shaking my hand. 'I'll see you later man, I'm gonna be up at the Fillmore myself, although Bill's a bit cagey about letting me in these days. I'm sure Chris has got it all arranged for ya. So I look forward to seeing you, there's gonna be some real good San Francisco jams going on tonight.'

I walked the few blocks back to Chris Brooks' place. When I got there the house was dead. Her kids were fast asleep in the bed. Chris had left a note, she was at a neighbour's just a few doors away. Judi had gone to the Fillmore. My name would be on the stage door and there would be someone there to meet me. She would see me later. Checking my money situation I found I still had $40 so I was in good shape. I stepped into the San Francisco night and headed for Haight Ashbury.

Haight Ashbury had once been a black ghetto section of San Francisco. To the locals who inhabited the place, the street where Haight and Ashbury Streets crossed was better known as just The Hate – a play on words, as the newfound philosophy was steeped in peace and love. If you weren't for peace and love then you were a part of the outside world, the place beyond Haight Ashbury, which stood for Vietnam, police brutality, racial hatred, multinational rip-offs and a bent Government.

I stood there on the streets of the ghetto outside the massive steel doors that were the backstage area to Bill Graham's Fill-more. Harley Davidsons were parked near the sidewalk. Two cops, totally alien to the society around them, were rapping into their radios. Nobody seemed to notice these space age troopers, armed to the teeth, as crowds milled around the backstage area hoping to gain entrance. Inside another cop, a black one, older, with a jovial smile on his face, but nevertheless an evil eye, kept a lookout for backstage passes as one or two lucky people stepped over the threshold from the street into the Fillmore. My turn came, I mentioned my name. He shook his head. It meant noth-ing. The door closed. Clang. I turned, walked across the side-walk.

The cops mounted their Harley Davidsons and took off into the night, yellow and red lights flashing. The sidewalk was awash with colour. Long-haired kids were dressed Indian style. Most male youths were shirtless as the night was warm and balmy. Lots of hand-tooled belts were in evidence, with blue jeans, cowboy boots. The blacks, who were the sole inhabitants of this area before the invasion of teenage runaways from all over America had arrived, mingled with the crowds freely, one or two of them clutching on to paper bags which held their cheap wine, manufactured without the hint of a grape. What impressed me more at that time was the interplay between the different races and ethnic groups. Absolutely no feeling whatsoever of tension, uptightness, difference.

When I made it to the backstage area, the small inlet door opened. A head full of frizzy hair, tied by a colourful rag, a girl in blue jeans and a tie-dyed T-shirt was talking to the cop at the door and then pointing to me. The finger that pointed to me then made a motion for me to step forward. I knew the face from somewhere, it was familiar to me, but I couldn't think where I'd seen it. 'Hey Eric,' she said in a Southern Texas drawl, 'Come on, come on, let's go, you're in.' As I walked towards her and took hold of her hand, her fingers covered in rings, metal bracelets on her wrists, I kissed her on the cheek, she dragged me indoors.

'Judi's around, she's upstairs somewhere, but she thought it'd be fun if I came down to meet you. I'm Janis, I sing with Big Brother and the Holding Company.'

'Janis Joplin?' I said. 'Oh yeah, I've heard all about you.'

'Eric Burdon of The Animals?' she said. 'I've heard about you.'

We both cracked up. 'Pleased to meet you, Mr Burdon,' she said in an even more exaggerated Southern accent. She shook my hand, pumping it. I felt something in the palm of my hand. I looked down, there was a purple dot. 'Take it, it's hot off the press,' she said. 'Owsleys, you'll love it, it's really good stuff.' I popped the cap into my mouth and let it rest between my tongue and the bottom of my jaw. The sweet smell of marijuana drifted down the staircase as we moved up the concrete stairs towards the main dance floor.

I peeled off my jacket, tied the sleeves around my waist and again stood and looked around the room. 'Wow, Janis, this is incredible, incredible.' 'Yeah, yeah, come on,' she said, 'Judi's waiting backstage.' One kid sat in the middle of the dance floor, a huge Alsatian dog on a lead sitting next to him, oblivious of the madness around. The kid had a pocketful of poster paints and brushes and he was carefully making psychedelic patterns on the dance floor, pushing people away so they wouldn't step on his work. 'Hey man, get off of my patch, get out of my way.' I stopped to watch him for a while. Janis stood there, hands on hips, looking at me. 'Oh come on, Janis, I'm a tourist, give me a break!' She laughed and stood next to me as we watched the guy unfolding his patterns in coloured paints on the dance floor. A strobe began to flash its harsh flickering light. A flower of evil within the hall of love unfolded before my very eyes. A team of male dancers, arm in arm, danced in a circle together. Upon their backs the evil, winged skull of death. Their colours proclaimed Hells' Angels, Oakland Chapter, California. They were all in perfect time, their huge steel-capped, buckled motor cycle boots moving across the dance floor in unison. A splash of red on the floor hit my eyes so hard it hurt. I squinted to get a closer look. It was a brighter red than anything else I'd seen since I'd stepped into the room full of colour, for this was the red of human blood. Some poor bastard was being kicked from one side of the circle to the other. I was horrified. Down to pure instinct alone, I moved forward towards the circle of dancing skulls. Janis grabbed hold of me firmly by the arms. 'Hey, no way, come with me, come on. Don't mess with those fuckers, they'll kill you.' Not all had yet been conquered by the philosophy of love and peace. 'But,' Janis explained, 'some of them are real nice guys. But when they're taking care of business, that's their thing, man. I wouldn't mess with them. You gotta take it easy. Come on, let's go to the dressing room and catch Judi.' It had taken us a good half hour to reach the backstage area and now we walked narrow corridors with rooms off to the left and right, filled with musicians tuning guitars, repairing amplifiers, roadcrews racing frantically through the catacombs.

I was introduced to some of the Grateful Dead crew, and Big Brother and the Holding Company who filed past ready to take the stage. One of the guys yelled to Janis:

'Janis, about 45 minutes, we'll see you out there.'

A long-haired, dark-eyed, good-looking kid leaned in the corner, wearing black leather Western chaps and a huge Western belt and cowboy boots. The lizard king himself. 'Meet Jim Morrison.' 'Hi Jim, how ya doing?' 'All right, man. You guys working here or visiting?'

'Oh, The Animals broke up, man, I'm just hanging out, checking out the scene. It's really great, I love it.'

'Yeah, I've just finished a tour up in Canada. The rest of the guys are in LA. When you coming down there, man? It's a good scene too.'

'Yeah, I mean to,' I said. He handed me a cold can of Budweiser. A familiar face pushed its way through the crowd. A hook nose, blue eyes, long white hair tied in a bun at the back, the beard and the smiling face of Eric the Head. 'Ah, so you finally made it at last huh?'

'Yeah, it's a trip, Eric, it really is.'

Chris Brooks emerged from the darkness of the room, a beer can in her hand. She came towards me. I kissed her on the cheek. 'See what I mean?' she said, looking as proud as an owl. 'Yeah, it's really fantastic,' said Eric the Head. 'Who can say that things aren't changing when you see something like this? Do you see any problems out there, man? Four thousand fucking freaks dancing together and no problems.'

'Well,' I said, 'the Angels are fighting.'

'Yeah, but the Angels are changing too,' said Eric.

'Yeah, that's what I heard,' I said.

'Sure we're changing things. We're gonna change the world with this. Life is chemistry,' he said, 'there's bad chemistry and good chemistry and in San Francisco right now we stand for good medicine – what the world needs. We aim to bring the Vietnam war to a stop. It's illegal and immoral. That's why I left England years ago. In America there's still a chance for change and revolution. If it's good business it'll work. Look at the way Bill Graham operates this place. It may look laid back and hippy dippy, but man he's making hard cash too and so can the musicians. They are all professionals, it's just a new way of looking at things, a new way of doing things. More open, more honest, back to the roots.' As he stood there preaching his new world philosophy, a circle of us gathered around him to listen. 'Why just last week, man,' he said, cracking up, 'we had some airmen come in here, in their uniforms too, from the air base down the road and somehow, we don't know how,' he laughed, 'they got rather high and the next day they woke up at the air force base to find the atom bombers splashed in graffiti, white painted slogans, "Hell, no, we ain't going" and "War Sucks". I mean, if that ain't change, if that ain't radical change, I don't know what is.'

The dressing room door opened. A huge, dark-eyed, wide Slavonic face appeared beneath a working man's cap. His sleeves rolled up, it was an extremely busy, no nonsense manager, Bill Graham, who stood in the centre of the room. He smiled warmly. 'Janis, you've got eight minutes, babe, let's go.' 'Yeah, it may seem hippy dippy,' continued Eric, 'but Bill runs a tight ship here. You'll see. Come on, let's go watch Janis perform.' As we made our way down the crowded corridors I walked shoulder to shoulder with Morrison. He told me how he'd studied film in UCLA before joining The Doors and that was his end objective, to make new-wave movies in Hollywood. I told him that I was deeply interested in film and that we should get together and talk later. 'Yeah,' he agreed, 'when you come down to LA we'll get together.' Eric the Head seemed to know every nook and cranny of the Fillmore. We followed his lead through the crowds, in the darkened areas and then suddenly splashes of colour would illuminate the walls and blast over my iris, as the mescaline tab that Janis had laid on me, ran through my system, energizing my brain and allowing me to soak up every vibration in the room. Eric took me upstairs and showed me the light show section of the room, which was barricaded off especially to accommodate the 16mm film and overhead projectors, where oil-based colours were mixed on to a glass hot-plate and pressed with a saucer-like glass allowing the colours to melt and mix and flow freely. They were projected through a lens across the room on to the far wall. The operator sat looking intensely into the bowl, oil colours at his left and right. To the beat of the music he moved the plate, adding the colours as he desired and in turn sent the whole room into a pulsating mass of hues. The light man, I could see, in the new world of San Franciscan psychedelic arts, was as important as a musician. His creation was the visual part of the music, he was the eye of the psychedelic experience.

Janis took the stage, bathed in white light. The psychedelic colours faded away from the stage area. On her feet, red high-heeled shoes. Above, a see-through minidress. As she stomped her feet and rocked the room I could see her nipples struggling to push their way through the material. Throughout Janis's performance I was impressed once again that the new psychedelic age made way for an old world institution. Ain't nothin' like a Southern Texas mama wailin' the blues, stomping her feet and commanding the attention of the whole theatre just like Janis did. She never ever would be recorded right. No magnetic tape anywhere in the world could capture a performer like Janis Joplin in the flesh. Eric rolled up a joint and passed it to me. I took a swift couple of tokes and then passed it to The Lizard. It came round again, my head was into the music, I was high, gone, completely at home.

Suddenly, something brought me back to earth. Some policemen pushed their way through the crowd. The joint came down from my lips quickly. I fumbled, wondering how I could put it out, getting ready to eat the damn thing. Eric the Head cracked up laughing. 'It's OK, it's OK, they're Bill's guys.' The two black uniformed cops stood alongside of us and Eric passed them the smoke. 'Hey thanks, man,' said one of them, toking heavily on the weed, the two of them taking a smoke break. I couldn't believe what my eyes were seeing, but I knew right there and then it wasn't gonna last long. You had to grab it while it was happening. The Lizard leant across and whispered in my ear over the music 'You gotta come down to LA, man, that's where it is. You can do your own thing down there, it's just way too radical down here. If you're into movies, man, that's the place to be. Frisco's a good place to visit, but I wouldn't like to live here.'

Grab it while you can. Sure, I knew it was on the cards. No surprise to me that a few weeks later in *Life* magazine I read about the proclaimed 'Death of the Hippy' by the hippies of Haight Ashbury in San Francisco.

My first residence in LA was a rented room in the massive old Tom Mix cabin at the foot of Laurel Canyon Boulevard. The house was base for several newcomers to the city including Frank Zappa and his gang, the Mothers of Invention. Directly across the street was the house once owned by Houdini, the magician and escape artist. Legend had it there were underground passages which ran the length of the Canyon from his house. The area was steeped in movie history. I loved it.

Tom Mix's cabin was actually a mansion designed to look like a Wild West cabin. It was so big I hardly saw any of the residents, except the Mothers working on their monstrous Harley Davidsons in the courtyard. I was to spend the next few years commuting between Los Angeles and London. While I was in LA, my mate The Pill kept an eye on Dalmeney Court for me.

I hardly ever saw my wife any more. But one cold, wet, miserable night Angie turned up at my door in LA. The wind was howling around the house, as we were at the highest point along the Canyon. The rain was coming down sideways when I opened the door. Angie stepped forward in a black mackintosh and soaking wet jeans.

'Hi. It's Angie. I've brought a friend.' The guy stepped forward, dressed also in a mackintosh. Their feet were absolutely soaked. They were obviously in trouble. Nobody walks in Los Angeles. I took them in and offered them tea. Angela rarely ever looked anything less than stunning, but I must admit she looked tired and haggard. Too much coke and too much lunacy, I thought as I poured out the tea. She came straight to the point. She and her new boyfriend had run out of money. They needed to get back to England desperately. She didn't want to go to the embassy, because if you went to the embassy that was a strike against you in the future. She had every intention of returning to the States. Could I help? 'Well, I'm not exactly overflowing with cash myself, Angie, but, I don't know. Let me think.' Suddenly I saw an opportunity that I couldn't miss. Sure, I'd give her the return airfare to England, for both of them, if she would sign a piece of paper relinquishing all marital rights. I got a blank piece of paper and two US 25 cent postage stamps and quickly made out a small agreement. 'I, Angela Burdon, hereby relinquish all claims and waive all rights, against my husband Eric Victor Burdon.' It was dated and signed by us both across the stamps. This wouldn't be legal but it would begin the procedure. Next morning I got her the cash from the bank. She was gone. Out of my life for good.

THIRTEEN
MONTEREY

The Animals were finished and I put a new band together. I had spent the winter on the West Coast and went back to London to look for musicians who would have a fresh approach to the new music being pioneered by bands like Grateful Dead, Country Joe and the Fish, Jefferson Airplane and Big Brother and the Holding Company.

In England they seemed to misunderstand flower power. I pointed out it was a political, radical movement trying to stop an immoral war in Vietnam. People were trying to make a stand. But in England it wasn't their problem. British hands were clean, for a change.

I went back to base myself permanently in California in 1967 with a band made up of Danny McCulloch on bass, Johnny Weider on guitar and violin, Vic Briggs on guitar, and my old drinking companion, the lunatic Zoot Money. Barry Jenkins from the revamped Animals remained on drums, and later in the year we were joined by little Andy Summers who had been with Zoot in the Big Roll Band and Dantalion's Chariot, on second guitar.

Meanwhile Chas Chandler had gone back to London to go into business as a rock manager, and his first artist was Jimi Hendrix, the brilliant young American guitarist. He was put together with two English guys, Mitch Mitchell on drums and Noel Redding on bass. As The Experience they quickly became a huge success in London and soon headed for America. They were co-managed by Mike Jeffery. I hadn't heard a word from MJ about my supposed contract with him so no news was good news.

I had a new manager called Kevin Deveridge, and Terry McVey was my road manager. One of the first gigs we did was the historic Monterey Pop Festival which was the event of 1967 and starred all the great artists involved in the new psychedelic movement. It was a celebration of the West Coast revolution which had spread to England and back.

Derek Taylor of The Beatles office handled most of the organ- ization and several English acts were chosen including, of course, Eric Burdon and The New Animals.

I had to go to England to sign contracts for the show. I was overjoyed at being part of the English contingent which left London for Monterey. On the same plane were Brian Jones, Jimi Hendrix, Chas Chandler and a host of press. It was a jovial crew, madness right from the beginning.

I was late for the flight. No problem. British Airways staff ran me out after radioing the pilot to hold the plane on the tarmac. They whisked me out on a jeep to the brand new 707 just in time. The slamming doors cut off the noise of the howling engines, and I faced a planeful of grinning freaks, already as high as kites. The whole first class section was a party.

Brian Jones stepped forward and pressed two white caps into my hand which I swallowed. I sat down out of breath. Across the aisle was Jimi Hendrix, grinning broadly, eyes wide. He pushed forward a bottle of Jack Daniels. 'Here, man, take a hit, this'll straighten you out.'

Any barriers between me, Chas and MJ were stripped away, as we chatted about what Monterey would do for Jimi. 'It's gonna break him worldwide, ya know,' said Chas, a big grin on his face. 'Yeah, and it's gonna do your new band a lot of good too,' said Mike. 'They're filming the festival. It'll be like "Jazz On A Summer's Day", only better.'

We finally got to the festival site and the vibes were amazing. Everyone you ever wanted to meet was backstage. There was Pig Pen of Grateful Dead trying to freak out Brian Jones. 'Is that guy for real?' he demanded pointing at fey-looking Brian. 'I'm gonna spook him!' But nothing fazed Jonesy. He just floated through the weekend on a cloud.

As for my performance at Monterey, I would say that I put on a respectable show. It wasn't great but it was all right. We drew most applause for our version of 'Ginhouse Blues'. We did OK, the crowd liked us, but it was a new band and we weren't really cutting loose, like we would further down the line. On Saturday afternoon, thanks to Ms Joplin, I came by a healthy lid of weed. I rolled up a couple of spliffs, stuffed them down my cowboy boots, hitched a ride in a black limousine over to the motel where Jimi and the guys in The Experience were staying. Everybody who was close to Jimi realized how important that gig was for him. It was his first public appearance in the United States since he'd left for England some two years earlier. But more than that, it was Jimi back on the West Coast playing to an audience with the best minds of his generation. If he was a success here tonight then he would make history as the first black/white act to make it big in rock'n'roll. Critics in America had already given him the title of 'The Black Elvis' and fate had put him on the bill on Saturday night, face to face, back to back, with The Who, a hardcore band from England who, like Hendrix, used violence and destruction as a part of their radical rock'n'roll act. It was tough billing for both bands, but that night both of them were to live up to their great names and blow the minds of 20,000 people at the Monterey Pop Festival.

Jimi was crouched down outside his motel room with several guitars spread out on the tarmac in front of him. At least one of his beautiful Fender axes would be sacrificed tonight. He crouched down in the sun, a silver conch belt around his hips, white calf-length boots, a gypsy waistcoat, a purple shirt, the box of coloured inks and oils alongside his guitars. He was quite alone. I stood there and watched a minute. It was like a Navaho dream – the warrior before the hunt. He stood up, stood back and admired his own work, whistling through his teeth gently. Across the courtyard of the motel, through an open door, in the interior of a darkened room, I could see the blond hair of Mitch Mitchell flopping about in the wind as on a practice pad. He sat up on the bed pounding the rubbers, making various runs through an imaginary drum kit. 'Smoke, Jimi?' 'Eh, oh yeah, thanks. How ya doing?' 'Oh, all right. Looking forward to to-night?' 'You bet.'

I put the spliff between my lips, lit it up. Jimi bent forward, slid his brush into the yellow oil and applied it to the white guitar. Yellow flowers, white guitar. I handed him the spliff. He put it be-tween his lips and heaved on it. It was between his lips as he said to me, 'You know, I hear they printed up a different colour tab of acid for every night of the week, but there's only three nights here, right, so they got three colours, red, blue, and purple. Pretty far out, huh?'

He turned, cleaned the brush, dried it and went for another colour, this time black on the white Fender. 'Yeah, it is, it's mind blowing,' I replied, not thinking as I looked at his long black fingers applying paint to the Fenders.

'Well, it's a pity there wasn't a fourth colour, you know, because four's a real important number, you know what I mean?'

'Yeah,' I said, staring at the four Fenders on the ground. 'Yeah, four's *real* important,' he repeated. I told him I'd heard there was an alternative concert after the main show was over, in a football field belonging to the college. 'Are you going up there?' I asked. 'Yeah, sure I am. There's got to be a place where we can really kick out the jams all night long, uh?' 'Yeah, it should be cool.' He took another drag on the joint. 'Oh God, this is good weed. Oh, I'm looking forward to tonight, man. I'm so high, living on my nerves. The spaceship's really gonna take off tonight.'

MJ came by to give me the day's update on the final positions on the starting grid.

'Good news, Eric. Jimi's gonna follow The Who instead of pre-ceding them. Don't ask me how we managed to pull it off. It was a big fucking hassle though.' He walked away smiling and rub-bing his hands together.

I thought of Chas. Great stunt, lad, great. He'd pulled it off. It was the position they'd wanted and prayed for. Jimi had just arrived and was in the corner of the canteen. With a girl on each arm he stood in the corner near the stove. They went to fetch him food, but he stopped them saying he wasn't hungry, he'd eat later. He made himself some space and sat down at a table. Next to him sat a young baby-faced wide-eyed black kid, Buddy Miles. Then came Noel and Mitch to join Jimi at the table. As I walked past Jimi said, 'Purple.' 'Purple,' I replied. He grinned. 'I'll see you later, have a good one,' I said and slapped him on the arm. I went out front and joined Brian Jones for the Otis Redding Stax set. It was wonderful. The night got cold, the clouds almost scraped the top of the stage. A nonstop, incessant downpour began. It didn't make any difference to anyone. The crowds stayed on and rocked all the way through Otis's set. This was the first time I'd seen Otis since I'd met him in Memphis and there was a marked difference in the guy. He was now surrounded by lots of heavy black minders and was purported to be totally into his blackness. Indeed, I found him very stand-offish to me, although when I'd first met him he was real friendly. But now, in front of this psychedelic freaked-out white rock audience he was breaking down, getting loose and actually made an announcement to the effect that he understood what the crowd was there for and what they stood for was love and that he had nothing else in his heart for everyone, no matter what the colour. He brought the whole audience *en masse* to their feet when he called for respect. Someone from the press corps contacted Jonesy. They wanted to ask him backstage to the Committee Tent. Would he introduce Jimi? He'd be pleased to, he said.

I wandered backstage to see how the lad was getting on. Downstairs, beneath the stage, there was a little tune-up, warm-up area which had been set aside with a couple of AC 30 Vox amplifiers so that the guitar players could quickly tune up underneath the stage before emerging. I climbed the stairs down into the dark cavern below the stage. Jimi was in a corner, plugged into one of the Voxes, a Fender round his neck, a smoking cigarette stuck in the wires. The large fingers moved up and down the frets, whapping and vamping away, testing the strings, seeing if the tension was right. Young baby-faced Buddy Miles was there leaning against the wall, arms crossed, smiling broadly, watching Jimi's every move. Noel Redding looked very smart in a wild psychedelic shirt, his well-tailored pants making his skinny legs look even longer and skinnier. He nodded, gave me a smile, shook my hand. Mitch, his hair still flying in the wind, loosened up, his arm exercises cutting the air like a sword fencer. Jimi stood there underneath the single bare electric lightbulb, his eyes closed, his mouth bent in a downward twist, eyes rolling up into their sockets, nostrils widening, arm muscles taut. He played an unending riff 'whackatacka, whackatacka, whacktacka'. Buddy Miles stepped

Rock'n'Roll warlord

forward and began clapping his hands, keeping a back beat. Mitch began gently to tap the sticks on the side of the wall. We were sitting there. Chas and MJ were in the room, they too beginning to slap in time to the back beat. We didn't realize it but we were getting louder and louder. Bill Graham popped his head round the door, 'Hey, shut the fuck up. We can hear you coming through the stage floor. Give us a break.'

Chas stepped forward. 'Hey, listen, you heard what the man said – we don't wanna blow it, just cool down a bit. OK everybody? You in tune, Jimi?' 'Yeah, man, yeah.' 'How you feel?' 'I feel great, I feel really good.' They were like manager and fighter getting ready for the match of a lifetime.

The Who were already on stage when I left to make my way to the press box, Townshend flying through the air, Daltry like a cowboy herding strays, lassoing the microphone in circles. Keith Moon, 'the lunatic', hammered away on the drum kit, a flurry of arms and black hair flying everywhere, The Ox, Entwistle, steady as a rock, thumping the bloody great strings on his Fender. 'My generation yeah, talking 'bout my generation, yeah . . .' I looked around. Jonesy was nowhere to be seen. Next thing I was aware of was that the stage looked like a bomb had hit it. It was enveloped in smoke. The drum kit exploded. Moonie went crazy, hitting everything in sight. Bill Graham thought it was a terrorist attack and went flying across the stage, aiming at everybody left, right and centre. The film crew couldn't believe their eyes. They too thought they'd been attacked by some San Francisco radicals. It took them all by surprise. Nobody knew what had hit them. The Who let go with everything. A violent explosion erupted across the stage. People in the audience were visibly shaken and stood there open-mouthed. They couldn't believe it. They'd never seen such radical rock in their lives.

Jonesy emerged from under the stage, moving like the Queen. The people came to their feet to give him a round of applause. He introduced Jimi as his friend from London. 'Ladies and gentlemen, from London, England . . . from Seattle, Washington . . . the first American appearance of The Jimi Hendrix Experience.' Jimi looked terrific. The whole trio did. Mitch sat behind an incredibly colourful drumkit. Jimi had pulled around him something that he'd stolen from one of the girls, a bright red feathered wrap. He made some mumbled remark into the microphone about 'I ain't no faggot ya know, I just wanna feel good, look good.' The audience went wild.

They jumped into the first number – 'Foxy Lady' – 'Look out comin' to get ya'. Let me stand next to your fire'. It wound the audience up tight like a steel spring. The most well-received songs of the set were Bob Dylan's 'Like A Rolling Stone' and 'All Along The Watchtower'. These Dylan songs sat well with Jimi, as if they'd been specially written for him. The slide guitar in 'All Along The Watchtower' sounded like a breeze cutting through the stone windows of some cold lonely castle on a windswept beach.

The grand fiery finale, courtesy of Jimi Hendrix's 'special effects department' was a hard nut to crack and Jimi knew it. How could he leave an impression deeper and stronger than The Who? The answer was simple. Fight fire with fire, and that's what he did. Unknown to the crowd, he'd had a small can of lighter fluid stashed in the top of his calf-length boot. At the end of the set he took it out, laid the Fender to rest on the stage floor, squeezed the box of lighter fluid which he held between his legs and lit it. He was pissing fire on to the guitar. An outrageous act and demonstration of 'The Lord Giveth and the Lord Taketh Away'. Whilst he was doing this, Mitch and Noel kept up the on-slaught of feedback and terrifying drum-thunder until the audience were hammered into submission. Hendrix picked up the burning axe, it was now smouldering, the plastic cover buckling, bubbling with the intense heat. He moved towards the crowd. He picked it up by the neck and smashed it on to the floor. The fire was extinguished, the blue-black smoke drifted up into the super-trooper lights, the massive bass feedback washed over the crowd and immersed them in rumbling waves as Jimi broke up the remaining pieces of the smouldering Fender and handed them to the crowd like a bull-fighter offering the ears to the President. He'd made it. He'd broken the balls of England and now he'd broken the back of the United States. The shooting star was on its way. It never stops until it reaches the ground.

FOURTEEN
ESCAPE FROM JAPAN

The New Animals proved a successful band, at least for a while, and we had some great hits like 'Sky Pilot' which we recorded complete with the sound of The Royal Scots Guards Pipe and Drum marching band. They happened to be touring America, and stopped in Los Angeles. So I recorded them. It was then mixed together along with explosions and machine-gun fire and sunk into the track. Big production! I intended it to be the world's first stereo single, plus live Sky Pilot along with one light show and strobe lights. It was devastating, riot was often the effect! The album title was 'Winds of Change'. Other cuts were 'Yes, I Am Experienced', 'San Franciscan Nights' and 'Good Times'.

We set off for a tour of Japan. I had enjoyed my previous visit to the land of the rising sun, but this one proved something of a disaster. To my surprise we were met at the airport by gentlemen in grey suits and white gloves who whisked us to a press conference.

'Hey, it's Mr Big,' said Zoot Money under his breath as the man from the agency arrived. Kevin our manager, shook hands with Mr Big who welcomed us to his country. He was five foot one, with a wicked smile and yellow skin. Gold teeth glittered as he smiled. There was something intimidating about him. I suspected the worst. Nevertheless, I felt confident that the tour would go smoothly as we had Terry McVey along as road manager.

Three days of boring press interviews were over and we got ready for our first Japanese gig in Osaka. We went there by the new 100 mph bullet train. The show went like clockwork. We had a wonderful time. The audience applauded in polite Japanese fashion but we could tell they were enjoying themselves. For the next week we travelled out of Tokyo to various big, well-attended gigs.

The whole band seemed to be affected by the Japanese sense of decorum and good manners, so one night, at the end of our first week, Mr Big invited us out for the customary slap-bang nosh-up. The band and members of the agency were seated round a large oblong table in the backroom of one of the best Kobe steak houses in the Ginza, Tokyo's main street. Mr Big, in his shark-skin suit, sat at the end of the table rubbing his hands together, his face folding up and squinting like a contented cat. He looked towards me and gave a slight bow.

'Tonight, Burdon, san, we have much action. Kobe beef good?' I smiled back, gave a short nod and said, 'Yes indeed.' I looked around the table, everyone's face was beaming and lit up and there was a cheer from the table as half a dozen beautiful young Japanese girls tripped into the room carrying eating utensils and *hors d'oeuvres*. Freshly laundered, crisp white bibs were tied to our necks by the delicate girls, who we soon found out were to sit next to each one of us, cook the Kobe beef on the table right there in front of us and serve each and every one of us individually. Marvellous – it's a man's world!

The next day I paid off the taxi and stood outside the building where our gig was supposed to be. The fact that it was in the downtown area on the edge of the Ginza didn't surprise me at all. I'd gotten used to the fact that in Japan venues could be tucked away in the strangest places. As the elevator reached the fifth floor I was surprised to hear Danny McCulloch saying, 'I wouldn't care, man, but there's not even enough room for the bass amp. Look it's terrible. I can't lie it on its side, it'll screw up the sound totally, probably wreck the amp.' Then somebody else came back with, 'Zoot, Zoot, is there gonna be enough room for your extra keyboard on that stage?' 'No way.'

The band bitched on in the darkness. Then I could hear Terry

McVey, the voice of authority. 'OK, don't lose your cool, man, we'll build ya an extension, a runway, we'll get it together, don't worry.' I called out into the darkness, 'Terry, Terry. What's the score here, I can't see a damn thing.'

'Hold on.' A torchlight beam danced its way towards me. 'What's the deal here? What is this place?'

'Well, the stage is a bit small and the room is much smaller than we're used to, but I think it'll be all right. It's what we are contracted to do,' apologized Terry.

I was so brought down I didn't even bother talking to the guys. I ran into Kevin on the way out. He looked like he'd been running. 'OK, Kevin, what's the story on this place? I mean, are we expected to work here or what? I mean, it's just not on. We're a band designed for playing to a reasonable number of people. That's what we've been doing here in Japan and it's been successful. Why suddenly are we working in a small club like this? Does Mr Big own this joint or what?' Silence ... Kevin looked at the floor, then he looked at me. 'Yeah, he owns the place, what difference does that make?' 'Oh, I get the picture,' I said. 'How many shows here? Twice nightly for Mr Big and his gangster friends? Well look, I want to see an English contract or I ain't working.' I headed for the Ginza. After walking a few streets in boiling anger I realized I was lost, I had no idea where I was going. Then on pure impulse I stepped inside a shop, looked around in the cool darkness waiting for my eyes to adjust from the sun outside. Then I saw it was full of swords and guns.

I bought a gas pistol, pushed it into my pocket and felt much better. It was silly, but I did. Kevin was in the hallway with Mr Big. Mr Big was full of smiles. Kevin just looked at the floor, making designs with his toes. 'Well, what's the score?' I said. Kevin continued to look at the floor. 'Well, they just don't seem to understand, I can't get it across to them, er, you know, we're entitled to and we need to see an English contract.' 'Well, you better get it across to them, Kevin,' I said. Mr Big, oblivious to it all, smiled, gave me a curt bow, clicked his heels together and said 'Tonight, much action. Later.' He turned and headed for the elevator.

'Was that it then, was that your meeting, Kevin?' 'I don't know what to say to you,' he said.

'Well, I know what to say to you,' I said. 'Look, I haven't worked in a club as small as this since the Downbeat in Newcastle years ago. I mean, what do you expect me to say? Just cave in and give in to it? This is not on. You're managing us, aren't ya? So get us out of it and get us into something else. As far as I'm concerned this is fucking blackmail!' I ranted and raved. 'Look, there's a restaurant across the street, bring the band over, I'll meet you over there and we'll talk it over.'

I entered the restaurant with the band. We sat down at a long table in the corner, away from the main eating area. Two of Mr Big's goons were there. Kevin nodded to the two guys. One of them walked over to our table and in good English asked if we wanted a drink. 'May I treat you?' he said. 'Drinks are on your honourable promoter. May I suggest Scotch whisky all round?' Our hands shot up in the air. Scotch whisky, I'd found out in Japan, was a sign that your host was about to propose some kind of deal. Six hands shot up, six whiskies were ordered. When the waiter returned to the table, seven glasses were put down in front of us. However, six whiskies were poured and one glass remained empty, except for some ice in the bottom. The whiskies were distributed around the table. The empty glass, containing only the ice, stood there on the table in front of us. Nobody said anything.

One of Mr Big's goons, the one who had ordered the whiskies, sat next to Kevin, talking to him in English, whispering in his ear. The other guy from the office stood at the table, next to us, silently eyeing the scene. I was just about to make a toast when this guy pulled his right hand from his pocket, clenched in a tight fist. It hovered over the empty glass. His hand opened and six 9mm bullets bounced inside of the glass until eventually they came to rest in the ice. Andy Summer's eyes opened wide and his leg under the table nudged me. 'Did you see that?' 'How could I miss it?' I said. I stood up, whisky glass in hand. I toasted the table, 'Cheers', threw the whisky back, once again angrily headed for the street. Walking at a fast, steady pace away from the restaurant, my sweaty palms played with the butt of the German gas pistol. Blackmail, pure bloody pressure and blackmail, that's all this is. I won't stand for it, I swore to myself, I won't! Some kind of action had to be taken. I called Terry. 'Are we gonna get paid?' I demanded. The answer was half the money was placed in a bank in America already. 'Yeah but what about the other half?' I stared into a glass of sake. I was intent on finishing the bottle.

Terry knew what I was thinking and feeling. 'OK, I'm gonna try and find Kevin and I'll let you know what's going on.' I took off and headed for the main elevators in the hotel. The doors opened on the fourth floor. Kevin stood before me in the corridor, his face as white as his suit. I thought he was adjusting his tie with his hands, but when he took his hands down to his sides I could see the huge second smile below his jaw. From ear to ear across his Adam's apple was a huge red welt. 'Christ, what's happened to you?' I said. I pressed the down button towards the entrance of the hotel. 'After you left,' he said, 'they took me aside in a corner. The band had gone, everybody had gone, and one of the guys, who'd put the bullets in the glass, took out a *samurai* sword and stuck it on my neck. The message was "You play or you die."'

I headed for my room, got on the telephone immediately and one by one told the guys not to leave their rooms, but to get packed and ready to leave on an early morning flight. Then I got Terry to check out Pan Am departures.

None of us slept that night. We just stayed in our rooms watching *samurai* movies till the screen went black. Stomachs knotted, nerves on edge, we waited for dawn. I was lying on the bed, Terry McVey on the floor, his head resting on the luggage packed and ready to go. I'd just nodded off when the telephone rang. 'Good morning, sir, it is 4.30 a.m. This is your early morning wake up call.' We were soon assembled downstairs in the dark deserted, foyer. Terry paid our bills. Taxis were called. Kevin, although somewhat subdued, went about his business as usual. The first taxi pulled up in the wet drive. We filed outside and watched as the two young Japanese kids from the concierge helped us load the luggage on to the roof and tie it down.

Then, quite suddenly, from the shadows across the street emerged three rather large, angry-looking, Japanese gentlemen. Their arms folded, they stood by and watched us quietly load up the equipment. It wasn't until the first taxi was ready to go that they made their move. The first Japanese stepped forward and said something to the taxi driver. The taxi driver had his foot on the brake and put the car into neutral. Terry McVey stepped forward, the usual cigarette dangling between his teeth. He snarled at the Japanese taxi driver. 'We're paying the money, you bastard. Don't take any notice of these guys. Now move, come on, move!' He kept up such a verbal onslaught the driver couldn't argue. He slipped into drive, took his foot off the brake and moved slowly forward. The three heavies were now yelling, and shouting, with their arms waving. They let the first cab go and moved in on the second one. Andy, Zoot and Danny McCulloch were on board and already moving before they could protest. Two underway, one to go. In the last cab were Terry, myself and Kevin. We kept up the onslaught on our taxi driver. We raced off to the airport.

Kevin was soon at the desk explaining he had only one credit card. Could they possibly overlook the situation, bend the rules and let us out? The three heavies arrived just as Kevin was explaining that we were being pressured into staying against our will. The girls at the check-in counter immediately saw the situation and began to issue tickets. The minutes slipped by, nail-biting, nervous minutes. The whole band sat in a circle on the hard shiny tiles in the middle of the huge airport lounge next to the check-in counter. It was definitely now 'circle the wagons, dig in and wait for the first wave of attack'. In the enemy camp telephone calls were made while the other two stood guard. After the processing of tickets and boarding passes had been issued, Kevin strolled over slowly, nonchalantly, briefcase in hand, towards the enemy. He returned and reported that none of them spoke English but guessed a representative of the Agency was on the way. The automatic doors slid open, and Mr Big entered the hall. He and Kevin met each other, just out of earshot of the band. They were deep in conversation for what seemed an eternity. Eventually Kevin made his way over back to our camp. 'Well, he says it's most unfortunate the way things have turned out and it's a great misunderstanding and he's sent for his boss. The real Mr Big is on his way.' Zoot cocked an ear, 'You mean he's not Mr Big?' 'No, no, his boss will arrive here in a few minutes.'

The automatic doors slid open again. The real Mr Big stood before us. He was even smaller than I was. Round, wired, prescription-type glasses. He was a frail man in an immaculate business suit, with a white stiff collar and tie that looked too big for him. Immaculate in his patent leather shoes he held a small rolled-up brolly over one arm and a briefcase. Two more heavies stood on each side of him. They moved across the hall towards their compatriots and began to discuss the situation. Then Kevin was called over. He left his briefcase behind, strolled over and sat down at the table to confront the real Mr Big.

The sun was rising and the sky began to lighten. It had been dark when we arrived and time was slipping by. It seemed we had been here for hours. Kevin returned to retrieve his briefcase. 'The story so far,' he said, 'is that they never had an English contract for us to see. But they claim that from the very beginning it was agreed and accepted to play these club gigs and they can't understand what all the fuss is about.'

The whole band was now gathered around, anxious to hear what was coming down. Zoot chipped in, 'They don't see what all the fuss is about? Christ, just take a look at Kevin's throat, and what about the bullets in the glass, what's all that about? And heavies outside of the hotel all night? God, I don't understand these people.'

'Yeah,' I said, 'remember, Kevin, you're the one that's wearing the slash from the knife around your neck.' 'Well,' he said shrugging his shoulders, 'you're right, I can't forget that and I don't intend to. I'll just keep talking to them until departure time, hold them off, keep them cool.'

I paced our small circle of baggage and fingered the pistol inside my pocket. But when I looked at the size of the guys who were watching us, I knew it was absolutely hopeless, I'd have no chance, not with a gas pistol, not against this wall of flesh. We all kept an eye on the negotiations across the room. Kevin stood up, retrieved his briefcase and walked over towards us. 'Well, we've got ourselves into a situation now where nobody can win. I mean, there's nobody who can really speak for either of us. They speak little English and I speak no Japanese, so what are you gonna do?' I turned suddenly to find myself confronted by Mr Big, the real Mr Big. He looked up at me through his wire glasses, his lips moving slowly over his huge yellow teeth. 'Mr Burdon, why you no want to sing in my club?' he said. 'Why you disappoint Japanese fan, why you want to leave now?'

So this is the way it was gonna be. Face to face. The blame all on me. I was boiling inside. I looked him directly in the eye as anger welled up inside of me. Not knowing where the words came from, I just let my mouth run away with itself. 'Why do I disappoint Japanese fan?' I said. 'Why do I refuse to sing? Don't you realize, sir, that I first came to this country not long ago, about a year ago. For years I had been brought up to believe that the Japanese were my enemy. Then on my first visit I realized that the Japanese were misunderstood. Why, on my first visit here I found out your people were considerate, genial, and cultured. I love your country and the last thing I would want to do would be to disappoint or hurt our Japanese fans, whom we respect from the depths of our hearts. But you have destroyed my image of the Japanese people. I have lost respect for you and for your country. I do not want to perform here and I do not want to say anything else. Do you understand?'

He stood there looking at me and then at the floor. To my surprise I realized that tears were welling in his eyes behind the frames of his glasses. The tears rolled from his cheeks, down on to the breast of his pinstriped suit. There was absolute silence. The girls at the Pan Am desk looked over towards us in amazement. Their mouths dropped. There were just moments of silence which seemed like hours, then suddenly three of the automatic doors leading from the street into the main checking hall opened. A tidal wave of Japanese school-children rushed towards us, each of them holding up a piece of cardboard and a felt tip pen. 'Autograph, autograph!' they cried and surrounded the band and our baggage. They surrounded the heavies and the Pan Am desk. Where they came from I don't know and I didn't care. I began to sign the autographs, one by one, as fast as I could. They kept on coming. Mr Big, the Assistant Mr Big, Kevin, the heavies, everyone, were enveloped in the sea of blue uniforms and smiling faces. Under cover of this human tidal wave we made our way down through the hall, struggling with our baggage, towards the check-out gate.

The whole experience with The New Animals had cost me dear. Despite it all, I was still hooked on rock'n'roll, still looking for the way ahead.

FIFTEEN
MONSTER MASH

On the return flight, conversations with Kevin revealed the full extent of the damage caused by the Japanese fiasco, for which I held him responsible. It seemed that during the tension in the early hours at the Pan Am desk, he had signed cheques to the tune of $250,000, securities to get us out of the country. Luckily for him we made a short stop at Honolulu, during banking hours. He had a chance to telephone and cancel the cheques. Now we were happy to be going home to a peaceful Los Angeles. Or so we thought.

It only ever happens for a few months during the summer, but when it gets hot, the millions of cars flying around the San Fernando valley create a smog that makes life unbearable. We arrived in Los Angeles from Honolulu when the city was in the grips of smog-out. It was hot, and even humid, really unusual, as LA is on the edge of a desert. I had often heard people talk about the LA smog-outs. This was my first experience of one, and I could feel the crap attacking the back of my throat as I left the concrete walkway for a taxi that would take me home to Laurel Canyon.

During the ride I made small talk with the black cab driver. When he allowed me to think, my mind wandered through the

Canyon and I remembered the people I knew there, and hoped would be home to greet me.

I'd pop round and see Alvinia, beautiful black Alvinia and then there was The Princess, the blonde up the street from her. Then big Bob, he was sure to set me right. I couldn't wait to get back to the people. I gave the taxi driver directions. 'Yeah, go on, all the way up, all the way till you can go no further, just keep going, until the concrete stops, that's my place, right at the top of the hill.' 'Up here?' he said. 'Goddamn, I never knew this road went this far, we're almost touching heaven up here.' 'That's right buddy,' I said, 'above the smog.' I clambered out of the yellow cab, and he helped me with my belongings. I paid him and tipped him well. I kicked in the front door – I was home. Terry McVey was still at the airport hassling over the remainder of our personal effects. I slid open the glass doors, walked on to the balcony which overlooked the Canyon, inky black below except for a few streetlights. My dog, who'd been staying with some neighbours half a canyon away, must have sensed my return. He came bounding up the hill, charging through the door, jumping all over me, wild and crazy, his tail wagging. Another car pulled up outside, it was McVey. He stood there in the driveway, dumped his bags, stretched his arms up in the air towards the sky and yawned. 'Ahhh, good to be back.' 'Yeah, innit.' I fetched the torch to show him down to his apartment below. We switched on the lights, checked to see if the place was still secure. Everything was OK.

I could hear music drifting up the Canyon from the house where Alvinia lived. I took a walk. Watchdogs behind their fences howled and barked and scratched at me as I walked the streets, Hip trailing along behind me, fending them off, over-protecting me, overdoing it to impress me on my return. I reached Alvinia's house. The door was open, it always was. A party was in progress. Wild percussive rhythms filtered through the door out into the street. I walked up the small, neat garden, stopping on the threshold. I hesitated for a moment, wondering whether I was intruding or not, then I realized there was no such thing at Alvinia's place. I stepped into the room and was welcomed by familiar faces. Hugh Masekela stood in the corner, a huge smile cracked his face. 'Hey, Burdon, how ya bin? Long time no see.' 'Likewise.' Pumping each other's hands in a soul shake, I turned to see the beautiful, tall, black Alvinia dancing in the middle of the floor. She high-stepped across the floor towards me, almost lifting me off the floor, her arms around me.

'Good to see ya baby, how was the trip?' 'Oh I'll tell you about it later,' I said. Hughie's closest friend and producer, Stu, was in the kitchen mixing drinks. I made my way through the crowd. Some people I knew, some I didn't, but all with welcome smiles on their faces. God, I was glad to be back. I'd just missed out on a fantastic dinner, but Alvinia provided me with something to take home. I wasn't hungry anyway, but she wrapped it in tinfoil for me. Her cook-ups were always a treat. Stu and I talked about the weather. 'Yeah man, it's the smog,' he agreed, 'real bad up here. Downtown, during the day, it's the worst, gets to your eyes and nose, everything. It's driving people crazy.' 'Yeah, talk about driving people crazy,' said another familiar face from the Canyon, whose name I could not recall, 'there's some weird stories going around.' 'About what?' I inquired.

'Well, it seems that a bunch of strange hippy types living out in the desert have been offing people down on the beach and making movies of it, you know, "snuff movies", and selling them to well-known people in Hollywood. Real bizarre.'

'Yeah,' said Stu, 'and the influx of young kids this summer, man, all kinds of runaways from the Mid West and East Coast, man, coming here in search of the Californian dream and tripping out on all kinds of shit, going crazy, robbing houses, man, it's getting weird, I tell ya. The cops are getting tough.' I sort of took in what they had to say, but it went in one ear and out the other. After Japan, back here in the Canyon seemed like heaven on earth. Living up in the Canyon you had the feeling that you were out of reach, and what went on in the world below just didn't bother me. Hell, we were above the smog-line.

Alvinia danced with the throng, distributing percussive instruments. I was handed a tambourine. Everybody in the room cut loose. The record player was turned up high and we made a hell of a din. I could have stayed all night, but I wanted to stay true to my plan and check out the rest of the people in the Canyon, just to see if everybody was there. Hip was waiting for me on the porch. He was anxious as well to go for walkies. I kissed Alvinia goodbye. 'You leaving babe?'

'Yeah, just wanna take a walk. I'm jet-lagged you know,

wanna get some fresh air while I can.' 'Yeah, before people start kicking over their cars and smogging up the air again for yet another hot groggy day in LA. Well, I'll see ya during the week. Bye, darling.'

'Bye.' I walked to the top of the block, hung a right, down the hill, second left, then up a steep slope towards The Princess's house – the fabulous blonde I'd befriended.

The Princess owned a wig store on Hollywood Boulevard and when she wasn't working at her wig store, she stripped for extra pennies in the Valley. We'd made friends through a mutual acquaintance, another neighbour of mine, Bob Gordon. I walked up to her front door, all the lights were out and the door was locked. It didn't seem anybody was at home. Then I noticed the sign on her front door. It read 'Moved due to negative vibes. Signed The Princess.' Strange, I thought. Well, she was a strange girl, that's what attracted me to her. I stepped back and took one more look at the house, the dog sniffing around in the bushes. 'Come on, let's go, we'll go round to Bob's and you can see your buddy.' Big Bob's huge dog Baron strolled up the hill in the darkness towards Hip, the two of them growling at first, then sniffing each other in recognition. I strode down the hill towards Bob's house. 'Hey Bob, you in?' A voice from the back. 'Yeah, come on in, it's open.' He was in the back of the house, an array of cameras on top of a glass table. 'Come on in, just doing a little maintenance work. Welcome home,' he said, shaking my hand. 'There's chilled wine in the ice box if you want some.' 'Thanks, I think I will.' His house overlooked Hollywood, a trillion shining bright lights twinkled away through the now settling smoggy haze. I stood there sipping my cool glass of wine, watching a police car, its red lights flashing, its siren moaning like a dying dog, making its way through the streets below. The two dogs sat on the porch and in unison howled along with the police siren. It was spooky.

'I went looking for The Princess, nobody there.' 'Yeah,' said big Bob, looking up, wiping a bead of sweat away from his beard, 'you know The Princess, she's a strange girl. She got into this weird trip, man, done a little too much cocaine, I think, but she's into a white phase now, man, she says she's changed her name, her lifestyle, her place of living, she's moved over to the Gower area where she's got a castle. She changed her name to Princess La

Lune, Princess of the Moon – are you ready for that? The chick is crazy, but I love her. I got a telephone number if you wanna reach her. I'll give it to you later. I'm sure she'll come down off her throne and talk to you.'

A strong Santa Ana wind was now blowing in from the east. We sat on the balcony together, smoked a joint and I told him of the ups and downs of my Japanese trip. We talked until dawn, the sun cracking the horizon, Bob looking out towards the Pacific like a great Buddha, smiling all the while as I told him about my exploits in the Far East.

He turned on the radio. A news announcement made us both sit up and whistle in wonder. 'Wow man, check this out.' He turned up the volume. A multiple murder had taken place in the Canyons, not too far away, in Benedict Canyon, the place I'd just moved from. Several people had been found, victims of a ritualistic black magic slaying. Amongst the dead were well-known faces in the film and society world of Los Angeles, including Sharon Tate, Abigail Forger, Jay Seabring and a friend of Roman Polanski's who had all been murdered at Polanski's residence in the Benedict Hills. Polanski was away in Europe filming.

The sun had now fully risen over the City of the Angels. It was strange to think that just a few hills away the police were still viewing the scene of carnage after the multiple murder, the slaughter of the innocents. The Coyote was on the prowl.

Los Angeles was suddenly thrown into panic. It was reported that a gun store in Beverly Hills sold over 500 shotguns in one day. Guard dogs were being sold in the San Fernando Valley for up to $1,500. German Shepherds became a prized possession. The area was changing. The forecast made by the inhabitants of Haight Ashbury several months earlier had become a reality. It was the death of the hippies. From now on any long-haired, blue-jeaned, laid-back individual was to become a target for the massed police forces in the United States. There were new and more powerful drugs about, even stronger than LSD. I didn't believe it at first, but it was true. MDA, a three-way mixture of sodium pentothal, methedrine, psilocybin, and p.c.p. (Angel dust), a horse tranquillizer, was now being smoked by people as a means of cutting themselves off from reality. Lone females in the town were scared to death. Carolyn Williams, ex-model, who I had met at a festival at Devenshire Downs, had become one of the lonely females in a town that had the jitters. Carolyn was on the phone continuously. I often spent nights over at her apartment, protecting her and protecting myself from loneliness. The cops on the street were trigger-happy. Hollywood at night was like a ghost-town. Welcome to the twilight zone.

I was at home alone one night when I heard a car outside in the driveway, someone leaning on the horn. I rushed to the front door. The car's headlights on full lit up my front door. I stood in the doorway shielding my eyes from the bright lights. 'Turn it down, turn it off,' I said. The car's engine died and the lights went out. I recognized the Classic 1957 two-tone Corvette. It was The Princess. She stayed behind the wheel. I walked up to the car and leaned in through the door. 'Princess, how ya doing?' 'Oh, I'm fine,' she purred. 'By the way, my name is now Princess of the Moon. I brought you a gift.' She turned to the passenger seat and handed me a weighty cardboard box. I wondered what was inside. I held it in one hand, opened the door with the other and guided her from the car into the house. She was dressed in white satin, white stacked high-heels upon her feet, white fingernail polish, white toenails and one or two black feathers which seemed to grow upon her chalk-white skin. Her breasts were practically bare, loosely covered with gold fishnet. Her blonde hair (or was it one of her wigs?) exploded like a dandelion. Her eyes, her blue eyes, were wide and dilated. I couldn't help keeping my eyes on her long lithe legs, which exposed themselves as she walked in the tight dress with a split up the back. She stepped into the house. Her perfume was intoxicating. She looked around the house. 'You alone?' she said. 'Yeah, sure. Come on in, make yourself at home.' 'I moved.'

'I know,' I said, 'I went round there. Closed due to bad vibes? What's all that about?'

'Oh, it's a long story,' she said. 'You see I walked by this house belonging to this well-known Hollywood personality. He has two beautiful prize dogs worth a fortune and they followed me home, honest, I didn't tempt them or anything, they just followed me, you know how it is with me and little creatures.' 'Yeah,' I said, 'I do.' 'Anyway, since then he's had these black art freaks following me everywhere and they cornered me one night in The Whisky as I was getting into my car and savagely beat me. They held a crucifix over my head and said they were sent to exorcise me by this well-known Hollywood personality, who shall remain nameless.'

'That's terrible,' I agreed, offering her a drink. 'Oh, I only drink water now,' she said. 'Do you have any water, I mean bottled water?'

'Yeah, I think so, I got some spring water from down the Canyon. Will that do?'

'Sure, with just a little ice and a twist of lime if you have it. You see, man, there's lots of bad things coming down in this town, lots of bad vibes.' I said I'd been reading about it in the papers. 'That's just the tip of the iceberg, baby,' she said. 'Just the tip. The only answer is to get totally into the white,' she said. 'Totally into the white. I'm into a white phase now and I'm never coming out of it,' she said, opening up her purse and taking out a small wrap of paper, laying out several lines of cocaine on the table with a $100 bill. She offered me a couple of lines of the stuff. 'Oh, no thanks,' I said. 'You go ahead.' She did, snorting the lines professionally off the table, licking her fingertips and then sucking on the rolled $100 bill which she replaced in her purse.

'Yeah, cocaine helps me keep my head together and helps keep me into the white. You see, after the experience with those black magic bastards and after what happened to Sharon and her friends, I decided the only way to protect oneself is surround oneself with the white light. It's the only way to fend off the bad vibes going on in this town. Most of the women are scared shitless and they think the answer is to buy dogs and guns. That's no way to protect yourself. Everyone is so scared.'

'Tell me about it,' I interjected. 'I got a girlfriend over in the Gower district who was a close friend of Sharon Tate, she's really upset.'

'I don't blame her,' she said, 'but we must find new ways to deal with this problem. It can't be dealt with by resorting to violence. Anyway, if you ever feel the threat, you can always come to my castle, it's totally safe. You must come over for dinner one night. I have several new friends over there I want you to meet, so you must come by. Now, are you going to open your present?'

'Oh yeah,' I said, 'I'd forgotten.' I fumbled with the ribbon, which was tied around the cardboard box. I opened it. Inside was a human skull. 'Wow,' I said, 'thanks a lot, that's wonderful, darling.'

'Er, Princess La Lune,' she reminded me. 'Oh yeah, I forgot, sorry, babe.' I placed the skull upon one of my huge JBL speakers, stood back and admired it.

'Do you have any candles? You must place a candle next to the skull, it's only right.'

'Of course,' I agreed. After placing the candle and lighting it she left. Her cool lips kissed me on the forehead. The Corvette reversed and sped away.

I walked back to the house, the dog outside barking at her departure. I went back into the living room, the candle burned next to the spooky skull, beyond it lay a mirror. I looked at myself in the mirror, a splash of red colour on my forehead where she had kissed me. 'Wow,' I said to myself. 'Freaky, freaky.' But I knew then that I was determined to stay. Nobody was gonna turn my dream upside down and get away with it. I looked at my watch, it was 2.30 a.m. I switched on the TV. A Mexican vampire glared at me from the set. I sat down on the huge red couch and disappeared into gothic old Mexico.

A new club had opened in town on Sunset Strip, a rival to the Whisky A Go Go. It was aimed at the jammers in town, the musicians. Some of them, out of work, were only too willing, for the price of a free beer and free entrance, to get up on stage and jam all night long. The club was called the Experience. On the walls outside the club, owned by Marshall Bravitz, a huge Jimi Hendrix head was painted. You entered the club by way of his mouth. When Jimi came to town I drove him down there and showed him the place. He thought it was as crazy as hell and laughed all the way back to my place up in the Canyon. He had some new demo tapes that he'd made in London that he wanted to play me. Returning to my place we put the tapes on the machine. He helped cue it up, adjust the treble and bass and we sat back and listened to the tapes. My mind was blown. It was incredible. I was awash with the psychedelic sounds that rolled from the speakers. The JBLs were hung by chains from the ceiling and I had two more speakers which were actually slave amps from our PA system which I used for more bass response.

On top of the speaker, to the left, which was near the sliding glass doors which led to the balcony, was the Princess's skull and next to it a lit candle. At one point the bass response from the tapes was so strong, the rumble from the speakers caused the skull to move across the top of the box, fall from the box to the floor with a thud, roll across the floor on to the balcony, across the concrete balcony and then fall into the bushes below. 'Damn,' said Hendrix. 'Wow, that was weird.' Fetching my rubber torch, with the recruitment of Terry McVey from downstairs, we searched the back garden amongst the ivy for the skull and never found it, not to this day. A story developed around the skull, that at night it flies up and down the Canyon, descending upon young females and giving them head. The flying skull became a standard joke between me and Jimi.

LA's paranoia and state of siege in the coming months did not subside, in fact it seemed to get worse. Both the straight world press, the underground press, those who speculated, those who guessed, those who knew, informed sources, all agreed that the story had not ended, even after a second spate of killings. At the scene of both crimes there had been political slogans written in blood on the walls of the house and even though the Los Angeles Police Department had several hippy types in custody, the real killer, El Coyote, was still on the prowl. People just didn't give parties any more and in Los Angeles that virtually meant the end of social life, as the whole town closes down at 2 a.m. and it's usual for people to leave public drinking places and return to their homes to hold parties.

Now if you ventured out across the door midweek, places like the Whisky A Go Go, which would normally be quite busy during the summer, were devoid of people, except for the Princess. Maybe her theory of surrounding herself with white light was working. On evenings when I was free I took the pick-up truck and cruised the Whisky parking lot. It was empty, except for the Classic 1957 two-tone Corvette. Inside, the staff, one or two punters, sitting back in the empty place, the music booming over the PA system, the psychedelic light show whirling. Even though the place was empty Elmer Valentine was trying to keep the Whisky alive and on the empty dance floor the Princess whirled, floated like a cloud, her white shimmering backless gown revealing her white powdered skin, the long arms and fingers stretching up towards the ceiling. Her head high, she danced on oblivious to the rest of the world in defiance of all negative vibes.

Animals' guitar player Hilton Valentine had arrived in LA.

He'd got sick of London, was bored and came over looking for work, anything, roadie work would do, he said. 'Are you kidding?' I asked. 'No, I'll do roadie work for the time being.' 'OK, there's nobody living with me at the moment,' I pointed out. 'I haven't heard anything from Angie in ages, so you're welcome to stay with me for a while, until you get your own thing together.' 'Terrific,' he said. After he'd slept off his jetlag I woke him up about 9.30 p.m. 'Come on let's go down the Whisky, let's go watch the Princess dance.' 'Princess?' 'Yeah, come on, I'll show you.' Sure enough, her car was the only one in the lot. We entered, sat down, said good evening to Elmer's partner and were given two Scotch and Cokes on the house.

Hilton was oblivious to what had been going on in the town, the changes, and hardly noticed that the place was empty. 'Ee, it's great to be back in LA.' As the night rolled on, one or two familiar faces, who dared to walk the streets in fear, came ambling in around 1.30 a.m. It was filling out a bit. I watched the Princess leave the dance floor, now too crowded for her movements. I followed her to the door. 'Hey, Princess.' She spun on her heels. 'Yes? Oh Eric, how are you?' She pulled the dark glasses down to reveal her dilated blue pupils. 'I'm going home, it's too crowded, I can't take it any more.' 'Er, listen, I got a friend of mine just come over from England – Hilton. We were wondering, if you weren't up to anything, maybe take you up on your invitation to drop by your place.' 'Sure, honey, I'll wait for you in the parking lot. You know my car.' 'Yeah, I'm in the pick-up, I'll follow you.'

We wheeled our way down a deserted Sunset Strip, the windows wide open. Another hot steamy night. The Princess in front in the Corvette didn't seem to care that every sheriffs' and LAPD black and white that we passed was stopped, its orange and red lights flashing as they shook down anybody on the sidewalk who looked like a black, a vagrant or a hippy. They were all suspects. She gave me the jitters as she pushed the Corvette over the speed limit down the Strip. We could be stopped at any minute. Hilton let his long hair hang out of the window, feeling the cool breeze coming in through the car, oblivious to it all. We turned left at La Cenica. We headed for the Hollywood Hills on the east side of the freeway complex. The two-tone Corvette disappeared, as if by magic, into a garage. The automatic doors closing behind it.

The Princess came floating down the street. 'Just park there,' she said. 'Anywhere will do. Kerb your wheels.' We had to, the street was very steep. And then I saw the castle where she lived. It straddled the top of one of the highest hills in this area. It wasn't a European castle, it was more of a mosque of white stone and stucco. Standing at the front gate looking up at the place, it towered above us like a huge mystical abode in some strange, far-off kasbah. There was a high wall, iron gate and iron railings all round. The garden was steep, with lots of foliage growing up the side of the hill. In this heat and humidity the garden seemed wild and tropical. One wouldn't be surprised to run face to face with an alligator in there. The Princess seemed to radiate neon-white light as she mounted the steps and we followed her up. The door was open. Islamic wailing music filtered down the staircase from the room above where candles burned upon other candles that had burned previously, causing the table to become one mass of lava-like wax.

Within the sea of frozen wax were several objects, like a high-heeled shoe, a plastic doll's arm and of course a human skull. 'Hey, by the way, Princess, your skull – it took a walk.'

'Did it now? Oh, it'll return some day,' she said. She went straight to her handbag, sat down, found a space on the table which had not been covered by wax, produced a small mirror from her purse and laid out lines of cocaine. She looked up from the mirror. 'I'm afraid all there is to drink is Perrier water and fruit juice, or you can make tea if you want.' Hilton volunteered. 'Yeah, I'll make the tea.' He strode into the kitchen. A small skinny naked black boy with a dog-collar round his neck appeared. He clasped his hands together and bowed slightly. 'I'll make the tea, sir. What brand do you want? Choose one from the cupboard.'

Hilton looked at me, his eyes wide with fear. He quickly returned to where we were sitting and joined us. Other humans emerged from the shadows of the long medieval dining room. A half moon shone through a narrow rococo window. A tall blond-haired creature of indeterminate sex emerged from the darkness and sat in the chair opposite the table covered in wax. He was dressed in a gold lamé shawl. 'Welcome to the temple,' he said. 'Thanks,' Hilton stammered, 'Thanks a lot.' We sipped on ice-cold water and I got a joint together. The Islamic music whirled on. The Princess returned, feeling much better now she had a

nose full of the white stuff and didn't have the hassle of the bad
vibes on the street. She went over to the fireplace, turned up the
gas-tap, threw in a match. The fire exploded into life. She turned
and smiled at Hilton. 'Hilton, would you like to see my mummy?'
'Oh, does your mother live here too?' he said. 'No, I meant
mummy, as in the Egyptian. I have a mummy in my bedroom.
Come, why don't you guys take a look.'

She put a long, white-powdered, skinny arm around Hilton
and led him off towards the bedroom. I followed. The bed was
circular, covered in satin sheets, white of course, a canopy draped
across the top. The walls were white, the carpet was white, the
telephone was white. In the corner, beside a window, another
white shroud hung from the ceiling all the way to the floor. Princess stepped forward, pulling back the white curtain. 'In here,'
she said. Holding Hilton by the hand she pulled him forward.
Upon a dais, also draped in white silk, was a small coffin about
four feet long.

Inside was the remains of a rotting corpse, a doll-like infant,
wrapped in swaddling clothes, its face ancient and in a state of de-
composition and yet with eyes that stared out wildly, up to the
sky. It had small vampire-type teeth. There were splashes of long-
ago dried blood smeared upon the teeth. Upon its head, a tiny
nightcap. Hilton stepped back in horror. 'Christ!' he said. He
bolted and headed towards the living room, possibly down the
stairs to the car in the street. I wasn't sure. I broke up with laughter. The Princess turned and smiled at me. 'Do you like him?' she
said. 'Princess, I love it, it's great stuff and it seems it's really
working for you, man. You could really keep any vibration at bay
with this stuff.' I put my arm around her tiny waist and kissed her
on the cheek. 'Is this what fear can drive somebody to, or are you
just a merry prankster having a good time?' She turned and
looked at me, her eyes widening. 'You've got no idea of the forces
that are at work here,' she said. 'This whole State is in the grip of
panic and everybody thinks that they can change it by buying
guns and vicious dogs. Fight fire with fire I say.' It was the first
time I'd seen her serious since I met her. She had always seemed
oblivious to everything. As we left the bedroom we stopped at the
top of the stairs, 'You see, guys like Timothy Leary have set themselves up as gods, leaders of a new faith and have taught us really
to examine within ourselves whether we are good or evil. LSD

and other sacraments were given to us to allow us to see beyond the normal make-up of man as we know him. With these sacraments we can even see into the animal world and relate to them as equals and they're very forgiving, even though all we've done is slaughter them from the beginning of time. There are dark forces running wild in this town,' she said, 'and I aim to combat them with the strength of white light. We've been hurtled into the future. Time has been accelerated. Go hang out at that new club the Experience,' she said. 'Keep your eyes and ears wide open round there. You'll get the real story. White,' she repeated, 'it's all in the white. The Beatles' *White Album*, have you really heard it?' 'Sure, I've given it a listen.' 'You've given it a listen or you've listened to it? It's negativity wrapped up in white.' She paused and looked at me. 'What's Helter Skelter mean?' she said. 'It's a kid's game in England. They have them in amusement parks, public parks and in fairgrounds, you know? You pay your penny and you climb this tall tower, sit on a rug and skid down a spiral metal slideway on your ass.' She hesitated, looked at the ceiling, clapped her hands together. 'A downward spiral,' she said, 'that's it, of course.' She wandered off towards the living room. I followed behind her. Wow, this chick has really flipped, I thought. Hilton sat in the corner, still shaken by the sight of the mummified baby. 'Come on, Hilton, let's go.' 'Yeah, yeah.' He was on his feet in seconds. I headed down the staircase. 'Princess, I'm off. Bye, see you at the Whisky in about a week or so.' 'Yeah, glad you could come by. Stay cool and remember, think white.'

In that strange summer of 1969 the police finally arrested the man responsible for the Sharon Tate killings. He was Charles Manson, whose followers had attempted to start a race war, linking their ideas to songs on The Beatles' *White Album* which, with twisted logic, Manson thought was somehow prophetic. I often wondered later whether I had bumped into Manson. I knew he hung around on the same circuit, and was part of the same LA streetlife. But I don't think he would have entered Marshall Bravitz's club the Experience, as he hated black people, and wouldn't listen to the music of the Jimi Hendrix Experience. And yet the Experience club seemed to be the only one that was doing any business during the period of terror, prior to his arrest.

The sidewalks outside the club were aglow with the chrome of Harley Davidsons. An LAPD car parked on the corner made the scene even more bizarre with its red and yellow flashing lights. I stepped through Jimi's mouth. Receding-haired, pot-bellied, jovial Marshall Bravitz was at the door. 'Hey, Mr Burdon, your first time here, isn't it? And Hilton Valentine, how ya doing?' We shook hands. 'Anytime you want to come by, remember the place is open to you, free beer, free entrance, if you jam.' 'Yeah, we'll keep it in mind.'

The stage was packed, spilling over with musicians, some of them well-known faces. It was loud, noisy and funky but the players were tripping over each other. There was no place to sit so we huddled in the corner. Marshall was going out of his way to kill business at the Whisky further down the strip. On stage a harmonica player was wailing. He was white with an Afro hairstyle. Marshall edged towards us.

'Any one of you guys is welcome to jam any time you want,' he said (in other words 'get the fuck on the stage or get out'). 'Yeah, thanks,' I said, 'I'll wander down to the stage and see if I can find a place.' I was glad when the end of the number came and several musicians drifted off the stage. I climbed the stage and walked towards the harmonica player, who was now pounding his harp on the palm of his hand to clean out the reeds. I walked up to him. 'Evening.' He looked up, his eyes wide, face innocent, he couldn't have been more than twenty-two years of age. 'Hi.' We shook hands vigorously. 'My name's Lee Oskar and I'm from Copenhagen.' 'Pleased to meet you, I'm . . .' 'Yeah, I know who you are. Wanna do a blues, man?' Before I could say anything further we were into it, wheeling away a blues jam in C. The crowd gathered in front of the stage, slapping their thighs, clapping their hands, one or two of them finding room to dance and shuffle around on the floor. Cries of more, more, more! We did an uptempo version of the same thing. 'Let's change the key,' I suggested. 'I can't, I've only got one harmonica with me,' Lee said. 'OK, see you again.' Off we went into an uptempo shuffle. The crowd loved it. We couldn't leave the stage. Afterwards I talked to Lee and told him that I'd like to get together with him and maybe talk further. He'd just carrived in America and we had a mutual friend in Stuey, Hugh Masekala's producer. Hilton and I left the club about 2 a.m. and made our way back up Laurel Canyon, back to the house.

Elmer Valentine's business down at the Whisky was getting

very slack. I always looked in there at least twice a week, just to let him know that I still supported his club, even though he knew I was jamming down at the Experience.

I was in there one night, stoned, wide-eyed, awake and on the prowl. The Princess was not in evidence that night. I didn't feel like going over to Gower and facing the freaks at her castle so around 11.30 p.m. I headed back up the Canyon. I drove round to Alvinia's place, all was quiet and dark. Damn. I headed up the street, past the old house where the Princess used to live. I was horny as hell and I was wide awake. I had to find somebody to relate to. I remembered a blonde chick called Maxine who lived nearby. She was always good for a laugh. I was always welcome there. I cruised around to her house. There was a light burning in a bedroom at the back. Now the drinks I'd had at the Whisky were beginning to mix with the chemical that was swimming around inside my brain. Not realizing how stoned I was and what strength I had behind the drug, I leant a little too heavy on the front door of Maxine's place and found myself falling through the door towards the carpet inside the house.

Landing on my feet, I saw the light still burning in the bedroom. Yet another door to go through. Without thinking I pushed forward, grabbed the brass doorknob, opened it and fell into the room, spreadeagled across the bed. 'Goddamn you, Burdon, you pig.' Clenched fists rained down on my back and head, then a bare foot pressed against my belly and chest and pushed me off the bed towards the floor. As I rolled off the bed I grabbed at anything to stop myself from hitting the floor with a thud. What I grabbed hold of was Lee Oskar's hair. 'Christ! You're a bastard. Why didn't you phone first?' Maxine stood up on the bed, the sexy silk nightgown revealing her huge tits. I stood up, I was so stoned I had no idea what I was doing. I guess I was out of control.

I grabbed hold of Lee by the neck and the hair and pushed him through the bedroom door, into the living room. The bedroom door slammed behind him. Without saying a further word I grabbed hold of Maxine, pulled her to the bed, disappeared beneath the blankets and made wild, frantic, animalistic love to her. In a short while I passed out. The next thing I knew, I awoke with the sun coming through the back window on my face. Maxine was fast asleep next to me on the bed. I was so ashamed. I pulled on my pants as quietly as possible. My shirt and shoes in my hand, I crept out of the house. Fast asleep was Lee Oskar on the couch. I got home to Briar Drive. I cursed myself out loud when I realized that in my hurry to leave Maxine's place, shrouded in guilt, I'd left my watch behind. Damn, oh screw it, I'll get it later. I wandered downstairs to bed, climbed in between the sheets and fell unconscious.

Next morning there was a knock at the door. I climbed up the stairs. I opened the door. Lee Oskar stood in the driveway. 'Hey, Eric, here's your watch. You left it behind, man. I'm sorry,' he said, 'I didn't know that she was your girlfriend.' Then both of us laughed. 'Neither did I,' I said. 'God, I was out of control last night. Come on in, Lee. Sit down. Make yourself at home.' Lee and I became instant friends. In a way he reminded me of myself, a lost lonely muso in search of the end of the rainbow.

Fear and negative vibes crept from the depths of the city below, up the hills towards Laurel Canyon. A note through the door told me that Alvinia Bridges had left for New York. Other friends had gone home to London. On a couple of occasions we'd been out of town on gigs and returned to find the house ransacked, the television, tape deck and other valuables stolen. We were very pissed off.

On top of all this the newspapers told us the Manson murder gun had been found two hundred yards from the place where we once lived in Beverly Glenn with the band. The cops still didn't know whether they had got all the killers in custody. It was grim. The desert was my place to escape and motorcycles and dune buggies were my new-found toys. I moved for a while to a house out in the desert with Steve McQueen as a neighbour. The desert was a great place for creativity. The band would spend weekends out there thinking about material for a forthcoming album. It was to be our last. The band began to drift apart. Danny McCulloch the bass player had written a song by the poolside and was convinced it was a psychedelic smash. I didn't like the song and felt I couldn't handle it. 'Why don't you sing it, Danny?' I said. 'We'll put it on our album anyway.'

He did and from the first time he heard himself on record on the radio he was *gone*. It was the beginning of the end of the second generation Animals. Danny was soon off to get himself a contract with Capitol and rehearse with his own band. With the front money he shipped his girlfriend out from London, rented a house on Mulholland Drive and bought a Rolls-Royce, vintage, of course.

Danny went into rehearsals with his new band soon after we completed our last album together. The summer died, the winter arrived with heavy rainstorms, mudslides and chaos. It was time to move but I couldn't yet relinquish the lure of Hollywood. I made a splendid choice for a new residence. It was Boris Karloff's old house on the Trousdale Estate. Karloff, due to his movie image, had always remained a dark shadow in my imagination. I was intrigued to find his house reflected tastes exactly the opposite of his image. It was dignified, white, bright, airy and tastefully decorated in Spanish style. A magnificent garden was off-set by a pool which had an ancient thirties blue and white striped canvas canopy over the barbecue area.

I came in off the road on a hot summer's night and was met by Lois, my current manager's faithful secretary and shown my new home. 'I'm sure you're gonna love it here, Eric. This is the kitchen, isn't it magnificent?'

Huge french doors led out to a Spanish courtyard. 'I'm sure it's gonna be a magnificent place to entertain, and you're gonna attract a lot of ladies,' she smiled, as she handed over the keys.

The first unusual thing that I noticed about the house was a small window placed up near the ceiling in the main wall of the house, opposite the large fireplace. It was too high for anybody to reach and too small for much light to come through. I wondered if it was strictly cosmetic or whether it had a purpose. I was alone, having a smoke, sitting by the fireside watching the logs burn, waiting for the Princess to arrive, wondering about that window. What was its purpose? The doorbell rang, she was outside, shimmering in the moonlight, almost translucent. 'Hey, Princess, come on in. Welcome to Uncle Boris' place.' A broad smile crossed her face as she stood there in the anteroom. I took off the white fur stole she had wrapped around her shoulders. She stepped into the main room. The logs were crackling in the fireplace. 'Mmmm, wonderful, I could smell them outside in the street as I pulled up. Oh, this is magnificent,' she said, spreading out her arms, spinning on her heel, taking a 360 degree view of the main living room. The moon inexorably moved across the sky as I passed my joint to the Princess. The blue smoke drifted towards the ceiling.

The two of us sat by the fire, watching the smoke twist and turn its way up to the roof. Before it reached the roof, it passed the small window. Suddenly the full moon shed a shaft of silvery light. 'Oh, wow, magic,' she said. 'What an effect.' Now I understood why Boris had had that small window installed so high and out of reach. A pleasant surprise. We giggled, our minds drifting towards memories of Boris. It was true, his spirit seemed to fill the house, even though he was long gone.

Later I had the pleasure of showing the Princess around the house. Everyone else had gone. We were alone. 'Truly magnificent,' she said. 'Even better than my castle,' and that was saying something. Something she didn't have at the castle was a garden. This one was magnificent with its Olympic-sized pool. I flicked on the light, the blue turquoise water illuminated the trees surrounding the pool. She immediately began to disrobe. 'Oh, I must, I must.' 'No, no, later,' I said, 'later, we must eat first.' I had to drag her away forcibly from the water's edge. Anyway, she hadn't seen the courtyard yet, a magnificent Spanish courtyard. 'Oh, if I lived in a place like this I'd just never go out, I'd just stay home all the time, in residence, accepting friends and gifts,' she laughed in the warm night air. After we'd eaten I showed her the one place in the house I knew would flip her out. It was the prayer cupboard underneath the main staircase leading up to the guestroom, just outside of my bedroom door.

'Oh, what a trip!' she said as I pushed open the door and handed her the candle so she could find her way into the tiny prayer cupboard. 'This is great, can I just sit in here for a while and meditate?'

'Sure, go right ahead. Feel free. Do what you want.' She was in there for what seemed ages. 'Hey Princess, you all right? You're still awake, aren't ya? You're not dying on me in there or anything?'

'No, no, it's fine, I'm just doing a little meditation and absorbing the vibes,' she said. 'Did you know,' she said from the darkness, 'that next week, according to TV Guide, I guess it's in sort of celebration of you moving into this house, no, no, it's a great coincidence, anyway according to TV Guide, next week on Channel 13 there's a Boris Karloff film festival.'

'You're kidding!' I said, 'Really?' It was true. Every night of the week there was a different Boris Karloff movie on TV. I left her to it and made my way through the house towards the huge TV in the main sitting room. Next week's *TV Guide* lay there alongside of the *LA Times*. Monday night, *The Dark Room*, well, isn't that a coincidence, I thought, we've already found that. Tuesday, *The Black Cat*, Wednesday, *Night Key*, Thursday, *British Intelligence*, Friday, *Black Friday*, Saturday, *You'll Find Out* and Sunday, one of my favourite Boris Karloff films, *Targets*. After leafing through the *TV Guide* and realizing she was still in there, I could stand it no longer. I wanted her body next to mine.

I went in there with the intention of dragging her out. I prised open the door, it opened with a creak. The candle was still burning, although it was now just about down to its last few flickering flames. To my surprise the Princess was on all fours in the corner. 'What are you doing?' She turned to look at me. 'Er, as I was moving around one of my shoes dislodged one of the floor tiles.' Using a fingernail file she'd worked on the loose tile and removed it. 'There's something underneath. It's not concrete, it's wood and it's hollow.'

'It's just a floorboard,' I said. I was now behind her, looking over her shoulder at the removed masonry revealing floorboards underneath. 'Yeah, but the rest of the floor, outside and inside of the cupboard is solid stone. Why should this be wood? And one of the floorboards is coming loose. Look for yourself.' I returned with my rubberized flashlight. By this time she'd actually removed some of the wooden floorboards beneath the tiling. Using the flashlight we discovered that beneath the floorboards was something metal. This was even more exciting. Then we both got a rush as we discovered a brass dial on a metal fascia. It was a small, steel safe. 'It's a safe!' she said excitedly. 'Boris's secret safe!' Now I was excited, flipping out. 'Let me see,' I said, pushing her aside. 'No, it's my discovery, give me the light.' We were fighting now like cat and dog to get to the new find. Who else, we wondered, had known about Boris's secret safe? When the Princess finally left the house that night we planned to do our utmost to find out what was hidden in the safe of Boris Karloff.

The following morning, with the aid of the flashlight, chisels and hammers, I removed more of the Spanish tiles and more of the woodwork to reveal the small green metal safe with its brass dial and fascia. Around 11 o'clock that night the Princess called me. 'Have you had another look at it?' 'Yeah, sure I have. I've been in there and uncovered the whole thing, removed about four or five tiles and the woodwork, I can see the whole safe now.' 'Well listen,' she said excitedly, 'I've been in touch with my friends who are members of the Magic Circle in Hollywood and they say that during the twenties there was a group of directors, actors and magicians, including King Vidor, Charlie Chaplin, Mac Sennett and several others, who all had a theory that the planet could be changed by way of the newly invented medium of the cinema. Of course everybody then thought that they were absolutely crazy, but now, with the advent of TV, and subliminal advertising experiments in the fifties, one can see that they weren't that crazy. Now my theory is that Boris's safe contains some of the minutes of their clandestine meetings. What else would Boris have locked in there?' 'Well, could be personal effects, family heirlooms, possibly gems, even money, I don't know.' 'Well, even so, it's an exciting prospect, isn't it?' 'Yeah, but we'd better keep quiet about it. I mean, after all, I am just leasing the house, the safe doesn't belong to us.'

'Yes,' she came back at me quickly over the phone, 'I'm sure that there are secret scrolls in there, something of great import- ance that Boris didn't want anybody to see. Obviously, that's why the safe was hidden so well, under floorboards, beneath tiling, in a prayer cupboard. Listen, I've got to work in that damn strip club tonight, but promise me, next week, the night that they begin the Boris Karloff season on Channel 13, you'll allow me to come over and in the meantime, I'm gonna do some research on it. OK?' 'All right,' I said, 'you're on. Next Monday night I'll make sure that the house is empty and we can begin work.'

Further investigation, when I was alone that night, revealed that the safe name and number was embossed on the front. I spent hours turning the brass dial, hoping that it would click in the magical combination and open the safe. Nothing, it just wouldn't work. Next move to the Telephone Directory, New York Information, try to locate the manufacturers and see if they could help me. 'Er, I've just inherited a house,' I gave them the story, 'and along with it a safe.' I gave them the serial number and all the relevant information. Unfortunately, they told me, their safe manufacturing division was no longer in existence, they were now strictly a security service. They gave me another telephone number in Zurich, Switzerland. Meanwhile the Princess had gone to work with a system based on numerology, using Boris Karloff's birthdate, his child's birthdate, and the number of films he made. She would break the code, she said. We were hot on the trail.

I contacted the people in Zurich. They said they would need papers, proof, that I was indeed the owner of the house and in turn the owner of the safe, before they could give me the relevant information to crack the safe, but they did tell me, however, that if the safe was blown by an explosive device the entire contents of the safe would be destroyed. The next move was to a music supply store on Sunset. I purchased two contact microphones, then I was off across town to a medical supply store to buy a doctor's stethoscope. I spent the next two days wiring up the pickups to the outside fascia of the safe, placing electrical leads all the way from the fascia of the safe, down the corridor, into my room, through my powerful Mackintosh amplifiers and Altec Lansing speakers, so that when the dial was spun every click and every move on the dial could be heard amplified several hundred times.

The Princess and I were jumping at the prospect of what the safe might reveal. We planned to get together at the house on Monday night for the first movie – Channel 13's Boris Karloff series. A big coincidence, the first movie in the series was *The Dark Room*. The Princess said that we should watch the movie and look out for clues. She was now firmly convinced that the safe held secrets to the control of the planet through films, TV and the media. For proof of this she said she'd just finished reading a book called *The Critoptic Society*, a book in which the writer claimed that the CIA, as far back as the fifties, had hatched a plan to control America by television and subliminal advertising. We viewed Boris's film with great interest. The Princess made notes all the way through. I found no clues or secrets held within the script or dialogue but the Princess was sure that even the title was significant.

After the film was over we tried every conceivable combination under the sun. Still nothing. The safe was not attached to the foundation. With a lot of effort I felt it could be moved. That evening the Princess had arrived in style with a stray black cat that she'd picked up off the streets of Beverly Hills, hoping that it would bring us luck. She also brought along quite a hefty parcel of Hollywood historical books, books that covered the history of all the great Hollywood horror actors and magicians, but nothing seemed to get us any closer to the cracking of Boris's safe.

Thursday rolled around. The movie that night was *British Intelligence*. Flipping through the *TV Guide* my mind wandered towards the safe cracker Eddie Chapman, who'd come from the north-east of England, had been a criminal during the Second World War and the British Army had bought him out of prison where he'd been serving time for safe blowing. They needed someone to crack certain safes and strongboxes behind enemy lines in occupied France. They'd give him immunity from prosecution if he would, as a commando, get to these German safes and strongboxes and crack them open on behalf of King and Country. I wished I had his skills. My mind was racing. Who did I know in the Los Angeles area capable of such a thing? It was true that I knew several people on the fringes of the underworld, but I knew no one with those skills.

Then I flashed on Eddie 'Boom Boom' Taylor. Boom Boom I'd met through my film contacts in Hollywood. He was a pyrotechnic expert in the movies and claimed that he could blow anything, anywhere. Once, for an album cover concept, I wanted to create a ball of fire over a lake, which seemed an impossible task. But Boom Boom claimed that he could do it with a gasoline explosion in the desert and had actually come up with a price. Maybe if I had a meeting with Boom Boom he could help me out. Friday night Channel 13 screened Boris's *Black Friday*. I invited Boom Boom over to the house. He'd been working on a major war film at Universal and admitted he was tired, but he didn't mind stopping by to participate in the good cocaine that the Princess had provided. Over a few lines I prodded and probed his mind all about the art of blowing up small hard metal objects.

'Now this is for a record cover,' he said, 'right?' 'No, not exactly,' I said. 'You mean you're talking about blowing a safe. I'm not gonna get involved in anything on that level, I'm making too much money to become a criminal!'

Of course he didn't know I was just leasing the house. As far as he knew I'd bought it, so when the Princess let the cat out of the bag, that it was Boris Karloff's safe, Boom Boom's eyes lit up with interest. I took him into the darkness of the prayer cupboard and showed him what lay beneath the loose tiles and floorboards. 'What do you think?' I asked. He looked at it with a professional eye. 'By the way,' I said, 'I contacted the company in Zurich and they told me that if the safe was blown it would destroy the contents, along with the safe.' 'Yeah,' said Boom Boom scratching his head, 'that's probably true, but they mean if you drill a hole in the front and explode it that way. Now with plastic explosives around the side, probably C4, there wouldn't be any problem.'

'Well, what do you think? Do you think it could be done?'

'Well, I suppose so, the hardest thing is getting the sucker out, you're gonna have to move much more of the floor, it's gonna be a messy job and I'm gonna need a lot of tools, and a small metal trolley with rubber wheels. You're gonna have to rent one.'

'You mean you'll do it?' I said.

'Yeah, I'll give it a shot, I've got nothing to do this weekend. But don't tell anybody, this is a secret, OK?'

'Damn right it's a secret, it's the secrets I wanna get to.'

We made arrangements to meet the next morning. We'd take my Chevy Blazer, go downtown, rent the necessary equipment and go up to the Mojave Desert. Boom Boom would secure the plastic explosives, wires and detonator from the movie set he was working on.

Bright and early, I went with the Princess to one of the many movie rental companies and hired a metal rubber-wheeled trolley and a small hand-wound wire operated tripod for lifting the safe out of the floor. By 10.30 a.m. we were on the road heading for the desert, drinking ice-cold vodka from the styrofoam container, listening to rock'n'roll tapes. I did the driving whilst Boom Boom and the Princess kept a look out for a suitable gully where the explosives wouldn't be heard, and we could crack the safe without anyone observing us.

'Right, pull up, stop, over here,' said Boom Boom. I jammed on the brakes, enveloping the Blazer in a cloud of dust. There was a small winding trail. Shifting the gearbox into four-wheel drive we made our way down the bumpy trail towards the bottom of a gully. I released the tailgate. The safe was in the back. Boom Boom assembled the winch. Gently he lowered the safe to the floor. The Princess took a walk several hundred yards around the perimeter of the gully to make sure there was no one in sight. I put the tailgate back into place and moved the Blazer to safety whilst

Waiting for the Princess at Boris' house

Boom Boom applied the C4 plastic explosive to the outer casing. He then laid the wires several yards over the top and around the corner of a large rock. He wired up the detonator. The three of us hid behind the rock.

Boom Boom turned his long peaked baseball cap back to front, a cigarette clenched between his teeth. He looked a me, his cold blue eyes flashing with excitement. 'OK, you ready, Princess? Keep your fingers and legs crossed and say a little prayer.' He turned a small key on the black detonator box. There was an unearthly silence. Then, suddenly, not a loud explosion, but more a loud pop! Directly after the pop Boom Boom stuck his head over the rock, I followed suit, so did the Princess. We could see a small black object shooting up into the blue sky. The safe spun in the air and then began tumbling and crashing towards the bottom of the chasm. Then there was silence. The three of us scrambled over the rocks. Out of breath we reached the safe. The Princess in her bare feet, high-heeled shoes in one hand, was the last to make it towards the small green safe. 'Well? What have we got? What's in there?' Boom Boom took off his baseball cap and scratched the back of his long shaggy blond hair. 'Not much,' he said. 'God-damn.' He threw the baseball cap in disgust to the floor. There was the safe lying there, looking up at us, perfectly intact, except for a few scratches on the side. In disgust Boom Boom turned, walked away and headed towards the pickup. Boris had beaten us, there was no way we were going to find out his ultimate secrets. The Princess was in tears. Boom Boom needed a drink. The vodka had run out. He started walking down the long dusty road towards the small town that we'd just passed, heading towards the nearest water-hole. I was left there, sad, dejected, looking at the safe, cursing it.

I could hear the ghost of Boris Karloff laughing down at us. It took us three hours to load the safe back on to the Blazer, and we drove back to LA. We found Boom Boom at the nearest bar and drove him back to Boris's house, just in time to catch the latest in the series of Karloff films on TV called *You'll Find Out*.

It took me weeks, working in secret so the owners of the house wouldn't find out, to restore the safe, replace the tiles and floor-boards. I locked up the prayer cupboard and forgot about its existence.

The last I saw of the Princess was at one of my gigs at the Roxy in Hollywood. Then she was gone. I heard she had been kidnapped by her own father, a rich farmer. She had been taken from the streets of LA at gunpoint and whisked away, never to be seen again. This followed an article on her in a national magazine about black magic.

As for her theories about Charles Manson and The Beatles *White Album*, she was right, as the court case proved. But it seemed one of her regular boyfriends, a screenplay writer, had chanced upon a conference on the Manson murders at the Los Angeles police department. He saw the information about the *White Album* chalked up on a blackboard of the tack-room at LAPD Parker Center and gave the information to her. He was at the time working on a documentary about 'the Family'. It seemed as if the Princess's real power, like Manson's, was LSD.

SIXTEEN
IN THE WINK OF AN EYE

By now I was penniless and living up on the hill in Hollywood, coming down after the early success of the New Animals. I had two years of lunacy. Bought a house. Had a couple of favourite cars. The old EVB trick. I was living with my girlfriend Caroline, and things had got down to the bottom of the bucket when she started to make and sell huge psychedelic pillows from door to door. She was hawking her wares in Beverly Hills when she met two guys who said they were interested in managing me. So off I went and met them.

My new managers were known as the Gold Dust Twins, Steve Gold and Jerry Goldstein. On all their artists' albums appeared in small print the legend 'Another Gold and Goldstein Happening'. It was a record executive at United Artists who tagged them the Gold Dust Twins. They epitomized the bullshitting Hollywood entrepreneur. They were both Jewish and from the East Coast. They were quite different in character and personality but when they came together they were ruthless and vicious. It was like talking to one brain with two mouths.

The reason I got together with them was to see if we could break an act called Eric Burdon and War. The deal was I'd give them talent and they'd give me the tools I needed to move forward as an artist. Eric Burdon and War was the brainchild of Steve Gold. When I first met him he was selling pop posters out of an office in Beverly Hills, along with his partner Jerry Goldstein, who became the producer of the band. We soon moved offices to Sunset Boulevard. After many hours of hard work and rehearsals within the space of a year we created a solid chart-orientated soul band. There was a new regime at MGM and we gave them their first gold album and single.

Gold, an ex-CPA and one-time stand-up-comic, had been turned on by Lenny Bruce and never looked back. Although he was sharp-witted and possessed a poisonous tongue coupled with a three-toned laugh, he somehow managed to fail in the theatre. Never say die! He turned his office into an arena and proceeded to jaw his way through the record industry; he believed greed was healthy. He began as a business anarchist and developed into a business terrorist, laced with a megasize helping of what 'Holly-weird' can offer. It ultimately led to fear, paranoia and megalo-mania on his part. There were many times I felt I was in the wrong place at Far Out, but they had something I wanted ... so I hung on in there.

They dangled a golden carrot to keep me in line. They kept promising me action in a movie about Jimi Hendrix. The film companies were interested. We had the footage. So once again I was close to something worthwhile. But of course it took me years, a lot of money and aggravation to find out that it was debatable whether they owned the rights to the film. They didn't own it, right from the beginning. They sold off the bits of sound-track they had, without telling me, to other film makers, who were producing a movie on the same subject.

So another rip off. But it's easy to steal from a performer, like taking candy from a baby, no big thing. Just a pity to see it, all because of the mighty dollar. Their idea was to keep me on the road, playing gigs and ensuring there would be a steady cash flow into the company.

In the beginning the concept of Eric Burdon and War took off extremely well. I came up with a radical plan to break the band in Europe. Little did I know the adventure would coincide with one of the major tragedies in rock history, the death of Jimi Hendrix.

By now we were into 1970 and the start of a new decade. New bands and ideas were coming along. Rock festivals were big business. That summer Jimi played at the Isle of Wight. It was the last chance his English fans would have to see him.

As far as I was concerned, things were looking good. Record-wise in the previous couple of years I'd had two Top Ten hits in America with 'Sky Pilot' and 'San Franciscan Nights'.

After my marriage finally broke up I got together with War, an all black progressive band. Our first album was called 'Eric Burdon Declares War' and we had a US hit with 'Spill The Wine'. We did another album before splitting up called 'Black Man's Burdon'. Goldstein did an excellent job as producer, whilst Gold made waves at MGM to free me. He also secured War a deal at UA. The Gold Dust Twins, it seemed, were on my side.

In September 1970, I wanted to put War into Ronnie Scott's Jazz Club in Frith Street, Soho. I loved the idea of a rock act playing in a solid jazz venue and showing what we could do. So after a tour of the US and Canada we flew into London to play one week at Ronnie's.

It was a prestigious gig and there was a degree of unity in War then which made us hang together. We threw ourselves totally into the job and got the jazz audience to move their asses. Even the Gold Dust twins had the business sense to see what I was trying to do. My theory was that as England was so small, if you could break London, you broke the whole country. The news would feed back to the States, and bingo – international success.

Come the opening on Monday night, the attendance was very good. The club was happy and so were the band. Steve Gold was ecstatic. Yet another of his 'personally managed' dreams was about to unfold before his bulging eyes.

Into the club on opening night came Eric Barratt, Jimi Hendrix's roadie. He stood at the bar sipping a pint, a concerned look on his young face, long black hair curling over his eyes. We started rapping. 'Where is Jimi, then?' 'That's what I've come to talk to you about,' said Eric.

It turned out Jimi wanted to get in touch. He had been holed up in his apartment in London for months, not going out or doing anything. The last couple of times I'd seen him had been under difficult circumstances, like the time I met him in Bel Air when he was beating up one of his girlfriends. I'd heard all kinds of weird rumours, including one that he had been set up for a kidnapping, organized by guess who? ... MJ.

214

I suggested that if Jimi wanted to see me it would be a nice idea if he came down to the club to sit in with me and War. I told Eric how sorry I was to hear Jimi had been sitting depressed in his room, not knowing what to do next. 'We've all been there, I know what he's going through. Tell him to come down. We do two shows a night. He's very welcome to bring down his guitar and sit in.'

Jimi came down the next night and was well out of it. He had his guitar with him but he was wobbling too much to play, so I told him to come back tomorrow night. So he left with his girl-friend Monika Danneman. He came back the next night and he had on his best psychedelic suit and looked immaculate. He sat at the table quietly with Monika.

I had a quick word in his ear and said I would call him up when the time was right. We played a whole set, and when it came to 'Tobacco Road' Jimi came on stage and plugged up and joined in. He made an attempt to lead the band, but there was no way any of the guys in War would let him do that. He ended his solo with a climactic finish. Much to his dismay and surprise the band kept on trucking. He wasn't the boss, he was the guest, and that really hurt him, I could tell. He got ready to leave the stage. I grabbed hold of him and said, 'It's not out there, man, it's over here.' He stood in that half-way world between the stage and the audience. Then he turned around, plugged in and started playing back-up chords, 'wacka diddy wacka diddy'. The guys realized they had won their point but we forced him to stay. We played 'Mother Earth' a Memphis Slim song.

He shocked Howard Scot, War's lead guitarist, into playing the best lead solo I've ever heard him play, which got a tremen-dous round of applause. Jimi came back with his answer to Howard, which was an absolute mind blower. By now we were running over time, and Ronnie Scott was making frantic signals for us to cut it.

There were congratulations all round back in the dressing room and we realized that Jimi had at last broken out of his shell, the first time he had smiled or played in months. Then he said he was going to a party. He just took off and was gone. He had no band. The Experience was gone, and the Band of Gypsies had folded, and whether he liked it or not Chas Chandler had been phased out of the picture leaving MJ in control.

After Jimi walked out of the dressing room at Ronnie Scott's, I never saw him again.

I went home to bed. Alvinia, who was in London for my show, came with me. We were both so beat, we climbed into the sack and fell asleep. Before I slipped off I remember thinking it was good to see Jimi back in London which had always been better for him than New York. Then the phone rang. Alvinia answered. 'It's Monika Danneman. She is with Jimi and he's so stoned he won't wake up.' Half asleep I suggested she give him hot coffee and slap his face. If she needed any more help to call me back.

My girlfriend, Alvinia, told me: 'Monika is a good kid, she'll look after him.' That made me feel better and I slid back under the covers. I don't know how long I dozed, but alarm bells began ringing in my mind. The first light of dawn was coming through the window, and it was raining outside. 'Monika's number, Alvinia, give me Monika's number, quickly!' Alvinia found the number in her handbag.

'Monika, it's Eric. Listen, just do what I say and don't ask any questions. Phone an ambulance now, quickly.' She came back at me with, 'I can't have people round here now, there's all kinds of stuff in the house.' 'I don't care, get the illegal stuff and just throw it down the toilet, do anything you can, but get an ambulance now, we're on our way over.' I slammed the phone down. Alvinia was already gone, out the door, yelling to me over her shoulder, 'I'll get a taxi, the address is there beside the bedside, come as soon as you can.' She was gone and the door closed. I felt much better now that help was on the way. I arrived in a mini-cab at a basement apartment in Bayswater. As my car pulled into the street I saw the flashing blue lights of the ambulance turning the corner. My legs and stomach went weak. I paid off the taxi. I looked down the staircase of the basement apartment, hesitated for a few moments. Straining my ears, I could hear the crying from within. Two women holding each other. The small blonde distraught, eyes red, tears streaming down her cheeks towards the floor. The tall black woman trying to comfort her. I stepped through the kitchen into the main living room, a small gas fire was burning, a white Fender guitar on top of its case lying on a table in the corner. The bedclothes were thrown back. On the bed I could see the impression of where the body had lain. Jimi was gone. I wanted to stop and cry too, but I knew there was no time, the police would be here soon and so would the vultures of the press. There were things we must do.

Keeping the girls busy was all I could do to save them from going to pieces. 'Monika, passport, where's his passport, Monika? The police are gonna want it.' She found it in one of the drawers beside the bed. On top of the drawers, next to the bed, a note in his handwriting. The writing was scrawny, scrawly, but nevertheless legible. 'The story of Jesus is so easy to explain, after they crucified him a woman she claimed his name. The story of Jesus the whole Bible knows, he went all the way across the desert and in the middle he found a rose.' Now a mixture of pain, sorrow and anger welled within me. 'Oh Jimi, Jimi, Jimi,' I thought, 'you've gone too far this time, you took it to the max.' Monika and Alvinia read the poem together. Now I felt a sudden sense of failure that I'd have to live with for a long time afterwards. Had I let him down? Had I been too hard on him? When he called I didn't come. I asked him to come to me. I thought I'd be doing the best possible. To see him smile again, to see him play again, that was what was important and we'd achieved that. But I hadn't achieved anything, 'cos he was gone. He could have had a wonderful life, he had so much to give. Would he ever forgive me? Was there anything I really could have done to prevent it?

Then we unearthed the plans that he'd left for Monika's paintings. He'd forced her, made her promise that she would use her skills to execute the paintings and drawings that he'd left behind. Yeah, it was a well-executed plan, Jimi, too well executed.

Later we were to find, whilst examining the sketches, that all the numbers, all the measurements, were in nines and sixes, nine inches, six millimetres, six feet, sixty-nine millimetres, ninety-six inches and so on and of course, he'd taken nine sleeping tablets, just to make sure. We got the message. Monika and I would swear together that we would try, somewhere along the line, to take his plans and try and turn them, if possible, into a beautiful movie, a work of art that would explain his ideology, his feelings, what he stood for. This was not such an impossible task, I explained to Monika, as my own company, my own partners, the Gold Dust Twins, had just completed the documentary film of Jimi and The Experience at their last gig together at the Royal

Albert Hall. I would do my best, I swore there and then, to make sure that it looked good and smelled good and would show him in the best possible light.

But for now, right now, I had to get his girlfriend out of the way before the press arrived. They were already at the door, standing in line, tape machines, cameras with flashlights, pen and paper ready in their hands, a mass of flapping vultures. The uniformed cops made their way through the crowd and down the staircase into his apartment. The next thing I remember was standing on the station at King's Cross, waiting for a train, to try and get Monika out of the glare of the harsh lights of publicity, up to the sanctuary of my mother's. Standing there on the station at King's Cross, Jimi's Fender guitar in one hand and his woman in the other.

Fist-fights broke out on the station between loyal friends and the press. I felt a great sense of relief once the train pulled away from the station and we headed towards Newcastle and my mother's sympathetic pot of tea. But the hurt inside was indescribable, the first time that death had ever really touched me in my whole life. Monika would stay at my mother's until the heat died down, then catch a plane to Dortmund, via Hamburg. I returned to London with a heavy heart to continue my gig and finish the week at Ronnie Scott's Club. It was gonna be awful lonely on the stage for the rest of the week.

The representative from the BBC told me I shouldn't be afraid, I could trust the BBC, and Kenneth Allsop was gonna do the interview. Surely he would give me an honest hearing? I agreed to talk. Stupid of me. In defiance of everybody and everything and all that Jimi stood for, I got stoned before the interview. Allsop took me apart, fried me. I can't recall what I said, nor do I care, I only care that my ego was stupid enough to allow me to speak publicly about the death of a friend, for my feelings I couldn't put into words, they were scrambled, disconnected, senseless, not words, just feelings pouring out. Allsop had a field day. Three cheers for the media. Another nail in the coffin of the dream. As I left the TV studio I recognized an executive from Polydor Records standing near the glass doors of the entrance-way. He grabbed me by the arm and looked into my stoned eyes. 'For that, for what you've just said, you'll never ever work again in England, son.' I left the BBC studio, leaving the music scene, leaving London, leaving England, leaving friends behind. Saying goodbye to a dream.

I had been gone from England for a long time. The sixties had ended with the deaths of many friends and heroes; Jimi Hendrix, Roland Kirk, Jim Morrison, Brian Jones and Janis Joplin. War had long since disbanded and I found myself in need of money. Word reached me that 'House Of The Rising Sun' was back in the charts in England. I flew back hoping to get a small advance from the royalties to set me up a new band and a new career. There was even talk of an Animals revival.

Back in London I found the place changed. The old dreams were over. New kids, new music, new attitudes. Punk rock ruled. The buildings were covered in graffiti including the old record company headquarters. The uniformed doorman had gone. I didn't know anybody at the company, except one of the oldest executives. 'Ah, Eric, welcome back. Some money? Well I'm sure there must be some. Let's go and see the accountant.'

We met the accountant. 'Ah, Mr Burdon. Yes "House Of The Rising Sun" is doing nicely in the chart. We've had a big promotion campaign on TV, you know.'

'Yes, I was hoping for an advance,' I said eagerly.

'Well now, let me see. According to the accounts, taking note of the original Animals contract, the inflation rate and cost of promotion, it seems you owe us £675. Feel free to photocopy the accounts.'

I was dumbfounded. I took the bus home to Fulham and remembered the words of the late Graham Bond. 'Yeah, you're gonna be famous, the whole world's gonna know your name, but if you take up the challenge of the blues, you'll never have any money.' Fame I had, but fortune had eluded me.

EPILOGUE

Bitter? No I am not bitter. Bitter-sweet maybe. At least I am alive to tell the tale. And the money, the hard cash generated during The Animals' heyday? Gone, slipped without a trace, like a ship into the sea in the Bermuda Triangle.

Soon after The Animals split we sent a representative to Nassau to investigate. To our horror the bank was gone. The people we had dealt with were no longer there and soon after a new government with new laws and different attitudes came into power.

As individuals and sometimes together, The Animals attempted to recover some of the lost revenue, bringing us into conflict with record companies, agents, management and sometimes ourselves. We employed lawyers and accountants but the law moves slowly and is expensive.

Yamita was the tax dodge set up by MJ through London and Nassau for the benefit of his artists. Various lawyers and investigators have made educated guesses that between one million and five million dollars went through MJ's hands during the period that he managed The Animals and Jimi Hendrix, including the three clubs in Palma, Spain, and others in Newcastle. Unfortunately, some years later MJ was reported dead, killed in a mid-air collision over French–Spanish airspace in 1973. No trace could be found and his secrets went with him.

I remain today a hard-working rock-singer doing live gigs all over the world. As for the boys in the band – I rarely see them. There have been a couple of reunion tours and even some recording but they have their lives and I have mine. As for Newcastle, England, I am a memory there now – it seems there's just no way home.

Maybe that is what keeps me singing. A voice alone in a sea of amps, lights, computers and gadget gimmicks.

I still believe in the human voice, it delivers the message. 'Oh mother tell your children, not to do what I have done . . .'